# Cellini's Revenge

## THE MYSTERY OF THE SILVER CUPS

### BOOK 1

# What People Are Saying About *Cellini's Revenge*

"This historical mystery intriguingly delves into Catherine's struggle to deal with the emotional and physical consequences of prison time; it also effectively relates her difficulty in grasping the idea that her beloved husband might have kept things from her. This is a first book in a planned trilogy, but it stands well enough on its own, and it's a breath of fresh air to have an older woman as the protagonist in a mystery story with such tragic beats." — ***Kirkus Reviews***

"As a long-time mystery fan, I have read my share of great mysteries. It takes a well-crafted read to get my attention. Cellini's Revenge got my attention from the first page. The author's writing style is compact. She is able to create rich imagery with few words.

"Most importantly, Cellini's Revenge does what all good books should do, and that is to create an emotional bond with the characters. Wendy Bartlett does this so well.

"To me the hallmark of a great mystery is that the reader simultaneously wants the story to end to find out 'Whodunit,' but also does not want to say goodbye to the characters.

"I cannot wait for the next book in this trilogy."
**—Helen Cameron, Ph.D, Higher Education Administration**

"A fascinating international mystery set in 1960s England with a 400-year-old riddle wrapped into it–plus a totally unexpected surprise ending."
**—Art Goldberg, journalist**

"*Cellini's Revenge* is a tale that spans the centuries. If you love historical mysteries, this may well be for you."
**—Stefany Reich-Silber, writer, editor, former librarian**

"Wendy Bartlett, a student of Italian Renaissance art history, has crafted a trilogy of historical novels based on the tumultuous life of Benvenuto Cellini, the most renowned metal sculptor of his generation. In her expertly paced *Cellini's Revenge*, twelve priceless silver cups made in Italy by the Master himself mysteriously re-appear in modern England. Life will never be the same for those who discover them."
**—Ruth Hanham, Professor/Writer**

A great read! Intriguing plot with a surprise ending....It's one of those books where you develop an attachment to the characters and you don't want it to end. Hope to find more novels by Wendy Bartlett in the future!
—**Bev Tisdale, Teacher's Assistant**

A fun read with interesting twists. The plot was intriguing, the characters interesting and colorful, the settings atmospheric... A fun, well-constructed tale.
—**C. Sweeney, Travel Agent**

*"I've read the Memoirs of Benvenuto Cellini, as sure as
you're looking at me now, and in Italian, what's more!
That chap, a pretty bright spark, taught me to imitate
Providence, which kills us all at random, and to love
beauty wherever it may be found.*

–Spoken by Vautrin, in Honore De Balzac's novel *Père Goriot*

# Cellini's Revenge

## THE MYSTERY OF THE SILVER CUPS

### BOOK 1

## WENDY BARTLETT
**San Francisco Writers Conference Award Winner**

**Kensington Hill Books**
Berkeley, California

**Kensington Hill Books**
Berkeley, California

kensingtonhillbooks.com

*Cellini's Revenge: The Mystery of the Silver Cups*
/ Wendy Bartlett – 2nd ed.
ISBN 978-1-944907-12-9 print
ISBN 978-1-944907-13-6 ebook
Library of Congress Control Number: 2020911699

*This book is dedicated to my two grandsons,
Leo and Charlie*

# ACKNOWLEDGMENTS

First and foremost I would like to thank Laurie McLean for choosing me as the runner-up for the Fiction category in the 2007 San Francisco Writers Conference Writing Contest, which was started by two amazing, hard-working agents: Elizabeth Pomada and Michael Larsen.

I would like to acknowledge the following people for their very kind help and advice throughout the writing of this novel: Very special thanks and my deep appreciation go to: Luis Lázaro Tijerina, my most eloquent, detailed, hard-working and encouraging editor; my wonderful line editor, Tiffany Watson; Lindsey Brodie for her endless original ideas; Steve Whittle for his important wisdom and detailed critique; Ruth Hanham, with her great knowledge of shipping in the 16th century, Nanou Matteson for endless help, Hap Allen for his wonderful cover ideas, Charlie Hopper, Marvin Spector, Marilynn Rowland, Joyce Scott, Sarita Berg, Doris Fine, Carol Nyhoff, Kishma Patnaik, and Darlene Harden, for their critique at least two years running,

Rezaul Bashir for his constant computer support, Christopher Rouzie for taking the author photo, Bob Diener for legal ideas, Arden Johnson, Christopher Peterson, Geri Lennon, Peter Bertine, Jeannie Pestell, Clare Langley-Hawthorn and Elizabeth Stark for great ideas, design and writing support, the rag-and-bone man from Norway, whose name has disappeared somewhere in a pile of papers, Jean Wilson who kindly showed me around Rottingdean, Julia Bell, for reading my manuscript and adding her insightful critique, Jane Brodie for her bright cover suggestions, Linda Starkey Queen and David Queen for great ideas in which English coastal town the story could take place, Michael Cole, Dept. of History and Art, University of Pennsylvania, Philadelphia, for ideas on where to find the fictitious value of Cellini's silver sculpture, to Thierry de Lachaise, Directeur du Département Orfèvrerie, Sotheby's. A big thank you is also due to all those who will participate after the manuscript goes to the printer: marketing friends, reviewers, and purchasers!

I would like to acknowledge and thank Stefany Reich-Silber, Charlie Hopper and Helen Cameron for their intelligent and thoughtful feedback on the 2020 edition. And I want to thank Joe Miller for reading *Cellini's Revenge, Book 1*, in preparation for the editing of *Book 2*.

Next, big thanks to my writers' group, all members along the way (Marilynn Rowland, Joyce Scott, Sarita Berg, Ruth Hanham and Dean Curtis) who have been there scribbling away and listening to my work for 27 years!

Special thanks to Ruth Schwartz for getting this updated edition to the final stages and making it real!

Lastly, I would like to thank all of you out there who listened to me, offered your ideas and took an interest in my novel, in particular to the memory of my mother, Ruth Bartlett, who listened for hours while I read it to her, and to Eileen Milsom, my very great friend, and to many others along the way.

# 1956: Sudden Events

**On the south coast** of England, four miles east of Brighton, stands an old village, long settled into the earth over hundreds of years: the smuggler's village of Rottingdean. Tunnels under the streets are evidence of secret sailing hauls from times long past.

On a November afternoon in 1956 in this coastal village, it seemed like a perfectly ordinary day. Intermittent white clouds lingered southwest before a blue sky, and distant seagulls swarmed over the languishing sea.

Catherine stood in the village greengrocer's queue and glanced up at her house on the hill, the last one at the top of Neale Street. She didn't see David's car coming back down the road to pick her up, but the walk back would do her good.

While she waited for her turn, Catherine looked through the pages of *The Daily Mail,* skipping the bold headlines about the news in Hungary and the Suez Canal, and instead, turning the pages of her newspaper and glancing at her horoscope. November 3, 1956: *"Sudden events will change the course of your life."*

Catherine smiled to herself. Life was so tranquil at the English seaside; nothing unexpected or sudden ever happened there. She didn't believe in horoscopes anyway. She folded the paper and stuffed it into her woven shopping bag. She ordered two large onions, a little flower of broccoli, and a bunch of carrots, complete with the green, wispy stalks, and held her cloth bag open for the greengrocer, who put them in carefully next to the newspaper. She laid two shillings into the palm of his stubby hand.

After the bustle of London, Catherine felt relieved to live in their lovely house by the sea. For her it was a perch where she could observe the slanted rain, the rolling, thunderous clouds, and sometimes, on a walk, the thrashing waves against Brighton's pier; where she could tuck herself into her favorite armchair while witnessing the daily drama of pastel colors churning across the lively sky. She felt calm and serene just now, remembering how David had finally said the night before that he was ready to have a child.

The endless waves in the distance gave a rhythm to Catherine's life. A black cloud lurked at the edge of the horizon. Two seagulls above Catherine banked against the wind and squealed their harsh notes. The cloud crawled across the sky with a blast of wind from nowhere, transforming the whole village from the sparkle of sunshine against the windows into the heaviness of a plunge into darkness. Villagers scurried for shelter as the rain splattered onto their red noses.

Catherine pulled the hood of her duffle coat over her head while cradling one bag of groceries under each arm. She nodded at their local policeman, their "bobby," as he hunkered down with his slight smile and splashed by on his bicycle. She hoisted the bulging shopping bags higher as she began to trudge back up the hill, her American leather loafers shielding her from the gravel and mud. A young boy rattled down past her at top speed on his shiny black broad-wheeled bicycle. A blind man with only one leg hobbled across her path on crutches, saying "Sorry" as he crossed in front of her; but she felt she should have been sorry. Surely he was the one who had fought in the war. A jumble of seagulls ahead of her on the ground scuttled away from the breadcrumbs the blind man had just finished tossing to them.

The war was really over, even if the holes around the bombed build-ings in the East End and Fleet Street were still there. Buildings all around the newspaper offices and local pubs had been burned and collapsed, leaving huge, gaping stories of death and misery. Catherine shuddered when airplanes flew over. Sometimes, even though she had not lived in

England until after the war, it was all she could do not to run and duck under a wall, a tree, a house.

It was not an easy stretch from the shops up the hill to their house. But she couldn't wait for David. Strange, with this sudden downpour, that he wasn't there yet.

Catherine climbed up past the few quiet, neighboring red brick houses with pointed roofs. The wind hummed roughly past her ears, almost like it was lurking behind the hills, ready to whisk itself and the leaning, long grass into a swirl of frenzy. Their neighbors had drawn their curtains, appearing to be gone for the day.

She turned onto the dirt pathway leading across the yard to their front door and was surprised to find that it was ajar. They never locked it, but she felt sure she had closed it firmly. David's old car was parked there in the yard. She nudged the door further open with her elbow, her arms still full, kicking it closed with her foot. It banged hollowly and she stiffened as she noticed a musty, unfamiliar smell in the hallway.

"Hello, dear," she called. He would be home from the usual Saturday London-to-Brighton train, had likely dozed off by the gas fire in the kitchen. She rested the groceries on the long hallway table and unbuttoned her coat. An eerie silence, heavy and dark, greeted her. She stood immobile and cocked her head.

"Hello, dear!" she tried again, a little more forcefully. The grandfather clock ticked, and the ocean hissed like a snake, far in the distance. Their cat, Alexander, brushed her leg, purring. She hung her duffle coat on the coat rack, slung her scarf over it, and picked up the groceries from the table.

"Darling, I'm home."

Catherine walked through the long hallway toward the little kitchen at the back of their house. The kitchen door was also slightly ajar. She knew she'd closed it, to keep the precious heat inside. Maybe David had just gone in and left it open for a moment. She stood awhile, hesitating. She listened. The cat's purring continued. She pushed the door open a little more with her foot.

More heat was escaping into the rest of the house. Catherine pushed the door further and edged in. Just as she was about to set her groceries on the table she saw a fleshy hand, lifeless on the floor.

Catherine's body was pulled down, like gravity gone mad. Her vision was suddenly blurred, her hearing muted, as though she were drowning. Her chest exploded and caved in, a burning, breathless anguish taking over her entire body. David was lying there on his side in a pool of blood.

"David!" The groceries dropped onto the floor from her arms, oranges and tomatoes rolling away like guilty balls of energy. She fell onto her knees and turned him over.

"David!" she cried, brushing the back of her hand across his short, fair hair, which draped along his marble-white forehead and above his frozen eyes. As she drew the back of her hand across the sandpaper stubble on his cheek, she saw the dark red blood that had soaked through his gray tweed jacket. The bloody fingers of his left hand were clenched like iron jaws around the knife protruding from his blood red button-down shirt. Instinctively, she reached over and peeled his fingers from the knife, pulling it from his body and letting it clatter across the floor amongst the scattered groceries.

"David?" she said hoarsely, her tears blurring the reality of the wet, red floor, and the stiffening, cold body before her. Her mouth hung wide as she realized that he would never hear her say his name again.

Catherine's throat was too paralyzed to make another sound. She quietly reached over and touched David's cheek once again, realizing that this rough growth of unshaven beard would be her last physical contact with him. The agony of that moment: the cold, lifeless corpse lying there that was once love, the silence that bounced back from her tears, the baby that would never be conceived, the life that died in her heart as she witnessed the end of every dream she had…all of it crashed in slow motion around her ears, like fog diminishing her brain.

Who could have done this to her husband? Who could hate him so? Who? Her watery eyes surveyed the kitchen for clues, but all was quiet. There were no signs of another human being; just the Cellini manuscript an inch from his other hand on the floor.

Drops of blood splattered her dress, and she looked at her hand, slightly smudged with his blood now. With her other hand she reached for his handkerchief, pulled it out of his jacket pocket and up to her mouth with a long, bitter howl, then pushed it up her cardigan sleeve. She stood up, inched backward, and ran back down the hallway.

Was the corner shop open? The public call box was broken again. The shopkeeper would let her use the phone. She yanked her scarf and duffle coat from the coat rack, which crashed onto the floor, and ran out the door and down the steep old cobblestone road, her shoes clattering on the wet surface. The clouds ferociously emptied their raindrops on her face, where they mixed with her tears. Not feeling the sudden cold, but hardly able to breathe, Catherine rushed to telephone the police. She finally arrived at the shop, her mouth dry, her throat tight, and panting loudly, banged on the door. No one answered. She pounded and yelled, "Hello? Hello? Help me! Please, I need to use your phone!" But the shop was quiet and no one answered her.

Dark clouds blew across the sky, like all the smoke in London's chimneys had gathered to spew their grit and anger right there on Rottingdean. Catherine covered her head with the hood of her duffle coat and leaned breathlessly against the mossy old stone wall. The swift change back into the usual damp November cold penetrated through her coat and into her arms as she stood there paralyzed, like she was supporting the wall.

The handkerchief, with David's initials engraved in blue, fell from her cardigan sleeve onto the bumpy cobbled stones. She saw the handkerchief in a haze. It seemed so far away. The distant ocean rumbled. The wind pushed against her hood. The handkerchief limped toward her in the wind like a drunken man, lifting and collapsing, dragging and inching sideways, but toward her. She ran to it, reached out and put her hand on it like a cat's pouncing paw.

She turned and felt the weight of her shoes, one in front of the other, carrying her away from the shop. She lifted her green wool scarf over her nose and, sticking out her bottom lip, blew her hot breath up to warm her cold nostrils.

The little hut at the bottom of their hill where the local policeman stayed was shut up. The few people out were hurrying home, heads down, hats and hoods up, eyes on the ground. Catherine trembled, not knowing what to do. She shivered with fear and shock, the wet handkerchief still in her hand. She placed it in her coat pocket.

Growing darkness turned the streetlights into shadows of moving monsters. The pub wasn't open yet. The shops had all shut. The bobby, hunched down against the ocean wind, cycled in the distance, thankfully in her direction. Catherine darted toward him, waving, shouting, "Help! Help me!" Tearing her hood from her head, her bun came undone and her long, red hair fell around her wet face.

"Help me! Please help me! My husband's been murdered!"

And as she looked at the bobby's concerned expression, for the second time her whole life caved in, for she and David had never officially married. But of course, the truth would come out and the little gossipy village would now know their secret, which they thought they had left behind in London.

# 1952: The Walk

**Through her upper** window in Kentish Town on a spring day in 1952, Catherine saw that it was a bright blue day. After the smoggy winter, smoke belching hard from the brick chimney pots all along endless rows of houses and from the trains on the tracks across the street, the clear warm day broke with the sounds of birds announcing the birth of spring. With her mother weakening rapidly, Catherine knew it wouldn't be long before they stopped their lifelong pleasure of walking on Parliament Hill Fields. Catherine yawned, stretched, and invited her mother on a walk through the rolling hills of the heath. It was a present to her mother. The war had made other presents too scarce, so Catherine invented free gifts, like she had as a child.

Catherine's mother struggled out of her chair, packed on a warm coat, grabbed her umbrella, and proclaimed, "I'm ready, Catherine. I love walking on the heath!"

Catherine let a soft, sad smile break from her face. She offered her mother her arm and they walked slowly out of the flat and toward the trolley stop on Kentish Town Road. They took the trolley from Kentish Town up to the corner pub across from William Ellis School and Parliament Hill Fields; then walked past the tennis courts and along the winding pedestrian walkway over toward the ponds and the ducks.

Catherine's mother looked up at her, her face beaming with delight; and as she did so she lost her step, twisting her ankle and falling forward onto the path. Catherine looked from her mother on the ground to see a tall young man running toward her mother, gathering her into his arms, inquiring about her ankle, and offering his shoulder. Stunned, Catherine allowed the stranger to help her mother. She felt a flutter of excitement as this man struggled with her limping mother, and there was also a subtle, inexplicable feeling of foreboding, a miniscule flash of a momentary dread.

David accompanied them on the trolley all the way home, helped her mother into the house, and settled her into an armchair. He then went downstairs to the pub next door and telephoned the local doctor in Kentish Town. The doctor arrived shortly afterward and checked her mother's tongue, took her pulse, and began bandaging her ankle.

"Are you Canadian?" David asked Catherine. His eyes were green.

"American; East Coast."

"Could this brave woman be your mother?"

"Yes. She's English, aren't you, Mum?"

"Of course, I'm English. Why else would I put up with this weather?"

They all laughed, including the doctor as he finished wrapping her bandage.

"We moved back to England and into my great aunt's flat here when my father died in the war," Catherine said. "He was American. My father was a soldier: a private in an infantry squad. A sniper killed him."

"I am sorry to hear that. As it happens, my mother's American. She lives in Brattleboro, Vermont," David answered. "My father was English. He died in France in the second wave of the invasion. He was a lieutenant in a tank unit."

"I'm very sorry," Catherine said.

"My husband's family comes from Connecticut, next door to Vermont," her mother said. "Fancy that!"

Both Catherine and David laughed together like shy teenagers.

David gently took his leave, but first he slipped Catherine a piece of paper with his telephone number at work scribbled on it, saying he worked as a journalist on Fleet Street, and to call if she needed any further assistance. Catherine mused that she might never have met such a man walking along in Vermont. In England, everybody walked:

Walking on Hampstead Heath was a friendly, almost communal occupation. Catherine smiled and thought she would hide the paper in the top drawer of her bed table.

It was two weeks before Catherine's mother started to walk again, hobbling mostly to the bathroom and back while Catherine offered her endless cups of tea and stacked piles of newspapers on her table.

Catherine's mother had been an activist in America before and during the war, and she continued to follow the politics of the British Left in England, if only to read about it in the papers.

"Look here, Catherine," said her mother, who was sitting in the rocker in the sitting room. "Isn't this the name of that lovely young fellow that brought me home from the heath? David Evans, it says. Let's see what he's written." She pored over the article about bombs being found in a schoolyard, and the children getting the day off while they were cleared away.

"Why don't we telephone him and tell him we saw his article?" suggested her mother.

Catherine blushed. She hadn't told her mother that she knew his number. She stood still.

"Go on, then," said her mother. "You can't hide it. I saw you take his number."

Catherine turned her back to her mother. She reached into her purse and pulled out the crumpled paper with David's number scratched on it, and went next door to the pub to telephone him.

# David's
# Cellini Manuscript

## Rome: Early in 1527

**Benvenuto Cellini** leapt from his horse, grabbed his sword, and ran after the man who had slashed the rope holding down his precious box of silver cups. Cellini was no coward; a good sword fight was a welcomed distraction from the intensely detailed silver work he had put into those twelve cups. The money he would collect from Cardinal d'Este of Ferrara would buy him many old, fancy swords, and perhaps a mansion. And now a thief had bolted with them.

"En garde!" Cellini yelled, drawing his sword and running closer to the escaping thief with all the power of a man at the height of his strength.

An Italian could not resist the call. The thief put the box down on a rock and drew his sword. But no one could outdo Cellini. The thief surely knew that. Everyone in Rome knew of Cellini's amazing swordsmanship. The thief glanced at the box, then stood with his legs astride, his arms spread, his sword ready, waiting, with Cellini's angry eyes now close enough for the thief to read the fury behind his sword.

For six minutes the swords clanged and crashed as the men grunted and dodged each other. Neither of the men, nor anybody else, seemed to notice the small ragamuffin who swept up the box and ran with it as fast as he could go to a wagon, which had stalled a moment on the way to the wharf. He deftly climbed aboard, and his father whipped the horse like hunger was chasing them.

When the boy and his father arrived at the wharf some time later, Cellini's temporary work hand, Caruso, was perched high above the dock in the crow's nest of the ship, nicknamed *The Warrior*. For the two weeks before the ship's departure, Caruso had watched the apprentices run back and forth carrying whatever their master silversmith, Cellini, had yelled for. They watched him work out of the corners of their eyes as they darted past, probably aching for the chance to design their own, to imitate those hand-size cups, to carve out the bulls and crabs around the outside and an astrological pattern of stars inside; and to make them shine until they glowed against the starlight.

Caruso now watched in astonishment and horror as money was exchanged for the box containing those twelve small silver cups that Caruso himself had proudly bound for Cellini with leather straps before dawn that very morning.

He yelled at them, but from such a height it was clear they did not hear him. The son and father turned away like hares being chased by hounds, and disappeared into the distance at a gallop.

Caruso saw the sailor with the eye patch hand the box over to Captain Rubiano. Caruso knew of Cellini's plans to deliver the cups to the d'Este family. Something had gone wrong, but Caruso, only a lowly seaman, could only frown as he looked in the distance up the long road from Rome that ended at the wharf.

Caruso knew that these unique cups had been put under lock and key every night with the other silver at Cellini's studio. These grand silver cups, sharper in the light of day than polished diamonds, sculpted with the large, artistic hands of his master, far surpassed those of any living silversmith. No matter how an apprentice might yearn to make even one like them, he never would. A master silversmith like Cellini had not been known throughout the world, though a million silver crosses with Jesus hanging from them had been made; though silver platters for kings had been ordered and gifted.

Temperamental Cellini had dared his art beyond his own imaginings; had pushed his art to the limits; had loved and cherished each small cup as it if were his offspring.

*The Warrior* was leaving at that moment. Ropes were disengaged from the wharf, and a few people waved amidst their daily trudge back and forth with heavy bags and boxes just unloaded from the Italian ship.

Two weeks later, out in the Atlantic, the listing ship hiccupped, promising to hang there a few hours longer and not go down. Three passengers and the underfed crew crowded into the few inadequate, wooden lifeboats. Braver crew members clung to the sides of the sinking ship, and some crept back onto the slippery deck while Captain Rubiano stood high in the air on the turned-up stern yelling instructions.

"Whoever brings up the box of silver cups shall be rewarded with half of them!"

That was enough to make Caruso climb back aboard the sinking ship. He figured he might die anyway, and if he saved the cups and lived, he would be able to leave the sea and begin a farm. His children and wife would see him more than every six months.

He put his foot against the railing sticking up from the water, falling onto it as the ship surged. His arms encircled the railing, the waves beating against the fallen monster. It appeared to roar as more contents inside shifted and slid downward into the jaws of the sea. Caruso hesitated. Maybe his life at sea was worth more than this risk? He could still just about grab onto the last lifeboat near the ship.

And what if the box of silver cups was under the water already? Caruso looked up. It was near the middle of the ship, close to the Captain's quarters, maybe in the safe, and still above water. As he lifted his foot from the railing and onto the moody deck, a splash against it shoved the last lifeboat away.

Caruso felt nauseous. This slanted world was making his eyes hurt, his head thump. He had never experienced anything like this in his whole sailing life. He held fast to the railing as *The Warrior* surged in protest against the angry sea. Would the vessel now shift and begin its descent? Caruso held fast, hearing the Captain's voice. Then he heard the splash.

"Help!" yelled the man Caruso hated and served, paddling below, thrashing, and going under. Caruso could hardly swim. There was no chance of him going into the cold water to save the man. The lump in his throat came in spite of his hatred.

Caruso held his hand out in a feeble, helpless wave, between a salute and a frozen statue's eternal goodbye. Caruso grasped the ship's rail again, with the saluting hand, and gulped in the cold, salty air as the bubbles boiled and the sea crashed against the ship.

The railing was slippery and treacherous. The water was lapping at Caruso's bare feet. The ship sank a little more. Could he get inside and capture the silver cups before it went down?

Where would he put the box, now that his lifeboat was gone? Maybe another lifeboat would appear from the other side of the ship. He pulled himself up and along the railing toward a door across the deck. He had worked on this boat before and felt sure he knew where the captain kept the keys to the safe. He climbed, hand-over-hand, toward the door. The boat lurched, and he slid back down to the water. He righted himself against the slanting exterior wall and groaned; then he swam the few yards toward the door.

The boat plunged and lifted with the fierce waves. Caruso reached out but missed the door and slid back. Panting, he reached out again, using the force of the boat's gravity to heave himself toward the door. His fingers finally latched onto the wooden handle, and he grasped it hard as the boat lunged downward.

# 1952: THE DRIVE

**Catherine and David** drove through green orchards of apple trees in Southern England. As they bumped along in David's colleague's Morris Minor, David delicately slid his rough hand around her shoulders, and Catherine felt a tingle. Her eyes shifted downward at the Cellini manuscript that he'd been writing, laying on the seat between them. He pulled over to the side of the road and parked. She had only been kissed by a few young men, but just now, she gazed at his lower lip, his eyes smiling kindly at her own lower lip, and she moved an inch closer to him. He leaned a few inches closer to her.

Catherine closed her eyes. She waited so long that her neck felt a twinge. She felt his warm breath on her nose, and she waited. He jostled himself, and the automobile creaked. The warm breath left her face, and the brisk spring air returned. She waited. This was astonishing. The other young men she had gone to the cinema with had been quick, with hardly a moment for her to breathe. His breath came back, and a delicate smell of morning coffee entered the space in front of her lips.

The warmth hovered longer this time. Catherine waited with her eyes closed. The warmth stayed. At last, his full lips pressed gently against her slightly parted mouth, and his grip around her shoulder was joined with a hand on her opposite shoulder, pulling her gently toward him. It was only a quiet, soft kiss, but then the breath came hotter again. This time his lips finally opened to meet hers exactly. Catherine's heart was beating so hard she thought he might hear it. She brought her arms up, placing her hands on his shoulders, on his green wool sweater, and melting toward him. She felt his heart beating against her right breast. A swirling feeling entered her head as she moved away, eyes still closed, to catch a gulp of air.

He said something to her very softly. It was that hot breath, but now it was all over her left ear. What was that? I love you? Could that be what David was saying to her? She moved away from him and looked at his profile.

David started the engine. The car jolted forward and cut the silence of newness and freshness and embarrassment. Catherine turned back and looked straight ahead, with an ironic smile. His arm brushed hers as he leaned forward, his eyes fast on the road.

David's grandfather's old farmhouse came into view. They stopped some distance from the wide front porch steps. He jumped out, walked around the car, and offered his hand to Catherine, who felt like a princess.

"My grandfather sold this farm just before the war. I still come here to remember him and our childhood adventures here," David said, his Cellini manuscript slipping onto the car's floor.

# 1985: The Basket

**The summer** in Vermont was beautiful and warm; sometimes very hot. Catherine, her hair white with a tinge of red showing underneath, prepared breakfast in her small kitchen. First she had a drink of cold milk, then she poured the last half of the glass into her cold, crisp cereal. She added finely chopped, mixed nuts and a few raisins and then walked back to her rocking chair and sat down.

In her youngest years in Connecticut, before she and her mother had to return to England, Catherine had spent hours at night face up, nose damp, eyes blinking, catching a shooting star through her small telescope, studying where the constellations were, even what star was covered by a cloud. She had read books in the library as a teenager and thought she might love to study astronomy.

David had taught Catherine about antiques, and she had taught him what she knew of astronomy. David had also tried to teach Catherine about astrology, as his mother had taught him, but Catherine only laughed and said that it was all unscientific, mystical, and superstitious. But she still stole that quick, guilty glance at the horoscope page, especially on a day that held promise or even foreboding.

She always watched David as he pored over the astrology section of the paper, as if he were memorizing life's instructions for the day. That was a part of David's and his mother's life that Catherine was amused by, and which she found she tolerated quite happily. Surely no harm could come from it, and Catherine hadn't protested much since she realized it was hopeless anyway. For her, it had felt like David was avoiding the burden of his daily decisions, using the horoscopes as a guide, which had allowed him to not have to plan his day. Sometimes, when she wondered what David was doing on a certain day, she checked the horoscopes in the paper and wondered if his day was coming together as the horoscope suggested. Catherine could pretty accurately predict his day before he came home to tell her all about it.

Catherine rocked lightly in her chair. She looked at the basket of David's old papers on the table, her gaze lingering a little longer than usual. It wasn't too hot this mid-summer day, just pleasantly warm and muggy, and maybe fine for a short walk.

Catherine pulled the basket toward her and put it on her lap. As she sat there looking at the basket of letters and manuscripts that some anonymous person had kindly sent to her in Vermont six months after she'd been let out of prison, she remembered how she had hated the Second World War. Those were terrible times in England: So many of her mother's friends had died in World War II; so many people everywhere. Catherine opened the basket, her hands sifted through the fading papers in it.

Catherine's memories were interrupted by a chorus of cheers from outside her Vermont window, echoing in waves back through the screen door into Catherine's ears.

Catherine sat back in her soft armchair. The television flickered. The murder mystery was on again. She sat forward as she watched the television for a few minutes. Too bad they had not had DNA thirty-five years ago. David might be sitting right beside her now. No, he would still be dead, but they would have found the killer with that new science, and she would never have gone to jail. She stared at the television. The murderer's hair was found on the victim's clothing. His own DNA in it had trapped him.

When she looked away from the television and over at the newspaper on the table next to her she read the headline:

**DNA Clears Man Accused of Rape**
**Freedom After Fifteen Years in Prison**

Freedom: She felt like she was still in jail even with all her physical freedom. The world believed she was a murderer when she was not, and could never have done that miserable deed. She imagined the headlines:

## CATHERINE EVANS' NAME CLEARED
### First Woman Not Hanged for Murder in England
### Wrongfully Accused of Husband's Murder

Catherine stared down at the piles of cut-out newspaper articles. How many times had she turned them over in her hands and wondered how those reporters had found out all those so-called facts? *Lies*, she called them.

A kind of time lapse set in as she sat holding the basket while the television chattered on. That heart inside her chest was hammering a little too much at this particular moment. Bad nutrition for twelve years had aged her, turned her hair white, made her teeth come loose, and lined her face before it might have otherwise in a woman only sixty-five years old.

Catherine stopped looking through the papers and looked for a long while at the painting opposite her, to the left of the curtains, and remembered how she and David had purchased it the same day they bought the house in the southern English seaside town of Rottingdean. At the time, it didn't appear to be anything more than a pleasant seaside town on a warm, English summer afternoon. Now the painting seemed to be another messenger, like the television program and the newspaper, nudging her to return to England to answer the questions that still lodged in her gut like a sleeping dragon.

Catherine looked down again at the basket and fingered through the papers until she got to the last one. As she peered at his typing on the old, crumpled paper, she saw a paper that had been sticking to its side. She sat straight up. How had she never noticed it before? She had always been in such a hurry and had never managed to reach the bottom. Something more urgent always interrupted her. Now she had time.

She read it slowly. Her mouth dropped open. There was the missing link, the answer she had searched for more than thirty years; right in her basket. *"Under the deck are buried six silver cups. This treasure is real."* A tidy little map was crudely drawn under his notation of exactly where the silver cups from her faded dreams were—in the cold earth under the small deck of their seaside house.

But the house was in England, and that meant a flight above those dark, emerging clouds. She wondered if she could gather the nerve to return to England to find those silver cups. She turned the map over in her hands. There was nothing on the back. She turned it again to look at the map. There it was: the place where the silver cups apparently had been buried.

Catherine held the paper under the light and chuckled cynically to herself. Her husband always fancied himself a fiction writer, not just a journalist.

She crackled the map in her fingers. An idea was forming in her mind, surfacing after a long lull, years of trying to forget it all. Hadn't David been writing something about Benvenuto Cellini and some silver cups? It was just a novel. It was his way of relaxing, he had said. Journalism was their precious bread, meat, butter, and milk.

"Oh, how insane: to kill a kind man for a bunch of silver cups," she mumbled. "Who did he tell about them? He didn't ever tell me. Oh, there I go again, talking to myself." She turned the map over and began again. "Maybe the killer's DNA is on the silver cups. Surely David's DNA is on the cups." She wondered if she had enough life left in her to get out of her chair, take an airplane to England, and find David's killer.

She slumped back in her chair and sat in silence for a while, then closed the basket harshly. "No! I'm not going," she mumbled. "I'm getting too fragile for this nonsense!"

Catherine stretched one leg and then the other. Her physical therapist was coming in an hour, for the last time. She was getting much stronger. She sighed and then took a huge breath, clenched her hands into fists. She stood up, put the basket down on the side table, walked over to the television and switched it off.

As Catherine raised one arm up and put it down, she heard all kinds of creaking. She put the other arm up, then down. It was even noisier. Her head twisted slowly back and forth, and she heard some awful crunching. Everything worked. She simply needed a little more physical therapy. Her new hip had healed well from her fall and operation, and it didn't hurt at all when she walked. Just in that one hip, she felt seventeen again when her weight rested on it.

Later on that evening, after her physical therapist had left, Catherine walked over to the window and stared out at the blustery trees and the streetlights twinkling through a slight Vermont summer rain. As she watched the rain, she thought of her mother, those last few letters she had sent to Catherine in jail; the fragile handwriting announcing quietly with each letter that her mother would not be her support much longer. The letters, in the end, were dictated by Mr. Bernie Ward, according to a little note at the bottom, and at the end was her mother's signature: so faint, so labored as to shout at Catherine: This is the end.

Catherine pulled the curtains closed, went to her bedroom, climbed into her warm bed, and closed her eyes. Her body sank down into a deep relaxation and sleep that brought dreams that sorted out her past, her future.

Up to now there had been no reason to go back to England. There was nowhere to stay. There was nobody to visit; just graveyards and graves. In spite of this, the thought of finding the murderer and the silver cups grabbed hold of her again, like it had when she had first returned to Vermont. The idea of going back to London took shape through the night. Catherine picked up the phone the next morning, lifted the receiver, and dialed the airline.

"Hello? Reservations, please." She booked a seat for August 14, hung up and mumbled to herself. "What shall I wear? I believe it could be quite warm in August." She laid her palm against her chest and vaguely noticed her labored breathing.

"I must do this soon, while I still have my health," she mumbled to herself. If she found David's murderer, she didn't quite know what she would do with him, but she was now determined to find him, if she could. If the silver cups could be found, and if they were valuable, they might lure the murderer to her, and she could catch him and clear her name before she died.

Catherine walked over to the window in the living room, toward the light. She cautiously pulled back the heavy green drapes she'd had sent over from England. There was some sort of birthday party next door;

young children laughing and chattering in their pink paper hats, cake smeared on their cheeks, mothers wiping it off.

The corners of the living room swirled and faded as she felt her suppressed anger growing again at the murderer who had put her in prison–that anger that remained just under the surface and sustained her now, as she willed herself to stay alive. She could hardly breathe. Blackness slowly enveloped her brain; she felt confused and slid like a waterfall down to the floor.

# THE TURTLE

**Caruso held** his sore arm. He lay in the wooden boat, too exhausted to toss the dead man overboard. He peeked at the body, now white; its swollen feet stiff and pale. Caruso's longing for fresh water was as strong as his need for companionship; now he had neither.

He put his bare, brown toes on the box of silver and laughed hoarsely. The ocean would carry him somewhere. Fearing he would die of thirst, he held back his tears, to preserve the water left in his body. His lips were peeling and bloody now as the sun pierced his bare head and shoulders. His sunburned knees stung at the touch.

The corpse was stinking after half a day. It was time to part with its company, such as it was. Caruso's loneliness had seemed tolerable with this kind man in the boat; even when he was dead. Caruso inched toward the body, and as he lifted the shoulders, the head fell backward; he heaved the body up and pushed it over. Within seconds the school of sharks that had been circling the boat all day began fighting, tearing the body apart, turning the water around the boat red. Then the silent, black fins went back to a quiet circling of the boat.

Caruso lay face down. His throat was so dry he desperately wanted to drink from the ocean. It was calm now. The sharks circled again and again around the leaking, wooden boat for another hour then disappeared.

23

Caruso's ears picked up a tapping sound, and he looked over the edge of the boat. His eyes were only a foot away from a small sea turtle. The greenish-gray creature blinked at Caruso and hovered nearby, floating. Caruso could hear the turtle nibbling against the other side of the boat. Perhaps small seaweed growths or barnacles were the attraction; whatever it was gave Caruso the extra seconds he needed to hatch a plan.

After the turtle's next peck on the boat, he flung his arms over, hardly noticing the stabbing pain this motion caused, and grabbed the turtle's head, holding on with the grip of a man who knows this is life or death. The turtle flapped his powerful flipper feet, pulling backward, pulling Caruso almost into the sea. Caruso wrapped his feet around the bench and held the turtle's head until he almost fainted from the pain in his arm. With one last, huge breath, he fiercely yanked and twisted the turtle's head, breaking its neck. The paddling waned to nothing and the turtle hung in the sea, but Caruso couldn't wait until he could tolerate his own pain enough to pull it up; the sharks would smell death. Caruso groaned as he pulled the dead turtle into the boat and then he collapsed, cracking a triumphant smile.

Thinking of the juicy eyeball he was about to devour, he dragged the turtle up toward his chest. His parched mouth almost watered. He found himself wondering where the boat was drifting as he scraped out the turtle's innards and laid them in strips to bake in the sun. Caruso used the laborious oar, one unmanageable paddle, to push and pull the drying flesh, then scrape off what remained until he had a turtle shell bowl with openings where the limbs used to be, which, if only it would rain, might save his life.

One of the turtle's eyeballs lay melting and disintegrating on Caruso's tongue, like liquid gold, saving him for another day.

Caruso scanned the horizon, hoping for storm clouds. The storm had already long passed; the sky was clear blue, the ocean glassy.

The quiet existence he now shared with the ocean made him dream of his noisy son and bedraggled wife. He was glad they were on safe ground and not with him as he watched the shark's fins arrive, circle, and depart. Were the sharks waiting for him to die? Had they already eaten his fellow sailors, miles beyond the horizon, and then swum to him for their final tasty dish? Didn't they know he had an eyeball in his throat and an upside-down turtle shell for the rain that must come? Their silence frightened him; what if he accidentally left his arm dangling over the side of the boat?

Then the silence was broken with a loud, banging crash against the boat which lurched up and splashed down, almost tossing him over the side. He grasped the edge with both hands as another thump from underneath knocked the boat from the stern, then the sides, then all sides and the bow. His waning strength could hardly contain the sudden necessity of gripping onto the boat. He peered over the edge into the bubbles left by the boat crashing against the water and saw a mass of huge fish that looked like the Dorados he had spotted before, from the deck of the ship. Now they punched his fragile home again and again until he felt sick.

There was nothing much in his stomach, and his arms were sore from holding down the turtle shell and the box with the silver cups, and from anchoring his body to the boat. The shark fins were back and circling. There were splashes and bubbles constantly around his boat, like they were fighting for the first bite of Caruso the moment he succumbed. He took a strip of raw turtle meat and tried to chew it to gain strength. He bit his tongue as the boat lurched up and banged down against the water. Surely these creatures had more staying power as a unit than he did as a starving, thirsty man. "Andate via, voi bastardi!" he cried.

The last time they knocked the boat upward, his glance hit on the horizon and he saw the dark clouds coming up from nowhere, increasing at a fast pace. The white caps were forming in the distance and moving rapidly in his direction. He turned the turtle shell upside-down.

As the whitecaps reached him, the boat began to rise and fall with the increasing height of the new waves. The fins sank below. The pounding stopped after one last, unexpected thump.

The wind howled like a screaming bird. Caruso knew this horrible storm would save him for a while more. He popped the turtle's other eye into his mouth and let it squish its sweet taste over his cracked tongue as he chuckled hoarsely.

Caruso held the turtle shell between his knees for three hours, grasping the sides of the tiny boat as the waves thrashed it up and down and swirled it around in circles. Caruso could only hang his mouth wide and laugh as the rain pelted onto his tongue and his parched throat opened and moved with this life-giving force from the sky.

Then the rain stopped; the ocean became smooth again, and the sun beat down on Caruso's neck. His legs covered the box while the turtle shell rested on top.

Caruso began to study the stars as the boat moved where it wanted. Each night a pattern emerged, and he seemed to be drifting in a constant direction with a group of stars to the left and another distinct group to the right. Caruso had not one notion of astronomy, yet he had the long, cool nights to study the stars and notice where they were in the darkness of the ocean. The days and nights informed his senses, but he felt weaker and weaker after he had devoured every morsel of the turtle. He hated the moment he licked the very last drop of water from the armpit of the turtle's shell.

By day he scanned the horizon for a precious cloud; by night he stopped fighting the rays of the sun. He had tried to catch fish. He had pushed himself to live. He had prayed for help. But after four more days, his limbs had lost their feeling. He lay prostrate, still covering the box and the turtle shell, but wholly unable to move and hardly able to breathe. At the end of a day that burned him to a dark red, Caruso thought once more of his family: his dear, patient wife, and his little son, and then his mind fell into a white daze.

The little boat rocked in the wide ocean and drifted for another two hours before the English ship's captain spotted it. A small boat was let down into the sea, and two sailors attached a rope to Caruso's boat and drew it to their ship.

# 1956: Prison

**As the living room** came back into focus and the voices outside reached her brain, Catherine realized she had just experienced another minor stoke symptom like the one she'd had at the beginning of winter. Foggy imaginings blended into her mind, and memories of the first months in prison began to swarm around her like it was yesterday. All that constant humiliation flooded back to her.

Just before Christmas, about a month into her prison term, the most sadistic guard had peered down her nose at Catherine, who had just finished pulling on her stale-smelling socks and cramped shoes.

"Remove your shoes," the guard bellowed.

Catherine's blue toenail raged purple from the last time Mary had trampled on her foot. No thunderous apology could have stopped the tears under Catherine's eyes.

Catherine had a hole in her sock: small, hardly noticeable, but that same stern guard grinned with her slanted mouth and yelled, "Take off your sock!" All heads along the line-up simultaneously shot toward Catherine like a machine had twisted them.

"What are you lot gawking at?" yelled the guard. "Eyes front!" All the women adjusted their faces forward.

"Wot's this, then?" The guard held out the sock for all to see. "Slovenly! We won't have that here, will we, missy?" The guard's face drew into an evil smile.

"No, ma'am," Catherine said, her toe bleeding. Her bare foot pushed into the cold stone floor. Her body shook no matter how hard she tried to solidify with the floor.

"Not only a hole, but a bloody toe!"

"Yes, ma'am," Catherine said, eyes front, staring past the large face, feeling the guard's hot, smelly breath, worse than a dirty sock, inside her nostrils.

The guard stood back and peered closely at the hole for the longest minute, then roughly tossed the sock back toward Catherine's stomach. Catherine caught it, and crushed it into her fist by her side.

"Twenty press-ups!" the guard sneered. "Now!"

Catherine stepped out in front of the line of women. She could hear the muffled twittering as she quickly lowered herself to the cold, stone floor and pushed her thin body up and down, her nose touching the floor, as required; the last five pushes upward burning her lungs to coal, tearing her arms to shreds. She got up, stony-faced, her heart pounding against her chest, and walked back to her place in the line, scooping up her sock from the floor.

"Clean that blood!" the guard yelled. "Now!"

Catherine ran to the sink and back, and scrubbed the spot of blood with a brush and an ice-cold rag until the floor was clean.

"Don't waste our time again. Get that hole mended by the next roll call or it's double press-ups."

"Yes, ma'am," Catherine choked, and ran back to the sink and scrubbed out the bloody rag.

"Back to your work, you layabouts!" yelled the guard, her squinting eyes tracking the line of women.

Catherine put her sock back on and glared for an instant at Mary.

That first month in prison was torture for Catherine: the way someone stared at someone else, the shift of their stance, a shoulder against the wall, all this meant something the others knew. She stifled the screams that beat in her head against the routine, the lining up, looking smart, putting on a show. Within the first week she had learned all of the survivor skills, had bared her teeth, shown her muscles, spat back. No one she ever knew would have recognized her. She checked the pimply faces of the women scrubbing laundry near her as she ironed. They kept their eyes firmly on their work. A flicker to check one's safety was all that was tolerated. Everyone shifted their eyes at the smallest squeak of a shoe nearby, at a loud yawn (which, too, had meaning), at a cynical laugh from around the corner, at the echo of the guard's footsteps looming nearer.

There were women with brown, bucked teeth, and with missing front teeth. Women with scars across their cheeks used their appearance to back their harsh voices, a threat of violence not far behind. How many times had Catherine given most of her disgusting-tasting peas and mashed potatoes to an Irish woman with her knuckle in Catherine's ribs? These bitter creatures seemed to have been born with bulging eyes, wild hair, and broken fingernails.

Some women tore the uniforms of their so-called friends, then collected regularly for the sewing they did, charging double for work at night. Catherine could still smell the women's old pads, used too long, blood dried and wet again. Some months she could have sworn every woman in the jail was bleeding on the same days, even the guards. Within a few days, Catherine had become a listless robot, following orders, suppressing memories of her former hopeful life, which had promised a kind of normalcy after the war that would never be hers again. Smiling was something she used to do. Now her face was frozen into obedience in a land with no hope, except the faintest ray of light so far into the future that it was better not to think about it at all.

What crimes had these women committed to end up there? Everybody knew; they whispered to each other, but no one ever dared ask. Some were crazy and repeated their stories to the walls. Catherine knew every word by heart. She never told her story to them. It had been all over the newspapers the day she went in. She knew they whispered about her. It was only known that she was a liar and a heartless killer. Very few women were in Holloway Prison for killing. Catherine had learned the art of listening. She learned not to react, no matter how they poked her and tried to pry out the "truth." But mostly, she learned the power she had over them, thinking she was a murderer, so for a long time she let them think it.

They had danced in jail sometimes, but Catherine had held back in the shadows. She would watch the other young women swing each other around, and maybe she would smile just to see them smiling for once, but when anybody asked her to waltz, she pleaded a stomachache. Dancing would only have reminded her of David's firm arm around her waist, his mouth upon her neck, his body pressed close to hers.

Catherine would gaze at the stars from her window of bars. Stars kept her company; they were her constant friends. They were harmless and predictable. She measured how long they stayed at the edge of her window and how long it took them to cross its opening from one bar to the next, and then move behind her prison wall. She imagined the ones she couldn't see. She watched these stars for twelve years, on the nights when the clouds had moved across the sky and left the sky dark enough to see them. They were company. They were a tangible past she could cling to and greet in the silent, endless hours while she waited for the day of her release.

The only thing she could never figure out all those years was why those men, probably detectives, had come to the prison and had asked her something about "silver cups."

Catherine lay on the floor and stared at the ceiling of her Vermont house. It seemed dusty just along the edge, with the sunlight pushing through the curtains. She inhaled quickly and realized that there was only one thing to do now: find the real murderer and get him imprisoned.

Before she sat up from the floor, she laid her hand against her chest. Her heart seemed to be beating normally again. She reached for her glasses, which had fallen off near her, and wiped her tired eyes. Putting both of her hands on the floor, she sat up like a sloth. She stood up and staggered over to the couch, trying to remember exactly what had just happened, then sat down with determination, pressing the muscles around her jaw.

Catherine lay down on the couch and imagined the silver cups: small, shiny, beautifully engraved, ancient, made by loving hands and eyes, beckoning her to hold them with tender hands, treasured with the same fervor as their sculptor must have felt.

Catherine sat up, quite alert now, and resolutely willed herself to go back to England one more time and find the silver cups and David's murderer.

# THE BATTLE

**All of a sudden** there was the sound of shoes trampling across the decks of the English ship that had saved Caruso. People were running and shouting. In the distance a ship of mighty proportions pointed menacingly in their direction. Caruso could see this new ship getting larger. How swift it leaned toward them, speeding with dozens of sails, billowing full-strength, the zigzag of the tacks changing direction every ten minutes, a full crew obviously at attentive command, bearing all weights with determination and perhaps the threat of a whip. Caruso swigged a drink from the water pouch around his waist and felt his lost strength flow back into his lean body. He leapt up and dashed to the bow, then back to the helm. It wasn't his Italian words that the crew heard, but the huge bellowing voice that alerted all hands on deck to face the threat and cock their ears for the English Captain's orders.

"All hands on deck. All hands on deck," yelled a red-faced man behind the captain. Before the next order was called out, the crew had climbed the masts and held the lines at the ready.

"Hard-a-lee!" yelled the Captain. His words were echoed by the crew all around the ship.

The men yelled at one another; the sails flapped with a huge roar; the wind grabbed the noisy sails from the other side; all the sails filled out together at once, as if they, themselves, were obeying the Captain's command; and the ship changed course. The captain must have known such a large ship could outrun his own. But a greater distance would give him time to assemble his crew and get ready for the inevitable battle. He could see it was a Spanish ship, the kind he'd heard about that ruled the seas now.

Caruso stood ready on deck at the Captain's side. Neither spoke the other's language. It was all said with the facial expressions: the raised eyebrows; the large, round eyes; the jaw protruding; the brows knitting. The Captain made a shape with his hands–the shape of a rectangle– then pointed his finger inside the cabin toward the Captain's quarters, and yelled, "Box!" Caruso knew what he must do. He saluted and ran across the wooden deck, into the ship and past the men scattering through it, hurrying to get ready to die.

As Caruso made his way to the Captain's cabin, nobody seemed to notice him. His eyes scanned the room for an obvious hiding place; he checked the vaults, under the bunk, under the desk; inside the buckets. He tried to read the Captain's mind; why was the box here, why wasn't it in the vault with the gold? He opened all the drawers; he looked behind some chests. He broke the lock on the big chest and riffled through the clothes on the surface. There it was, intact: unopened, with a tool next to it, probably at the ready for the moment the Captain might find some privacy to inspect his treasure.

Caruso grabbed the box, then wrapped it in a dark piece of clothing and tucked it under his arm. He left the quiet cabin and entered the noise of impending battle.

The Spanish ship was bearing down upon them. Once again, the Captain's hoarse voice roared to change tack and the ship hesitated; shook; then keeled to the other side so hard that Caruso could hardly move, with only one hand to hold the rails. He struggled past the crew toward the Captain. The Captain pointed to a boat containing two crew members who were at the ready to lower it into the sea. Caruso didn't know if he was supposed to give them the box or get in himself. He leapt from the ship into the small wooden boat wearing only his baggy pants and coarse red shirt. His feet were bare and hardened. He watched the Captain signal for them to lower the boat. The Captain gestured to Caruso and smiled in a resigned manner.

The boat was lowered with the three men in it, pushing it back from the side of the galleon. It swung several times, then hit the water. He kicked the box under his seat and grabbed the oars, wondering why the captain let three men get off the ship just before the battle. It seemed there might be a high probability that the Captain might want to be rescued, and the three men could then have pulled him into their little boat once the ship went down.

Caruso looked over at one man, whose black eyepatch had slipped upward over his forehead and whose vacant eye socket fell back with its thin eyelid. The other man's shoulders were hunched and brown. With only his britches on and his shirt tied around his waist, he managed to keep his wool knit cap on his hairless head. His dark eyes with those deep wrinkles surrounded by thick brown skin must have seen many an ocean. Each man studied the other. Their lives now depended on one another. Who would succumb? Who would prevail? Caruso shouted something in Italian, and the others got to work with their oars.

The noise of pre-battle still echoed in Caruso's ears, but grew fainter rapidly as the wind blew the sounds the other direction, across the ocean.

Caruso could see both ships now on a collision course. He looked at his companions.

"It'll be the end of them all," said one man.

"Be the end of us out here in this empty ocean," said his mate.

Caruso smiled only with one side of his face. He didn't need to translate, even if he could. He knew exactly what was about to happen.

The cannons began to boom and fly back and forth between the two ships. The ships heeled to opposite directions, trying to avoid a crash but getting close enough to shoot the fatal blow. Caruso could see the hole that a cannon had made in their ship, low down near the water. If they tacked again, the water would rush into it. Did the Captain know where it was? He must know they were hit. He wasn't tacking, but the Spanish ship was and bore down onto it, pulling alongside. Men were jumping across from one ship to the other, bearing knives, shooting guns. Other cannons struck their ship, and the water rushed in; the crew jumped, not into the Spanish ship, but into the ocean.

# 1985: To London

**The taxi** Catherine had ordered was just on time. The driver carried her old, blue, heavily-stitched leather suitcase into the car and then came back and offered her his arm. Catherine was annoyed at her left hip and lower back for being uncooperative, but her new gold-topped antique-caned umbrella was an ally; she set her jaw, and quite adequately made it out to the taxi.

After settling into her seat on the plane she smiled at the well-dressed gentleman next to her. He must be British, she thought. He hardly smiled back, just peered more closely at *The London Times*. Her head soon nodded forward, and the next thing she heard was the announcement that their plane was landing shortly.

The flight attendant helped her with her bag. Catherine stepped out of the plane door directly to her waiting wheelchair and another attendant who said, "Welcome to London. It's a lovely day." The English, she remembered, were all about the weather. As it changed every hour, it was always the latest and most topical news, and you hardly needed the radio for the weather report. It was a cozy, mutually shared misery. But today it was lovely. That meant it hadn't rained for an hour and the clouds had parted for a spot of sunshine. The weather in England was relished, one moment at a time. Catherine peeked through the window at the beginning of the ramp before the attendant pushed her wheelchair up. Indeed, the day was perfect.

The wheelchair—which she had requested, just in case—was rolling permission to glide past lines of tired travelers, pulling and pushing their suitcases. People of all colors and sizes dashed in and out of her focus. Neon signs flew past her: Information, Midland Bank, and Money Exchange. At every turn, at the luggage area and on the way out, finding a taxi driver, people seemed happy to help her.

Catherine's hotel was called the Churchill Bed and Breakfast. It was just across the street from Hyde Park. It was a little past noon when she arrived. A middle-aged, chubby man in a cap opened her taxi door for her.

"Thank you, young man," she said. As soon as the luggage was de-livered and she had tipped the man and was shown to her room, she climbed into bed and pulled herself under the soft covers of the flowery bedspread, felt the cotton sheets against her skin. Her conscious mind went blank as she dreamed of clouds. It was teatime when she awoke.

The sky was now gray. After a brief tea and scone at the hotel, Cath-erine ventured out the front door and hailed a taxi. She climbed in and went on a brief ride along the wide street to the corner past the Marble Arch underground station, and started down Oxford Street, where she told the driver to drop her off. From there, she could wander in and out of many different kinds of clothing shops. Mostly, as she walked along, she saw her new walking shoes and the tip of her umbrella on the cracked, uneven pavement. She finally stood by a bus stop and waited for a double-decker bus. She was determined to take one last ride in these buses right along Oxford Street, and take taxis for the rest of her stay.

Catherine stood like a flimsy feather blown by the energy of youthful young women who swept by in smart, colorful clothes, high-heeled shoes; a cigarette in one hand. She struggled into a doorway and watched the hoards pass up and down Oxford Street. Red double-decker buses lined the street. The tall black cabs looked petite as they squeezed in between the buses.

She looked over at the nearby bus stop sign. It seemed there were at least ten stopping schedules on the post. One would be hers, but it was daunting to imagine how she was going to push through the throngs of people just to get close enough to the signs to see which bus went where. The empty taxis looked inviting and easy. No: She would ride the bus one more time. A brief gap opened through the crowd. She hitched up her shoulder bag, tapped her umbrella loudly, and pushed her body across the rapidly closing space to the bus shelter, which was crammed with people holding shopping bags.

The bus arrived. She waited until a number of people pushed ahead of her, then held the rail at the bus door entrance and pulled herself up the step to face the driver, who looked at her impatiently; and as she did, she felt a hand gently touching her elbow and adding just enough energy to get her up. The British were in a hurry, but they still had a reverence for older people, which Catherine found shocking and wonderful. She glanced briefly at the gentleman behind her and thanked him. Then she started to fidget with her coins, finally holding out her palm and letting the driver pick out the correct amount. He handed her a ticket.

Sitting down in the seat reserved for the handicapped and the elderly, Catherine decided she deserved this seat. She was sure it would be her last bus ride.

She only noticed the kind gentleman's shoes as he walked past her. They seemed familiar to her, reminding her vaguely of shoes men wore in the fifties in England: black, laced, with tiny fake holes on the sides; "brogues," weren't they called? She settled into her seat.

This bustling London brought back old memories of David, and her throat pinched, her eyes went watery. How could it be that she was having this deep memory in front of these strangers, who probably just saw a lady in her fifties with bleary eyes? A woman across the aisle, not much older than Catherine, smiled at her like she knew. That woman, too, knew a lot. She knew about memories that never faded, wouldn't die, couldn't be left behind.

After only a few blocks in the very slow bus along Oxford Street, Catherine decided she might as well walk a bit. She held on to the seats and the handrail by the door and climbed down slowly to protect her new hip. She could hear the fuming of the passengers trying to get on, having to wait it out. There were people pushing behind her, desperate to get off, but she dared not look back.

"Sorry," she said, finally stepping onto the sidewalk and stopping to take a breath. She hailed a taxi back to the hotel.

As she got into her taxi she glanced at the one that pulled up right behind hers. Wasn't that the man with those black shoes getting into a taxi just behind her? Probably not: These English men all seemed to look alike anyway. She tapped the taxi's barrier window.

"The Churchill Bed and Breakfast, please."

# CATHERINE'S HELPER

**Apart from** the meals she might eat at her hotel, inexpensive cafés would have to do for Catherine. She'd been to quite a few in her youth. The casual roughness was almost comforting: tea, fish and chips–basics to get her by, especially on a cold day. In the evening, the local pub was warm and cozy and had a "loo." The hotel was going to have to do for a few more nights, then she'd find something to rent by the week.

The second night she wandered over to a nearby pub called The Duke of Kendall for some steak and kidney pie. There was a piano player quietly playing old songs across the room. They said they were all out of steak and kidney pie, so she made do with a cold pork pie full of bits of fat. In fact, she was so hungry she ate two pork pies, along with a glass of water. She sat at the bar and checked her face in the mirror. Her hair was such a mess. Every time she had rounded the corner of a building the wind had seemed to grab her hair and tussle it about so much that she gave up and decided it was okay to look like everybody else did: windblown.

A friendly Cockney man sitting to her left looked at her glass and said, "Here, let me buy you a drink: You can't drink wa'er now. It's a pub, innit?"

"Oh, thank you. But I don't mind water."

"You're American. Nobody English drinks wa'er in a pub! Come on now. Let me buy you one!"

Catherine tried to say no, but the man put his hand up as if to soften her protests and said to the bartender: "And one for the lady, here, mate."

So she wouldn't hurt his feelings, Catherine sipped her warmish beer, and soon enough they were talking amicably. Before she knew it, she could see that this man, Christopher, was taking an unusual interest in her story. She looked at Christopher sternly over her beer. He would do: small, quiet in the way the English were taught. He stayed at a respectful distance. She listened to him chatter on and felt that he could be trusted. His Cockney accent reminded her of all those women back in Holloway Prison.

"You know, I do need someone who can help me go to unusual places and dig for a treasure in the dirt. Do you think you could do that?"

"I've got a good back, I 'ave."

"Then you will help me?"

"I'm on the dole now," he said. "I reckon I could help you out: Not much doing for me right at present. Another one?"

"No, thank you. I'm only halfway down this one!"

They talked a little more, then Christopher said conclusively, "I 'ope I can serve you well, Mrs. Evans."

"I am so pleased. Thank you!" Catherine said. "Now, there's a house on the south coast of England. That's where we're going to do a bit of digging."

"I think I can manage that," Christopher said. "And, like I said, me and me mum live in the East End. We can visit 'er first if you like. She'd like that, if you won't mind our humble home."

"What a lovely idea. I wouldn't even mind if we went right now." She squinted at him: Perhaps he was in his mid-thirties after all–maybe mid-forties. "And, by the way, I've stayed in all kinds of homes. I've lived a long time, and when I lived in London, times were hard. It was just after the war. I remember all those bombed-out lots near your mother's house in the East End. Not a pretty sight. I made trips especially to see it." She sipped, but her eyes never left his face. "My husband worked at *The Daily*

*Mail,* so he was always in your part of London." Upon squinting again, she decided he must be a young-looking thirty-five-year-old.

She now had one loyal teammate. She needed one more: someone with eyes good enough for peering endlessly at microfiche, and a suspicious bent that would help Catherine sniff out the facts and realize which ones were lies.

"Now, let's go meet your lovely mum," Catherine said.

Christopher hailed a cab and opened the taxi door. He offered her his hand. She shoved her umbrella onto the floor with one hand and took his outstretched hand, raising her leg slowly and carefully, while Christopher gave a polite shove on her back to keep her moving into the cab.

"Mind your 'ead," said the driver.

Christopher jumped in and slammed the large door. "The East End, mate."

"No troubles," answered the cab driver as he turned on the meter.

Driving through London on this sunny day in a taxi was like a movie for Catherine. The taxi weaved its way through Piccadilly Circus, through the huge red neon lights of the cinemas, through black iron-fenced block gardens with horse chestnut trees, past Holborn Tube Station and the narrow one-way lanes just large enough to squeeze a taxi through, but hardly wide enough for a lorry. It seemed to Catherine that they must have gone around ten roundabouts and past twenty pubs. She mused how there was something deeply British about the pubs, the refuge from the rain and fog; the steak and kidney pie; the large half pints of beer; everyone tipsy, chatting about football scores, politics, even cricket matches in Australia, New Zealand, and India. If you didn't want a beer, the fish and chip shop was nearby, and they would wrap the fish and chips up in a big newspaper that was wet with grease when the last chip was swallowed. Catherine remembered closing time at their pub in Kentish Town, how all the drinkers would stand outside at 11:10 p.m. and have one last "fag" before making their lonely way home to their dreary rooms or exhausted wives.

Times had changed in London, but she noticed that Greek and Turkish restaurants along the route still held their own with their delicious lamb moussaka and feta cheese and tomato salad covered in olive oil. The school children in uniforms and berets of blue, green, or maroon, all wearing striped ties to match, hung outside their schools for the lunch break.

As they neared Brick Lane, Catherine noticed more Indian restaurants. Everywhere she saw Asians; men wearing black suits and ties; caned umbrellas, Scottie dogs, red buses, endless rows of brick houses, zebra crossings with flashing orange lights, more pubs on every corner, with names like the Longacre Pub, the Golden Lion, and the Angel.

The cars were still small but had changed from the black cars of her youth to blues and greens. Mostly, it seemed to be more crowded, teeming with people from all parts of the old British Empire, and all in a great hurry. The taxi driver took shortcuts, steered through narrow lanes that even a scooter might have trouble squeezing through, pointed out famous pubs, and swore at people charging across in front of his taxi, mumbling that they should cross at the zebra crossing. So many buildings had been built over from the fifties. It hardly looked the same at all.

After forty-five minutes the taxi pulled up to a long row of brick-walled flats with doors all needing paint jobs. The black necks of the streetlights curved like swans and looked like ancient gas lamps.

Christopher helped Catherine out after she paid the taxi driver and opened the unlocked front door.

"Mum! We've got a visitor!" he yelled.

Christopher's mother, a chubby woman in her late fifties, white hair disheveled, came to the opened door and wiped her hands on her apron.

"Come in, don't loll about. How'd'y do, then? I'm Maureen."

"Nice to meet you, I'm Catherine," Catherine said, stepping inside. Maureen backed away and bowed slightly. Christopher automatically began relieving Catherine of her coat.

"Come and have a nice 'ot cuppa tea, love," Maureen said. Catherine hadn't heard a woman speaking Cockney in years. Again it sounded so familiar, like the clipped words that came from the mouths of the women in prison.

"That's exactly what I need right now." Catherine followed Maureen down the narrow hallway to the kitchen. It was a spacious room with a rectangular table large enough to seat eight. There was a wooden cupboard on the wall with a dozen different-shaped soup spoons hanging from it.

There was no microwave. The refrigerator buzzed a little with its round corners and its feminine '80s quality.

The kettle was on low, hardly whistling, ready for the teapot. A yellow birdcage sat in a corner; Catherine could just see a matching yellow canary sitting on the swing. She went straight for the armchair next to the birdcage and sat down with a *whoosh*.

Maureen bustled about over at the stove, then turned to the table, teapot in hand.

"I dare say, Mrs. Evans, you do remind me of somebody." She poured Catherine a cup of tea. "I can't quite put me finger on it, but I think I met you ages ago."

# Maureen's Suspicions

**Maureen held out** the bowl of sugar, and Catherine took two square lumps. Maureen stood close to Catherine and poked her face forward, peering at Catherine's lined face. "Was you ever in the East End before, a long time ago like?"

Catherine gulped her tea straight down. "Do let's have another cup of tea," she said. "I've longed for your nice strong home-brewed tea. It's just not the same as in America; must be the weather."

"Whatever 'appens, it's always on account of the bloomin' weva," Christopher said, picking up a small pad and pencil and drawing a picture of the fake flowers on the sideboard.

Maureen poured a new cup for Catherine. Maureen's spoon clinked against her teacup as she stirred in the sugar.

Maureen was now standing right next to Catherine's chair, her teapot resting on the potholder in her left hand. "Yes, it's that profile that rings a bell, way off in the past somewhere. You sure we haven't met before?"

"No, I don't believe I've met you," Catherine said, although Maureen was looking shockingly familiar to her now. "But I'm very pleased to meet you now. I'd love a scone and jam," she said, hoping to change the subject. Christopher reached over, grabbed the jam, and put it closer to Catherine's edge of the table, while his mother lifted the plate. "Help yourself, love," Maureen said, and went on cocking her head and peering at Catherine's profile.

"I used to live in London in the fifties, after the war," Catherine said. "But up in Kentish Town, you know." She could at least tell them that. She noticed that Christopher was drawing the flower quite accurately.

"That's it!" Maureen exclaimed. "I knew I'd seen you. It was in the papers. That scandal, beggin' your pardon, ma'am. A murder trial. She was guilty and went to prison for a lot of years. Oh, I say, could you be that very woman?"

Catherine felt like a deer frozen in a car's headlights. She studied Maureen's plump face and penetrating eyes. There was definitely a strong familiar feeling about her, but Catherine could not place her for sure. Then Catherine began to smell the past, the prison, the agony of her loneliness. Before she could answer, Maureen continued.

"Mrs. Evans, if you really want to know, and I am not sure you do, the real reason I recognized you weren't nofink about them *Daily Mirror* photos. I was in jail wif you for a short while, me dearie." Maureen added, "I wasn't guilty, neither. But I don't expect you to believe that."

"What?" exclaimed Catherine, dabbing her mouth with the napkin. "*You* are the Maureen from jail? I would never have known." The canary started twittering. "And, of course I believe you're innocent." Catherine studied the other woman and put down her scone. "I am that woman. But I didn't kill David."

"'Course you didn't," Maureen said, busying herself buttering her scone. Catherine looked up at Maureen. Here was a woman who believed her. "Mrs. Evans, love, I am the woman who sat in the visiting room next to you that one time staring at that strange man."

Catherine looked hard at Maureen's face, and as Maureen turned toward the stove, her profile gave her away: that pug nose, not noticeable from the front. Even with the white hair, it was the same arched line of eyebrow. Catherine shifted her glasses. "Come here. I have to see your face more clearly." Maureen stepped forward and bent down. Their eyes were not more than three inches apart.

"Yes. You are really that Maureen!" Catherine said. "I am shocked! But here you are! What happened to you in the end, once you got out of prison, Maureen?"

Maureen shrugged and looked down. There was a long silence, the kind Catherine remembered back in the U.S.: shocking memories, thoughts; regrets. Probably Maureen's silence was about trust. Catherine was in no hurry.

"It's just heartbreaking," Catherine said, to cover the moment of stunned silence, "when I think of all those years in that prison, that laundry room, those other poor women in there. Twelve years gone." She retrieved her scone. "If my husband were alive, he'd have died to see what I went through because some policeman jumped to conclusions instead of doing a thorough investigation."

Maureen sat down in a straight-backed chair next to Catherine and put her hand on top of Catherine's hand. "They said I murdered me husband," she confided, gently lifting her hand from Catherine's, "but it isn't true. I did kill him, the rotten drunken sod, beggin' your pardon, but it was in self-defense, pure and simple." Maureen pounded the table lightly. "That man was always drunk, always hitting me round the face. I hardly ever went out for the shame of me black-and-blue face. Sent little Christopher to do the shopping down the road, I did."

Here there was another lull, during which Maureen's eyes sank back into a dark hole and she moved the creases between her eyebrows. She looked back at Catherine. "One day, I thought he was killing me, hitting me up the side of me head with that 'ammer. The kitchen knife was right there. I don't fink I even knew what I was going to do, I just did it. I couldn't 'elp it, could I? Self-defense, they said it was, after all that fuss."

Catherine looked at Maureen sympathetically, but didn't reply. She remembered the story.

Maureen stood up and walked to the sink. "Do you remember when you first came in 'ow you fainted?" she asked, wiping her eye with the back of her hand.

"Were you there?" Catherine asked, digging back so far into her memories.

"I called to the other women out in the kitchen and we all fanned you and lifted you onto a cot and listened to your heart. Just probably fainted, but I'll never forget your young face: so sad," Maureen said. "They said you were dying of a broken heart. I see you never did, but, my dear, you did look so sad." Maureen held out the sugar bowl. "Sugar, me love?"

"Yes. I remember waking up and seeing a sea of faces, so kind, all those women. You'd never know they'd committed horrible crimes. We all seemed like normal people to me. I guess I was normal, too, to you all, but I was no murderer." There was a quiet moment in the kitchen. "I remembered all those faces after I came around," Catherine continued. The canary started chirping louder.

"Perhaps I'm growing old," Maureen said. "Me memory is playing tricks on me. I can't remember if it was a dream or if it really happened. But do you remember that man who came once at visiting time? He seemed to be quite tall, as I remember. That day he came and sat opposite me and never said a bloomin' word. I remember, if it weren't a dream, he wrote a note to me. It only said *NO TALKING*, in big, printed letters. Well, it was ever so nice just to have a visitor, whoever 'e was, that I just went along, didn't I?" Maureen shifted her apron.

"It must have been right after that when he started sitting opposite me, off and on for years."

"It was just that once with me. Wasn't long after that, I was out of there, wasn't I?"

# CATHERINE'S ARREST

"**Everybody** knew my case," Catherine said, behind her teacup. "It was all over the newspapers when they hauled me off to jail. I've had a look at them all, especially *The Daily Mail,* where David worked. Lots of photos." Her mind slipped through a long tunnel of time into a place long past.

"Come along, Mrs. Evans. You're wanted by the law."

They grabbed her arm and brusquely escorted her into the waiting police van. No one saw the twitch under her left eyelid. No one saw the extra huge breath she took when the reality of that moment pressed into her unwilling brain. She had always considered the policemen one of England's better accomplishments, remembering how one tall, lanky young policeman had leaned down to David's father's old car window and said, "I'm sorry, but I am afraid you are driving the wrong way down this one-way street." No gun bulged from his hip: just a truncheon; no piece of paper declaring a fine was handed over. She could never imagine that polite man slapping handcuffs on anyone. Here now was evidence that he could and did. This policeman said to her, "Sorry, madam. It's required." At least he apologized. She was, after all, innocent until proven otherwise, or was that just American law?

Her mind fluttered from her sore wrists to her house disappearing from the side of the van and the neighbors' hands in their flowery dresses of the early fifties, perched upon their innocent hips. She turned her head away from their home. She would be back soon. The gravity of their mistake would be proven, and she would go home with no further fuss.

She could hardly remember the trial at the Old Bailey. Her eyes had scanned the strange wigs. She felt sorry that they had to wear them. But tradition in England always won over practicality. A blur of people were shouting outside the courthouse with signs, it seemed, indicating that they thought she was a killer. She remembered the loud crash of the judge's mallet and the jumble of words from the barrister's mouths that were so posh she could hardly understand a word, except "m'lord." Her handkerchief was sopping wet. Weren't they yelling "death" outside? Could it be about her? Wasn't that a tomato they threw at her when the trial was over? Was that a dream? Would the English do that to her? Surely the mistake was clear? Of course her fingerprints were on the knife. She had pulled it out. Of course she pulled it out. Wasn't David still breathing? Wasn't he still warm? Was he? She couldn't remember now.

Sometimes, Catherine remembered, she would lie on her bunk and wonder why Mr. Smith started visiting her there in prison. And who was Mr. Smith to Catherine? As she floated into a dreamy state, her mind filled with questions with no answers, night after night, year after year.

Mr. Smith had come and sat in front of Catherine on subsequent visits. By then Maureen was out of jail. He had also held up to her the small sign that read *NO TALKING*. Catherine hardly ever looked at him. It was a welcomed break in her routine, so she sat with him once every few months for almost twelve more years. Mr. Smith never said one word to her.

Catherine knew why she and Maureen had never spoken of Mr. Smith's one visit to Maureen. Maureen was different from Catherine. She talked in a raw fashion. There were class cliques in Holloway Prison for Women. Catherine was shunned by everybody because she was American, but mostly, it filtered into her ears somehow, because she had married an Englishman.

Of course, they had not married, but that was still Catherine's secret. There weren't enough men after the war for the English women who had been supporting the war effort with their newly won workers' privileges in munitions factories and airplane companies. Maureen had been one of the ones who snubbed Catherine: turned her back, didn't smile.

# THE LANTERN

**The huge** Portuguese ship bore down upon the little boat. Caruso stopped rowing. It was pointless. He didn't fancy becoming a galley slave, but the chances of survival were down to nothing. He waved at the ship that slithered alongside them. Two huge ropes were slung overboard from the ship and instinctively, Caruso slid a large loop under each end and yelled in Italian something that ensured they were slowly raised up and onto the deck. Caruso grabbed his wrapped container of the silver cups, but it was seized immediately by orders of the Portuguese Captain. It was the last Caruso ever would see of it.

Caruso studied the stars again. It seemed they must be sailing north. Certainly it was colder now. Caruso stood aloft at the very highest mast on the ship and spied the darkest clouds he had ever seen spreading rapidly across the sky from the northwest, until the daylight shivered and almost disappeared. He and the others furled the sails in preparation for the storm. Men shouted all around him. Some words he could understand. The rest he could read on the terrified faces of the other men. The white caps rushed toward them and then the waves took on a rolling motion that made their large ship into a toy, tossing and turning at the tip of the now-huge waves—the kings of the sea.

At last, through the thick fog there was a light. It was another ship; there were pointing fingers; the Captain made them turn the ship and sail toward the light.

The ship angled its sails such that the light brightened, beckoning them closer. Surely the light was a ship at anchor.

Caruso was drenched and shivering. He squinted his wet eyes, blinked back the cold wind upon his eyeballs and yelled, "Nooooo!" with all his might. He pushed the sail to turn the boat away from the now-evident rocks just ahead.

The roar of the cracking hull echoed through the boat as men jumped into the foam: men who'd never learned to swim, who had never felt the salty sea in their throats and who had never stopped breathing for so long under water. The boat shattered and roared at its own demise as the incessant waves beat against its remaining bulk. The yelling simmered down to gurgles. The boat crashed once more, emptying its contents onto the rocks; then sunk whimpering below the bubbling foam, the un-caring waves.

The bow of the ship shattered, and the sea rushed in. Caruso tumbled from the ship as it crashed on the rocks, jutting out into the ocean from the very tip of the land of England. The box of silver cups flew out of the ship on its first impact: out of the cabin, through the swinging door, and against the upturned deck. Then at the second crack of the ship to the rock, the box was catapulted across the sky, soaring as if it were as light as a bird and landing solidly under the cliff in a crevice two inches below the highest tide mark.

Caruso's bare feet jarred against an underwater urchin. His raw hands reached for safety, slipped. He fell backward. The ship backed away into the bubbles. The waves pushed it underneath and threw it once again against the rocks. He was knocked down as he reached out with bleeding hands to grab a rock. The sea pulled him back with its ferocious energy. His sight blurred and failed; then he blacked out, and fell into the sea, head down. As the salty water filled his lungs, he was carried into the deep by the undertow, his shadow blending and splitting into the raging current.

Very early next morning the villagers ran to the shore with their ready wheelbarrows. The young, hearty boys waded into the waves, jumping, searching; diving with their eyes stinging from being open in the murky waters. Each boy came up with treasures: boots, pans, knives, ropes, carved bits of wood, flags, a helm, a mast, sails. It was this plunder that would save them through the next hard winter when all they might have to eat was fish and potatoes.

The family waited in the traditional place–the barn behind the old tavern. It was like an open secret in this village. The bounty made its way to London by cart over the roughest of roads.

It would be almost four centuries before the curious eight-year-old Carey, a slender child with blond braids, whose father had forbidden her to stay away from the rocks and the giant waves, was born down there in Cornwall.

The Portuguese ship had broken into a million parts, crashed up against the rocks of Cornwall, and sunk, snuggling up to centuries of rotten, waterlogged skeletons of ships long smashed and drowned. The rest of the debris floated along the rocky coast, bumped and crashed into flickering, wet rocks, and finally gave in to the pull of the murky, sandy bottom.

Over the years, crabs came to explore the box, its leather strap, its metal, rusting sides, its orange hue. Every day the tides covered it briefly then let it be, exposed to storms and sun.

How many times the waves had crashed and smashed against that rock in over four hundred steady years, while generations of children ran in the early mornings, every fall when winter hunger threatened, and gathered up the remains of the wrecked ships, never seeing the rock behind them where the box blended with the orange and green rocks around it; where they never glanced long enough, so eager were they to see what could readily be seen.

The ragged children stood above the spot for generations, a hand held above the eyes, scouring the sea for the treasures of the past jettisoned from ships, also crushed against the solid rocks, whose function seemed to be to increase the earnings of the poor who lived by the sea at the southwestern tip of England.

They pointed to there and there and over there, as the waves rolled in and out, but below their feet the box remained, grew barnacles and moss; rusted its chain and lock, settled deeper into the crevice millimeter by millimeter, until no rogue wave could have shifted it at all.

The children waited until early summer and swam among the rocks, but they looked down into the sea, through to the sand. Their bare feet pushed against the treasures languishing on the sandy bottom, and each child watched the older children for almost four hundred years and copied them. Not one child looked up in all that time. One day a young girl wandered alone down the steep cliffs to the shore. Carey was her name. She hardly ever disobeyed, but she felt that at eight years old, she was almost old enough to go to the beach alone.

# Maureen Is Chosen

**Catherine grasped** Maureen's hand. "You're the one I'm looking for."

"Who? Me?" Maureen asked, wiping her other sticky hand along her apron.

"Do you have good eyes?" she asked Maureen.

"I've got grand eyes. Nobody hardly ever wore specs on my side of the family, did they, Christopher?"

"No, Mum," answered Christopher, shading the flowers in his drawing.

"'Course, I've got me back-ups," Maureen added softly. "You never know if the light is dim."

"Well, that sounds fine. If you have any sense of justice at all, would you please consider being my eyes? I can't read very well now. I like the way you saw right away who I was. Could you make time in your day for a few hours' research for me?"

"Well, I dare say, Mrs. Evans," Maureen replied slowly. "I'm not that much of a reader meself—just *The Sun* and *The Daily Mirror,* and a glance at *The Guardian* headlines, 'course." Maureen grabbed a copy of *The Daily Mirror* from the table and flipped to the horoscopes.

"Let's just see what I should do now. It says: 'Jump on the bandwagon, Virgo. This is the break in your boredom you were seeking last month. Another opportunity like this won't come 'round for another seven years.' Well, 'ere it is, then." Maureen looked hard at Catherine then said, "I'll do it." Maureen sipped her tea and laughed, then gave Catherine Evans a little push on her shoulder.

"'Ow's that, then, love?" Catherine smiled a broad smile. Her other teammate was in place.

"If it eases your mind, I'll pay you up front," Catherine said. "Who knows if I might drop like a fly at any moment, and if I hadn't paid you…" Maureen put her palm up and waved Catherine backward.

"No, no, I couldn't," she began.

"Yes, you could," Catherine said. "I have a great feeling we're going to be true partners in this venture. Let me pay you at least a hundred pounds each in advance, and then at least another hundred each on a weekly basis. Every few days or once a week we'll settle up for the anticipated week. How does that sound?"

"Well," began Maureen, as she walked back to the table and picked up her cup. Her little finger stuck out as she raised her cup thoughtfully. "We'll just wait and see."

Catherine pulled out her purse and laid down five twenty-pound notes in front of each one. Maureen put down her cup. Christopher sat motionless with his hands knit tightly in his lap, his eyes wide.

"Go on, they won't bite you!" Catherine said.

Maureen reached daintily and picked up her notes, and Christopher slid his notes off the table into his lap.

"When do we start?" Maureen asked.

"I believe you've already started. What I'd like you to do next, Maureen, is to check back to the horoscopes of 1956 at the library. It'll help jog your memory."

"Well, what a fine how d'you do! She's going to pay me to go to me own library!" Maureen said. "That's where I read the papers every day. I buy them, too, sometimes, I do. Not a ten-minute walk from here, our library." She folded the twenty-pound notes in half, then half again, and pushed them down her dress front and into her bra.

"You won't regret it," Catherine said, accepting her third cup of tea and clinking cups with both Maureen and Christopher.

"The best of British luck, I say!" Christopher said. "Cheers!" They all drank their tea like it was beer.

"There might be some way we could use DNA to find the murderer," Catherine said, as she settled back thoughtfully, her teacup dangling in her fingers.

Maureen stood up and walked over to the sink. "I'll just wash up, then, and be off right away. Can't believe I'm getting good lolly to do wot I love."

Christopher sat looking down at his notes scribbled around his drawing.

Maureen took off her apron, turned, and stared at Catherine. "Apart from the library, what else can we do? What exactly are we looking for then, love?"

Catherine opened her handbag and pulled out a photograph of David with his arm around her, both so young. She pulled out her handkerchief and wiped her nose, then stuffed it up her sweater sleeve.

"This is all we have to go on for clues, unless we can get back into the old house and find other possibilities. We might find some old silver cups, and we just might discover David's murderer."

Maureen picked up the photograph and reached over to the side table for the magnifying glass attached to Christopher's keys. Catherine watched as Maureen skimmed the postcard-sized photo of David take the day before his murder. She skimmed back and forth. There he was, smiling, with his arm around Catherine. There was no hint on either face of foreknowledge of the imminent disaster about to befall them.

"Hmm," Maureen said. "What?" Catherine asked.

"Hmm, is all I said." Maureen put the keys and the magnifying glass down and stared off into space. "Who took the photo?"

"Just the shopkeeper on the corner," said Catherine. "We asked him to. It was the day before David died." More silence. Maureen picked up the magnifying glass again and peered at the photograph, then moved it up to the corner of Catherine's own handkerchief, sticking out of her sleeve. "'DE,' it says here."

"Yes. David Evans. It was in my bag of things they gave back to me when I got out of jail: such a small remembrance. I carried around with me for all four years we were together. I am so grateful to have it."

Maureen jumped up. "Don't you see, me love? Look 'ere!" She handed the photograph and the glass to Catherine.

Catherine squinted as she moved the glass slowly across the photograph. "That's how I remember him, that lovely smile."

"Now look 'arder, Mrs. Evans. Look at his clothes. Look at your 'ands, your sleeves. Look! Look! It's right in front of us!"

Catherine moved slowly, squinting, and there it was. Poking out of her sleeve in the photo was an embroidered handkerchief.

"Could it be the same handkerchief?" Maureen asked.

"Why, yes, there was only one like that. I gave it back to him right after the photo was taken. I remember it was chilly and I had just borrowed it from him. I dabbed his nose with it, too. My own handkerchiefs were all in the laundry. He stuffed it in his suit breast pocket just after I folded it back up. I only brought this back to England with me for a remembrance; never used it in Vermont all those years."

"This is our DNA sample, Mrs. Evans!"

Catherine searched Maureen's face. It was hard to imagine that this handkerchief could be that useful. "I can't see how it could have DNA on it other than David's and mine. I've only washed it once since then! Took it out just for this trip."

"You're probably right about the DNA," Maureen said. "Don't you think we ought to get it tested if we can anyway?"

"Let's see how things go. It doesn't seem likely, but then again, you never know."

# OVERNIGHT AT CHRISTOPHER AND MAUREEN'S

**How could she** refuse? An invitation to spend a night at Maureen and Christopher's house was the break from the hotel world that Catherine needed to bring her down to earth.

Catherine cut her beef at their supper table with an extra firm sawing motion, and chewed with vigor as she told her story to Maureen and Christopher. "All those people got hung just weeks before my case came up. It's a miracle I'm alive to tell the story."

There was sympathy emanating from their eyes, so unlike the suspicious eyes and the judgment she had feared from her American friends. Every time the truth had shot to Catherine's tongue, trying to tell her friends what had happened to her, she found herself in a state of paralysis. None of her friends had been to jail, had had their minute liberties torn from them, had to eat tasteless food, had been grateful for even a crumb of attention from somebody, anybody. No friends of hers had to always be on guard for fear the truth would be discovered. No friends smiled with a well-worn mask when people in the news were sent to prison for dubious crimes. No friends had to live with people who were sane one day and crazy the next, who threatened them with smuggled scissors, stole their food, drove them crazy on purpose with a rhythmic knock on the wall in the middle of the night. No friends had ever dreamed so hard of escape that they chipped into their walls with their fingernails to begin an imaginary escape.

Catherine smiled ironically at those days of wanting to emerge into another world that, in truth, had its own kind of prisons: prisons of poverty, psychological terror, and the need for secrecy that there was no path to leave from, no tunnel to dig out, no person who would understand.

Later on, one by one, those old friends in Vermont held her hand and gargled their final breaths, never knowing that Catherine, to whom they had entrusted their very last moments alive, had been a prisoner in England. No one would have believed her story; that lingering doubt would have hovered between friends like a misty ghost.

But Maureen was different; and Christopher, too. Their sympathetic faces nodded and their mouths opened in disgust and incredulity as each word poured from Catherine's long-sealed lips. They let her chew and swallow and mull over her next sentence.

"Ruth Ellis killed her lover outside the Magdala Pub in Hampstead—just went and shot him in front of all his friends. I went around there one evening with David about that time; he was interviewing someone.

She was the last one hung in England for murder, around July 1955. I'd have been next. They gave me fifteen years and let me out early for good behavior. Good behavior, my foot!" she spluttered. "I was just depressed and sad. Injustice always made me furious, and here I was, wrapped up like some gift, parceled, stamped and sent off to Holloway Prison for something I didn't do!" Catherine banged her fist on the table and her fork flew out of her hand and off the table, clattering onto the kitchen floor.

"Never you mind, Mrs. Evans," Maureen said. "Justice will be done this time. I can't bear injustice, right Christopher?"

"Me mum's mean as a boxer if someone's done a friend a nasty injustice."

Catherine looked from Christopher to Maureen. Why were these people so different? They understood her from some place inside that no one she'd ever met had been able to venture.

Maureen offered Catherine a hot water bottle and said there was another one up between her sheets already. Catherine remembered the cold nights in jail, especially before they tore the old castle-like jail down, never enough blankets, just the dark eerie wet winter air blowing through the bars. What a joy a hot water bottle would have been then! The rough bedding had been icy cold on her feet. She had to pull herself up into a tiny curled roly-poly bug and blow on her cupped hands to get warmth onto her frozen, dripping nose. She had a cough for twelve winters. There was a lone plane tree outside her window that bared itself every fall and remained so, teasing her with its raindrops dangling, pretending to be buds, then dropping to the ground. Those drops would never turn into buds. But somewhere in late March or early April little bubbles sat up on the branches and stayed there and in May tiny leaves poked out to remind Catherine that there was another winter endured and gone and soon she would stop coughing.

Even in Maureen's spare room, Catherine had to pull the covers over her head to warm up her cold nose. How could it be the end of August and be so cold? In jail, her nose was red and dripping most of the winter, starting in September. Her handkerchief was lodged up the sleeve of her cardigan for immediate intervention. Every woman there was armed similarly, with a handkerchief up each sleeve. Vermont was cold outside, but at least there was a pleasant temperature indoors during the night. The fireplace was still warm through the night, and the wall heater automatically switched on below fifty-five degrees. She lay there, the light burning through her blankets and eyelids, the wind rattling the falling leaves outside, her toes frozen and wiggling half the night.

How kind of Maureen to let her spend the night there. Too bad she was still paying those high prices to hold her room at the Churchill Bed and Breakfast. The sharp contrast of her attempt at keeping warm versus the perfect temperature she was paying for there made her wish she had cheaper lodgings somewhere else. Paying so much for a room just because she felt so close to dying was becoming embarrassing to her own sense of values.

The next morning the teakettle whistled downstairs. Soon there was a knock on her bedroom door and Maureen tiptoed in with a large white cup and saucer on a tray.

"Here's your tea, then, love," she said quietly. Catherine poked her face out from the covers.

"Thank you, my dear. It's such a wonderful British tradition: a nice hot cup of tea to start the day."

"Breakfast in half an hour!" announced Maureen, wiping her hands on her flowery apron. She closed the door gently.

Catherine wondered how she was going to get her cold fingers out from under the covers, to reach over and pull the tea next to her pillow. After a minute or two, she realized she was going to have to sit up for this treat. Maybe that was the only way the British were coaxed from their beds into the damp, cold shock of the morning air. Slowly she shifted the blankets, sat up, and reached for the tea. The cup was warm as she encircled it with her thin fingers.

After breakfast, while Maureen did the washing up, Catherine announced her plan to Christopher, who was sitting staring at his twenty-pound bills. "Now, young man, we're off to the train. Time to visit my old house near the beach. Would you please hail us a cab?" Maureen would be off to the library to continue her research.

"Right you are, Gov–I mean, Mrs. Evans," he said, as he leapt up, jamming the bills into his front trouser pocket.

# AT THE BEACH HOUSE

**The day** was gray and windy, nothing unusual. Now and then, the sun peeked out from behind a cloud and warmed Catherine like the hot breath of a lover, but it didn't last long. Catherine had prepared for this breezy experience and had dressed with long, woolen stockings, a snug, warm blue wool coat, and a cashmere scarf. They climbed into the taxi to the train station.

On the train, for the next hour or so, Catherine sat in complete silence, staring out of the window. Christopher sat across from her reading *The Daily Mail.* All she could see were the backs of brown English brick houses. Some windows were still bricked up from the historical tax on windows. Lines of red shirts, white underwear, and white sheets flapped in the wind. Red and yellow flowers in window boxes took the place of longed-for gardens.

Catherine remembered how she was drawn to the beach house in Rottingdean's architectural beauty, with its two grand windows facing the sea from the sitting room. The small deck just outside the kitchen was an invitation for tea and scones and laughing with friends.

One day, while holidaying in Brighton, she and David had wandered into the antique shop near the beach house.

"Let's buy this painting!" she said lightly to David, who was admiring an antique silver plate. "If we can't afford a house like this, we can at least look at it on our sitting room wall!"

David's eyes sparkled as he looked at the small watercolor. He paid the vendor, took the wrapped painting under one arm, and offered his other arm to his wife.

"By the way," he said, turning back to the vendor, with his handlebar moustache. "Is this house local?"

"Yes, indeed," said the vendor, pointing out the door. "Just up the street to the top; left side on the corner. You can't miss it."

"Thank you very much," David said, as he reached for the door, offering Catherine the exit as the doorbell jangled, then taking her arm again. Off they went to explore the local streets, their new painting under David's arm.

Catherine could still remember the salty air and the wind gently blowing her long, curly hair. She was absorbed with considering where she would hang the painting in their Kentish Town flat as they climbed up along the cobbled stone road to look at the house.

"For sale. knock hard, please." read a sign nailed on the closed car gate. They neared the wooden fence surrounding the house, looking back and forth from the house to the sign. Their faces turned toward each other.

"Shall we just see how much they want for it? We can't possibly afford it, of course, but let's ask anyway," Catherine said.

They nodded to each other and David opened the squeaky gate, gesturing for Catherine to walk in. They walked across the dirt yard to the brick path and up to the large front door. David hesitated then knocked in his usual gentlemanly manner. After waiting two long minutes, he ventured to knock harder.

A small man, perhaps in his early forties, held the curtain ajar at the side window. "Coming," he called from the inside of the house.

"Good afternoon," said the man, opening the door and peering gently at them through his thick glasses. "May I be of any help?"

"We saw your sign," David said.

"Oh, yes, me sign. I spent two hours painting that sign. Do you like it?" His small, kind eyes moved upward so he could look David in the face. He glanced at Catherine and looked back down.

"It's a lovely sign," Catherine said.

The man muttered something to himself then said, "Me name's Bernie Ward. Do you want to buy me lovely 'ouse, then?"

"Well, we think it is a lovely house and we would dearly love to buy it, but...," David said.

"Good," said the man. "Come in, come in."

The open door enticed Catherine and David inside. The old grand-father clock held a majestic presence in the front hall, and the flowery wallpaper behind it was as tasteful as old wallpaper could be. It wouldn't have been Catherine's choice, but the leafy pattern was art deco and subtle at the same time. The man led them into the sitting room. "As I said, I'm Bernie Ward," he said. David and Catherine in-troduced themselves, too.

"I suppose you'll want the tour?"

"Yes, that would be most appreciated," David said as Catherine squeezed his hand.

The kitchen was large and looked out over the little wooden deck and the gentle rolling waves of the sea in the distance. Far below she could see the old promenade under the cliffs. The breakfast nook was big enough for four, and another wallpaper of red and yellow flowers enlivened it. But it was the view of the sea that most charmed Catherine and David.

They made their way slowly upstairs behind the proud owner, along the smooth, shiny banister. White curtains and heavier green drapes cov-ered the windows. There was a canopy bed in each of the two bedrooms; and there was a water closet, just a small room with only a flushing toilet, which was so unusual, said the owner, to have upstairs. "Quite new," he said, gesturing with his hands.

"This is a beautiful house, Mr. Ward," she said. If there was a heaven on earth, Catherine had found it.

They went back downstairs and stood near the front door, ready to say goodbye. "We love your house, but...," David started.

"Well, then you must buy it!" Mr. Ward said. "We aren't in the position...," David replied.

"Nonsense! Nobody's in the position. You want it. You love it. I need to move to me flat in London. The wife's been dead two years now and

I'm too lonely here. You take it and we'll work out the payments so you can afford it."

"Oh, David!" Catherine exclaimed.

"Maybe I'll get that evening job teaching English and we can somehow pay for this," he said.

"There you are. It's done. Let's shake on it then." Mr. Ward held out his right hand. David placed his firm hand into it and they shook.

They walked together down to the solicitor's office on High Street. Mr. Ward's lawyer drew up an agreement proclaiming David owner of the house the following day: no down payment, and no payments due until David got his job.

"I can't wait another day. This is the answer to me prayers," Mr. Ward said, again shaking David's hand.

"We don't know how to thank you enough for this opportunity," Catherine said, offering her hand. Mr. Ward hesitated. A woman's hand apparently had never crossed his in business. This was men's talk. He stretched out his palm nevertheless, and they shook delicately. He turned red. "Well, the furniture and linens and the dishes–them's all yours."

"Oh, Mr. Ward! You're very kind!" Catherine said, as she watched the lawyer write that down.

"I'll be on me way tomorrow, back to me flat in Kentish Town, Leighton Road, if you know of it, so you lovely people can move in right away if you like."

"Oh, we live in Kentish Town on Leighton Road. We're neighbors! Well, not for long," Catherine said. "But my mother lives there, too."

"Blimey," he said. "It's a small world." He took out his handkerchief and blew his nose.

As Mr. Ward exited the solicitor's office, he told them he'd leave the front door key on the kitchen table, "...if I can find it," he added. "Haven't locked it in twenty years. Cheerio, then, and the very best of British luck to you!"

They spent the night at a local bed and breakfast, then went to their new house the next day and hung their new painting in the kitchen nook.

"Oh, David, I can't believe this! It's a dream come true. Listen to the crashing waves."

Catherine's memories faded as the train slowed into Brighton station. Christopher alighted first, then offered Catherine his hand. The steps were almost too big for her, but slowly she managed, her umbrella hanging from her wrist. They walked arm in arm along the platform, over to the taxi stand outside, Catherine raising her umbrella to protect them from the light drizzle. Christopher signaled a taxi, and he and Catherine climbed in.

They drove about four miles north to Rottingdean, along the marina and the coastal two-lane highway, then left on High Street and left again on Nevill Road, aiming up the hill. The rain had stopped, and Catherine and Christopher stepped out of the taxi into a hazy sunshine. The sound of the small, rolling waves in the distance gently touched Catherine's ears and brought back the happiest and saddest days of her life all at once.

"Ah, Christopher. Listen to the waves! Nature's own rhythm, day in and day out."

The narrow, old road was paved now and easier for Catherine to manage than the cobblestone would have been, despite its charm. As Catherine shuffled a few steps further up the road, she could see that the old place looked run-down.

"Do you think we ought to wait it out?" Christopher glanced up at the sky.

"Not at all. Look, it's going to be a fine day after all, isn't it? Come. Used to be all slippery stones. Now it's paved, and there are more electric lights, I see."

Christopher offered his arm, and she slipped her hand through it and slowly walked up toward the house. Christopher took up a quiet, whistling tune.

As they made their way toward the old house, Catherine remembered the night before David was murdered: how he had caressed her whole body and made shivers out of places she hadn't even know were being held in abeyance; how he had asked her to open her eyes and be there with him, how she had felt that this man had suddenly become someone else; how another side of him had blossomed. The autumn wind had thrashed outside and the waves crashed. A power surged through her body like none had ever done before and roared into her arms, her fingers, her mouth; her being. In that exquisitely close moment David had whispered urgently that it was time to have a baby. Catherine could hardly breathe or talk. Her arms held onto David like she was now a part of him, a part of his body, as his body was a natural part of hers, while the energy of all the oceans shot from his body into hers.

Catherine remembered how she used to almost run up and down this road. And now here she was, tottering along with an umbrella in her right hand and a younger man of thirty-five propping her up on the left. She tried to remember when she'd stopped running, but there wasn't a day she could point to. It was way before the summer her hips started screaming. And when had she stopped dancing? Wasn't it when David had died?

# PETER

**As neglected** as the house appeared, as they neared it, Catherine's heart fluttered as if she had seen an old friend, a tender friend who had aged: a few more lines, dark patches beside the nose and eyes, a cane perhaps, an out-of-style hat.

The brief shower had dampened their coats and shoes. Her legs were cold. The small, distant waves rolled in one on top of the other, breaking into white bubbles over the pebbled beach. A small black dog ran ahead of a couple walking arm in arm on the pathway up to the grassy hill beyond. The sun slipped over the top of a cloud to brighten the sea, but a slight rain briefly filtered down and Catherine remembered the rainbows she'd seen up here long ago. The rain stopped.

Maybe she was being foolish, intrusive, un-English, dropping in unannounced like this. She slowed to a stop. Christopher stood still, holding her arm, while her strange fears ebbed and flowed with the sea. Did she want to drag others into this old story? She turned to retreat.

"Come now, Mrs. Evans. You didn't come all this way for nothing," coaxed Christopher, turning her right back around in a circle. They continued their slow pace forward, reached the house and stepped through the gate, walked up the steps and stood at the front door.

Voices of laughter filtered through the air from inside the house. Christopher knocked. The laughter subsided. Christopher knocked again, firmly. After a long pause, a woman peeked through the peephole. "Who's there?"

Catherine straightened her spine and stared back into that peering eye. "It's Mrs. David Evans, or rather Mrs. Catherine Evans."

There was a silence. Catherine and Christopher looked at each other and stepped backward a pace. "...and Christopher, my helper," Catherine added.

"What do you want?" said the muffled voice behind the familiar door.

"I would like to ask you a favor," Catherine said.

"What kind of a favor?"

Catherine couldn't really talk to a little peephole and ask the favor that way. "Could you open the door just a little?"

Christopher stepped back a little further. The door creaked open, and a woman with hair turning white peered through the narrow opening. Her narrowed eyes examined Catherine and Christopher.

"Please could we just have a word with you?"

"Right, then. I'm listening," she said, but the door stayed as it was.

"Well," Catherine said, leaning toward the crack in the door. "I would just love to see your whole face. I'm kind of hard of hearing, and I have to read lips. I can't really talk unless I can see your face." Catherine lifted her eyebrows and tapped her umbrella a few times.

There was a clicking as the woman opened the door wide and peered at Catherine, and behind her, Christopher, whose head was bent downward, his feet shuffling a little, his hands behind his back.

"Well, we've traveled a long way to get here, and I'm very tired, for one thing," began Catherine.

"Yes?" said the woman.

"I used to live in this house," Catherine said abruptly.

The woman stared at Catherine's face, squinting, her lips puckered; lines cracking around her mouth. "What did you say your name is?" she asked.

"Catherine Evans."

"Did you say Mrs. Catherine Evans?"

"Mrs. Catherine Evans, yes."

"Well, my name is Angela Evans, Mrs. Angela Evans," said the woman. She pulled the door open wider.

"You must be David's wife," Catherine said to Angela Evans.

Catherine looked into her eyes: kind, reserved; sad.

"Well, yes, I was his wife," Mrs. Angela Evans said. "It was only in name, you know. You were his one and only true love–let's make that clear. Please come in." She stood back and opened the door wider, gesturing for them to enter.

"I've always wondered what became of you after you went to Vermont," she said, "and here you are." She gazed behind Catherine, and then waved Christopher into the house, which was still lovely despite being somewhat frayed at the edges. They stepped inside, and the other Mrs. Evans closed the door.

"Who is it, Mum?" said a man's voice from the sitting room. A fluffy cat appeared around the door. It looked just like David and Catherine's old cat, which brought even more memories flooding back for Catherine.

"Just a moment, dear," she answered. "Hang your coats here, then," she said to Catherine and Christopher, gesturing to the coat stand at the side of the door.

Christopher helped Catherine take off her coat and put her umbrella in the umbrella stand. Catherine remembered that umbrella stand. The grandfather clock shocked her like an old friend she had long forgotten. Her eyes scanned the old, familiar wallpaper, those sanded wooden doorways, and even her old Persian rug sweeping down the hallway. She withdrew into a stunned silence while she imagined David, kissing her goodbye, hugging her hello, right here at this old front door.

Christopher took her arm as they followed Mrs. Evans down the hallway and into the sitting room. A small gathering of people were sitting around an antique coffee table.

"Come and sit down and have a cup of tea and some cake," Angela Evans said. "It is my birthday so you might as well join in the party. It's almost over, anyway."

Catherine eyed the company. It wasn't his child Mrs. Evans had had. That was what David had said. He'd married her out of pity. That was what he had said.

"These are my grandchildren, Henry, Oliver, and Cassandra," said Mrs. Evans.

Here sat three grown children of this very son of Angela's, all with David's eyes: David, alive again in this very house she had last seen him.

"I'm Cassandra," said the young woman, holding out her hand to shake Catherine's hand. Cassandra had David's green eyes which Cassandra held in a steady manner just like David had done.

The couch was covered with fading rose patterns: the tall windows had thick, peach-colored drapes now; the lamps were still their old lamps, but with new lampshades; the maroon carpet was also the same one, but even more worn now. Catherine's rocking chair had remained the same.

Henry walked over to Catherine and held out his hand.

"My name's Henry," he said. He nodded slightly. His eyes, too, gleamed with the gentle side of her David. It was like David stood there before her, reminding her of the day she had first fallen in love.

"I'm Oliver," said a young man, smiling.

"Out you go for your hike," Angela said, motioning in the teenagers' direction. They nodded politely at Catherine as they filed out the back door to climb over the hill.

Catherine looked over towards the kitchen door where David's son, the father of these children, was rustling with plates and a freshly boiled tea kettle.

She leaned towards Angela. "I would like to ask a favor of you, if you don't mind."

Dishes clattered in the kitchen where the quiet man in his thirties had retired. "Yes. Go ahead then," said Mrs. Evans.

"But, first, I must tell you that I didn't kill David. I have said it so many times, but I will never stop saying it. I have come back to England to find the murderer."

"I always knew you didn't kill David," replied Mrs. Evans. "I don't know who did, but I knew you loved each other and you could never have hurt him."

"Thank you for saying that. I am truly touched," Catherine said, closing her eyes for a moment as if a prayer had been answered.

"I also would like to dig a hole under your deck, with Christopher's help. We think there is something there that belonged to David and me when we used to live here."

"That's strange. What is it you'd like to dig for?" Mrs. Evans asked.

"Something David wrote about. I just recently found out about it, sorting through his things in a basket of his belongings someone sent me. I am hoping to find clues to discover David's real murderer."

"I sent you that basket years ago." Mrs. Evans shifted in her chair and took a sip of tea, then paused. "Never looked through them much. It just stayed in the attic until you were released from prison, and I thought you had the rights to it and that bank account they froze. Had your name on it, after all."

The man came back from the kitchen and lingered in the doorway.

"This is Peter, Mrs. Evans." Peter took two long strides and held out his hand to shake Catherine's. Catherine stared into his eyes and held too long onto his warm hand. Peter had the face of a kind person. Catherine could hardly stare at him, but he was so much like David for some reason, she felt like walking quietly into his arms. He had hung in the background; had an observant air. His stoic face seemed to hide his thoughts. He was so British in his mute presence. She now held all her own emotion inside, smiled thoughtfully like the British-trained person she knew how to be, and nodded. Confusion swarmed in her head. Christopher stood behind a chair. Peter backed away, hardly taking his eyes from Catherine.

# THE CUPS

**"I'm not so sure** I want to unearth the past like that," Mrs. Evans said. "What could there be under the deck? Can't be anything worth digging for."

"We really would be grateful to you, if you wouldn't mind," Catherine said.

Angela Evans looked at Christopher. Then she eyed Catherine like she was a child. Catherine shifted in her chair, took a sip of tea, and fiddled with a crumb on her plate. The hush in the room blocked out the rumble of the sea.

"I suppose your man can dig in the earth. Whatever you find, it's yours. After all, I got this lovely house all these years ago by being David's legal wife. The least I can do is let you dig a hole under its deck!"

Catherine stood up with unusual energy, a smile creeping across her face; a feeling of triumph unmatched by any other in years anchored her feet to the ground.

"Christopher, what are you waiting for?" She turned to Mrs. Evans. "Mrs. Evans, do you perhaps have a shovel we could use?"

Mrs. Evans looked up, her mouth open. "I didn't realize you meant right this very minute; but, of course, a shovel. Peter, please get it from the shed."

Catherine followed Christopher the hallway after thanking Mrs. Evans for the tea. Christopher helped her with her coat.

As they stepped out of the door, Catherine noticed the sky was even bluer. Catherine held the old, wooden handrail with one hand and Christopher's arm with the other. They worked their way around the corner of the house, down the stairs at the side of the house and to the back of the house, where the deck was jutting out from the kitchen.

"We done it, Mrs. Evans, ma'am. Let's have a go at this treasure, then."

Peter came from the other side of the house and down the path, handing a short shovel up to Christopher. It would do.

"Do you need help?" Peter asked.

"No, thank you," Catherine answered, watching how Peter moved, how his long legs were in the exact proportion to his body that David's had been. "We'll let you know if we do later. Everything seems fine for now."

Peter slipped by Christopher and angled around Catherine with a slight bow, set a chair down on the ground with a smile, and disappeared around the corner. At least she didn't have to stand in the cool breeze.

She pulled the old map out of her handbag and studied it anew with Christopher, now that the real deck was in front of them. The X David had marked on the map was on just about the top of the peeling deck, if it was accurately drawn.

"Here it is, Mrs. E., right where it says 'X' here on this map."

That meant it was next to them. Catherine looked at the ocean and the pebbled beach down the hill. Nobody saw the tears rolling down her cheeks, pictures of happiness flooding her memory.

"Go ahead, then, Christopher." She lowered herself into the chair.

Christopher grabbed the shovel and went straight to work, whistling as he went.

"Right, then, Mrs. E.," he said as he plunged the shovel into the damp earth. He worked at the edge of the deck, just a few feet from where Catherine sat. She had imagined a warm, sunny day for this venture. Now, as she watched Christopher dig where the map had indicated, she pulled her coat around her shoulders and shivered. The gray rain clouds had blown westward, and the sky was turning blue. But the sun was still behind a large cloud that was taking too long to make its way across the sky toward France.

Christopher's boot echoed on the shovel's edge, his breath puffed regularly, his face determined. He bumped his head on the underside of the deck as he dug deeper. The pile of earth grew larger as Catherine watched Christopher dig into its eternal depth.

"Dig there, please, Christopher," she said as she pointed to the back of the small cavern he had dug.

"Right you are, Mrs. Evans." The shovel hit something hard. "I've hit on something 'ere," Christopher said. He gently shoveled the dirt away, finally scooping it away with his hand.

When Christopher came across a solid metal box lid, he came out from under the deck and propped the shovel in the pile of dirt, leaping into the air.

"I think we found it!" he bellowed.

But it was a rock, dark and wet. Christopher frowned for only a moment, and then dug a little further to the right. Catherine sighed. The wet earth smelled red, the sky frowned, too, and waited with her. The clouds hovered, shimmering, asking for permission to move on. Christopher was puffing and tapping and grunting while she waited and wondered if this was really just total insanity, and thought that they were acting rather like children, digging for treasure. The more she thought about it, the more she felt she was just embarrassing herself and Christopher. She would give him a minute more and then call it off. The ocean crashed in the distance. A seagull sat on the railing and watched Christopher dig.

Once more, Christopher's shovel hit something hard.

"This time we've got it! We've got it!" he yelled, out of breath.

Catherine was surprised and jubilant, but could hardly do more than tap her umbrella against the post and shout, "We have found it! Well done, Christopher!" She clacked her umbrella against the shovel.

"It's a box or sumfink: lookie 'ere." He brushed away the dirt, tossing it behind his back so that Catherine saw it flying out from under the deck. "There's writing on it. Wot's that say there? I can't make it out. It ain't English: looks foreign."

Catherine leaned over and shielded her eyes, standing up to get closer and take a look. "Just a minute, Christopher, I'm not as young as I used to be."

Christopher jumped up and took her hand as she stood over the hole and peered in. "Can't see it, really," she said. "I'd have to get on my hands and knees, but I don't think I can really manage that, Christopher. Could you dig it out? Then we can see what it is." She backed away, breathless, and with one arm back, then the other, sat down in her chair.

"Right-o, Mrs. Evans. I don't want you breaking your neck just before we find the real treasure 'ere." He picked up the shovel and removed the dirt from the perimeter of the box, until there was room to loosen the box. He pushed and heaved and angled the shovel deeper under the box. The box shifted.

"I've got it!" he yelled. After another ten minutes of prodding, pushing, and pulling, he grunted and freed the box from its hole.

The metal box was about four inches wide and four inches tall, and about fourteen inches long. He opened the rusty top. Catherine looked into the box.

"Cor blimey, wot 'ave we got 'ere?" Christopher said as he reached in and pulled out one of the objects wrapped in yellowed newspaper. He pulled off the newspaper, noticing it was dated 1956, and held up a tarnished silver cup. He turned the cup over and over in his hands.

"Let me see the signature on the bottom," Catherine said.

Christopher held it quickly to his eyes and then held it close to Catherine's glasses.

"No, no, further away." Christopher moved it back a little and then a little more until she said, "Stop!" and held up her skinny pointer finger.

"Turn it to the light, Christopher. I can see better in the light. Not that there's ever sun in this country. Let me see now. Good. That's it!" Catherine squinted and cocked her head. She reached out and pulled the cup from Christopher's hands toward her. "Looks like Italian, same as the top of the box," she said, peering at the lid.

Catherine put the first cup down, picked up another cup, unwrapped it, and slid her fingers around its tarnished exterior, buried so long in the dark earth. David had touched this cup, moved it around his palm, studied the engravings; and perhaps kissed it. He had breathed deeply, maybe clouding the reflection of his contented smile as owner of this precious antique. Christopher laid out four more wrapped cups on the ground.

It looked like there was enough room in the box for about six more of those small cups. Why would David bury them beneath the deck? Maybe he did it because they were to leave on their planned trip to Italy— for safekeeping? Why didn't he lock them in a bank vault? She might never know.

# THE SPARKLING OBJECT

**Catherine spit** on her new handkerchief and rubbed the curve of the cup to bring out the old shine and the inscription. There was a horse with wings. Rubbing it again, she read part of a word: Sagittari... She was a Sagittarius, he had told her. Maybe he had planned to give her this cup anyway. A warm feeling shot through her hands to her heart. David had died just before their anniversary: She decided this was his present to her; to them. She clutched the cup to her heart for a solemn moment.

Christopher picked up another cup and held it up for her, the second one slipped into her right hand, then she reached out her left hand and let the cup, which felt like an old friend, rest on her palm. She held them both out at arm's length, like she was weighing them. They were like twins, only it seemed the new one had a different inscription. She handed her Sagittarius cup back to Christopher and squinted at the new cup.

She shifted the cup delicately around her palm, spat on her now-blackening handkerchief, and rubbed across the inscription. "Leo," it said, along with a drawing of a lion. David had been a Leo. She remembered him saying that to her. He had sworn that Leos and Sagittarians made great couples. It seemed so in their case, whether or not she believed in astrology herself. Catherine felt a warm presence surround her. If spirits existed, David's was right there, caressing her cheek with a kiss, giving her a feeling of relief and a sensation of an end to a long story. But there was more to find out. The clues were adding up: the old, embroidered handkerchief, and now the cups and a link with astrology. The newspaper they were wrapped in had a date: September 4, 1956.

"Where was I in September 1956? We were planning our anniversary trip to Italy in November. That's a long time ago, now. Perhaps ten long years after you were a twinkle in your father's eye," she said, nodding at Christopher.

"I don't fink me father ever 'ad a 'twinkle' for me," Christopher said. "I think I was just a bloomin' mistake."

"I expect your father was a human being with all the urges that every man has to procreate." Catherine held her umbrella against the gentle English late-summer sun, now finally poking through the clouds.

"He may not have had a conscious 'twinkle,' but underneath it all, it was there, don't you think?"

Christopher shrugged his shoulders.

"'Cellini,' it says on the inside of the box lid," Catherine said. "David was writing a book about him years ago. He was a famous silversmith in Italy hundreds of years ago. We could check it in the library." How lucky that Christopher had a mother to beat all library researchers.

Catherine looked along the beach and the coastline and realized they would have to go back to London quite soon. The sun that had peeked from behind the gray clouds was quickly hidden again, leaving a silver signature.

She stood up, with Christopher's help. He picked up her black umbrella, closed it, and handed it to Catherine.

After Christopher shoveled the dirt back into the hole, he gathered the box into his arms and left the shovel stuck in the earth. "You go first, Mrs. E., and if you fall backward, I'll drop this box and catch you."

"I'm not falling, but I'll be slower. You go ahead, Christopher. I'll be awhile." She waved her umbrella at him. He turned and went to the stairs. Catherine took a few tentative steps then tumbled forward onto her face.

Christopher dropped the box of cups on the steps and ran over to her.

"Mrs. Evans, Mrs. E., are you all right?" He grasped her thin arm and steadied her as she struggled to stand up.

"It's no use, Christopher. I think I've twisted my ankle a bit. Go get some help from Peter. I'll just sit here and watch the ocean."

Christopher hesitated, then turned and dashed to the staircase, grabbed the box, and leapt up the wooden steps.

Catherine gazed out at the horizon and rubbed her swelling ankle. She turned and looked at the shovel, and just then the sun peeked out from the clouds. There was a sparkle, a glint, a shiny object poking out of the newly covered hole. She turned and shoved herself onto the ground and crawled like a tortoise toward it, moaning each time she knocked her ankle. She lay down slowly and reached out to pull the sparkling object from the earth. It was a pair of old-fashioned, thick-rimmed glasses, the kind David always wore. She leaned down, not taking her eyes off them, and drew them up close to her own glasses. She kissed them tenderly, stretched over and put them into her handbag, grabbed the post of the deck, struggled to stand up, and, grasping the railing, limped back up the stairs and around to the front, just as Christopher was arriving with Peter to help her.

When the three of them reached the door and got themselves inside, Mrs. Evans offered Catherine a hot cup of tea and they sat down together. Catherine's ankle was slightly swollen.

"Another cup?" asked Mrs. Evans after a while.

"Well, if it will heal my ankle, of course!"

"It will heal anything," Mrs. Evans said, smiling as she poured another cup for Catherine and herself. Peter entered with a bandage and wrapped Catherine's ankle like an expert. His eyes briefly penetrated hers as if he were asking a question, then he left the room.

# REVELATION

**"My David** was the sweetest man to ever walk the earth," Catherine said. "He was a gentleman with me every day of our lives together." Catherine felt a loud silence fill the room. Mrs. Angela Evans sat up straight and tightened her lips.

"I'm going to have to tell you something you won't want to hear." Mrs. Evans fidgeted with her cup. Catherine blinked rapidly. "You knew David married me because I was pregnant," she said.

"Yes, of course I knew that," Catherine said.

"But he didn't tell you that my baby was, in fact, his baby also?"

Catherine silently stared at Mrs. Evans. "I'm sorry," she said, putting her hand up to her ear. "I didn't quite hear what you said." She stroked David's initials on the old handkerchief with her thumb. "Or did I?" she added.

"Yes, I'm afraid you did, my dear. My son is David's son. We were never engaged, and he didn't love me like he loved you. It was an accident. We were young and foolish and it just happened. He very kindly married me, and then left me because he didn't love me. He was afraid he'd get pulled in by his baby. We told people he'd left for India and never came back. I wasn't in love with him either, but the good man supported us all those years."

"You've got to be joking!" Catherine said, with a shrill note bordering on hysteria. Mrs. Evans sat stern and silent, staring at Catherine.

"He never told me it was his baby," Catherine said. "He just said he married you out of pity!" She regretted her words the moment they were out, but then, she meant them. It was the truth.

"Well, it *was* pity, but again, it was his child as well," Mrs. Evans said. "And then there was the money."

Catherine didn't really feel like knowing any more about this kind of mystery left behind by David. Not for the moment: one day; maybe soon. Not right now. But Mrs. Evans continued.

"David had a good sum of money he had inherited from his father," she said. "And he gave every penny to me and the baby. It was still hard on me when he left, but that enabled us to survive fairly comfortably." Mrs. Angela Evans put her hand to her chest and slowly sat back in her chair.

Catherine looked down, wished she could knit; wished she had never flown to London.

"I am in shock, please forgive me," Catherine said, casting her eyes away from Mrs. Evans.

Mrs. Evans leaned over and handed Catherine a tissue. "I never thought I'd have to tell you all this. Never thought I'd meet you. I didn't mean to be secretive, except that David and I agreed to keep it a secret as long as I took the money. He had arranged for the bank to send me cash once in a while all through our son's younger years."

Catherine knew only the David who worked too hard and who had scrimped with her to get by. Catherine felt guilty for her lack of generosity and spirit of understanding and forgiveness, all of which she'd thought herself such an expert at. David: with his angelic smile; his bright, loving eyes. David: harboring secrets he should have told her. She had a right to know. For a moment, a flicker of a memory arose in her: Had she turned a blind eye to all this? Wasn't she just as bad, with her angelic smile for him? Catherine felt a little sick and excused herself. She walked haltingly down the hall to the "water closet."

Standing in front of the toilet, staring down at it with a nauseous feeling, she cried and wondered how all these years later she could find a degree of hatred toward the only man she'd ever truly loved.

However, it didn't seem fair to lay her disappointment onto Mrs. Evans, who had borne the secret all these years. She joined Mrs. Evans again and reached her hand out to her. "My dear, I never knew. I never suspected. I am so sorry."

Mrs. Evans reached her own hand toward Catherine's and leaned forward as they touched; Catherine's other hand gently covered and enclosed the hand of her stepson's mother, who, Catherine realized, had been silent and courageous her whole life. Between the women were two perfumes, a little strong, but perfect for people drowning in sad memories so pungent.

"If I had known, I would have helped. I can't understand why David kept it a secret. I thought we were always so candid; so honest with each other." Was she always so candid with him, she wondered?

"My dear, it was I, really, who swore him to secrecy," Mrs. Evans reassured Catherine. "I didn't want to ruin your unofficial marriage. It was, as you know, such a scandal in those days. It was for you mostly. Men weather these things in their way, but a woman's life is ruined with too much information. We always want to get involved, don't we?"

Catherine didn't answer. Did men weather it? Had David weathered it? He'd worked until he dropped, socked his earnings away for their future home, and stole some change to slip to Mrs. Evans, so alone, and a single mother with a small, dependent baby.

# AN ANCHOR

**"Did you ever** tell your son that David was his father?" Catherine asked, settling back with her hands folded.

"When he was eighteen; he was shocked and silent for three whole days. I am sure you have noticed how like David Peter is?"

Catherine nodded and smiled a little. "Yes. I felt it before you told me. I saw it in your grandchildren's eyes." She turned her head toward the door Peter had exited. "I feel we are like sisters," she said to Mrs. Evans. "I never had a child with David and always felt sad that we had waited so long. Now I feel like I, too, have a son." Noticing Mrs. Evan's serious expression, she added, "I mean a stepson."

The two women sat in silence as Catherine contemplated her knuckles and ridged fingernails.

"Well, I suppose we ought to be getting along," Catherine said. "It's a long way back to London, and we must get there before dark."

"Do say goodbye to Peter and his children," Mrs. Evans said.

"David's son and grandchildren, hardly children now," Catherine mumbled.

The two women stood up slowly, and Catherine busied herself with her handbag, her handkerchief, and smoothing down her dress. She put a little weight on her bad ankle again.

"You know, I do think that tea has cured my ankle. It feels like it's almost back to normal. I think I will keep the bandage on anyway, if you don't mind."

"Please do," said the other Mrs. Evans. Catherine slowly led the way down the hall toward the front door.

"Henry," Mrs. Evans called, walking behind Catherine.

"We're home!" replied a voice at the front door that sounded exactly like David's.

Henry came to offer Catherine his hand. Its warmth melted Catherine's heart as she looked into the soul of this young man who looked so like David.

"We must get to know each other," Catherine said. "I knew your grandfather very well."

"I know. We don't have to hide anything," Henry said. "I know all about him. So does my father. I am very pleased to finally meet you, Mrs. Evans."

Then Peter came and shook her hand. His eyes were his father's. His stance, even his lopsided smile, was his father's, and he probably didn't even know it. His hand was warm. Catherine could hardly bear to let it go.

Christopher stepped outside, the box tucked well under his arm, and bowed slightly as he backed away.

Catherine smiled and fingered her new handkerchief. She thought about David's initials on his old handkerchief, about the possibility of his DNA still being on it.

Was David really so secretive? He never told her that Mrs. Evans' baby was his own; he hardly ever mentioned the silver cups. And he'd never told her much about his inheritance from his father.

Catherine folded the handkerchief and pressed the folds several times with her fingernails, as if to iron it into a crisp crease like she used to do. She remembered ironing all his handkerchiefs, sprinkling water over them and pressing the heavy iron onto them, his shirt collars, and his trouser creases. It was her way of holding up his handsome turnout and his image for his job. She was there wherever he went. She was there with him at the pubs as he raised his beer mug and interviewed the famous for the next day's headlines. The creases in his trousers as he sat on the barstool were her presence, her contribution to their livelihood. She had loved to iron. It was meditative. She would listen to the wireless and look out their Kentish Town window at the bustling commuters hurrying along Kentish Town Road against the rain toward the Tube station.

Peter stood at the front door, his hand again reaching toward Catherine. She looked straight into his eyes: David's eyes; David's son. Just before she delicately stepped away from the front door, their hands touched once again. Catherine felt she'd found in him an anchor she didn't know was missing in her life.

# 1908: CAREY

**George**, the old man in the village with the wheelbarrow, somehow knew of the shipwrecks. Word of mouth arrived faster than a train. George was at the scene with his children and grandchildren, and the beach was scoured before the villagers had had their morning tea. The grandchildren were in their teens by now and climbed the rocks to look down into the shallows and the waves rolling in over them. They even dragged out strips of wood broken from the hull of the ship; but only after the true valuables were scavenged before the villagers inevitably arrived.

Sometimes George was blamed for putting the swinging lantern around the donkey's neck on the rocks to lure the ship to its doom. This time he had said he'd had business that day in a faraway town. But one couldn't help but notice his business was always completed and his cart was empty, just asking to be filled with plundered treasures. It was rumored that he gave each child or grandchild a farthing for anything they dragged up the beach to his cart. Anything of true value he might reward with two farthings or a penny.

At ten-years-old, Ronnie was the most agile and daring, and he didn't mind the freezing salty water over his head as he lunged to the rocky bottom and pulled out shiny objects, or leather cases, or plates that had not broken, or a full pair of shoes, tied together with leather laces. Ronnie was known around the village for his bravery and his daring eyes that spotted treasures others could only wish to see.

Only one treasure seemed to languish over the centuries, for Ronnie and George's grown children had always looked out to sea, to the far rock where the ships crashed. From the top of the rocks they couldn't see under the ledge of jutting rocks underneath where they stood. The bounty always rumbled and rolled up to the huge rock and hovered there until it was claimed, save the one treasure that had been rolled and knocked around that huge boulder when the world slept, until it snuggled in its home for centuries, forgotten, settled in like a hermit crab inside the rocks, tucked in forever.

Carey picked her way among the rocks, pulling her long skirt high over the surf. She glanced up at the steep cliff high above her. The tide was just coming back in, and the rocky beach sparkled in the summer sun. As the sea swarmed in and around her ankles, Carey jumped to clear the bubbles. Her leather shoes, full of salt and sand, squelched against her bare skin. She'd empty them later. A rectangular shape in the rocks just under the water beckoned her nearer. The clouds raced across the sky. The wind kicked up the waves. In the distance the white caps rose and moved rapidly toward the girl. The shape had disappeared, but Carey kept her eye on the spot where she'd seen it. The waves got bigger. The wind tore against her dress.

Carey was soaked to the waist, but she didn't turn back. The tide had turned, but she had plenty of time still to push through the deepening water, crunching over the tiny pebbles underfoot. She stood, eyes rapidly searching, while in her peripheral vision she saw a huge wave bearing down out of nowhere. She grabbed one of the large boulders that had crashed down the cliff thousands of years before and held its slippery rough surface, pushing herself behind it just in time. The rogue wave shot all around her and into her nostrils. The salty water drowned her mouth and throat. She coughed and choked, but held fast to the jutting rock. What if another wave came and dragged her out to sea? She looked again to where she thought she'd seen the unusual shape, but it was covered with water that seemed to stay there, high and getting higher. She decided to go back, to time her retreat with the next wave. Just then, the clouds parted and the shape of a box in the rocks became quite clear.

Carey pushed her way up the rocks under that thrashing sky, her arms finally grasping the slippery box. Another giant wave was racing toward her. She quickly pushed her legs and wet dress through the water and waded back around the rocks and sand, struggling up toward the dry beach. The wave opened like a giant hand and pulled at her shoulders and her legs, almost prying the box loose with its itching fingers, ready to pull it back into the sea and the rocks—its home for so many years.

Carey fell to her knees, grasping the box as if it were a baby. The wave died, and the sea backed away into the deep, leaving her a moment to get back on her agile feet. She ran the rest of the way up the sand and stones to a safe place where, panting, she tumbled to her knees again and let the box crash to the ground.

When she recovered, she sat up and began to push her palms across the box, now rough with growths of barnacles and seaweed. She turned the box over. A rusty chain held it closed. She drew it to her nose and sniffed. It smelled of seaweed, a familiar aroma dear to her. Carey sat down in the cold sand, her clothes soaked, and tried to open the box. The green moss made it slippery to her hands and seemed to hold the top closed, resisting her pull. She opened the rusty fastener with difficulty, using two stones against it. When she finally opened the box she saw twelve small, black cups, one inside of the other.

Toys! Here were lots of little cups for her straw and cotton dolls to drink from. As she sat in the pebbles and sand, she brushed and rubbed them with her wet dress. The cups were old and tarnished, and their exterior engravings were hardly decipherable.

She saw the horse-man and his arrows. She saw a crab. She put them side by side and played house, each cup for one of the twelve children she planned to begin having when she turned fifteen.

Carey pulled them out and pretended to sip from one. She studied the pretty engravings on the sides: all different. They were almost black. She rubbed the outside of one and it stayed dark. As she licked her pointer finger, stuck it inside the cup, and ground it around the bottom, the smallest hint of silver shone through.

Carey was delighted. She would go home and clean her treasures and have the best tea party her dolls had ever had. Putting the cups inside of one another and laying them into their box, she then closed the lid and gathered her bounty under her arm. She stood up, leaving the rusty old lock in the sand.

This was her secret treasure; hers and her doll family's. She climbed back up the path between the rocks to her house on the cliff.

Carey took them into her barn to the far, private corner, past the cow and the horses, past the chickens and their little yellow offspring; into the hay she had built up in her special corner where she kept her dolls. Her mother's voice called to her.

"Coming, Mummy," she yelled back. She wondered where she would hide her treasure. Her mother would probably take them away from her if she knew Carey had something that might not be hers to own. Perhaps she would bury it after dinner, behind the outhouse where the earth was soft.

Carey put her box down and covered it with hay, assuring her dolls she would return for a great party. She scampered across the yard, chickens squawking in her path, and went into the old brick house. Their straw roof needed mending again, but it wasn't leaking yet, so the wooden buckets were stacked in the corner in case her father couldn't fix it in time for the winter rains.

Carey stood with her hands behind her back, looking as innocent as she could, while her mother reached out and brushed seaweed from her daughter's skirt. The seaweed gave her away this time. She wished her mother had been too busy to notice, but perhaps the light of the day had shone into their house just at that moment, lighting up Carey just for the time it took her mother to see her dampened daughter.

# HIDDEN AND SAFE

**"Come,"** said Carey's mother, so Carey didn't have to confess what her mother already knew. "Let's change your clothes before you start coughing and keeping us up all night again."

Her father stood open-mouthed, looking at his wet daughter, the seaweed clinging to her dress, her leather shoes; her bedraggled hair.

"Carey, me love, whatever have you done with yourself?" he stammered.

"I stumbled, Papa, right into the surf."

"Not from the cliffs, I fear, love?"

"No, Papa. From the sand and stones. I was afraid. I got rolled in a wave I didn't see until it was too late."

Carey especially hated lying to her father, who was a gentle person, while all the fathers near their farm seemed so bad-tempered to her. But, just this once, she needed to keep her special secret.

"Run and change into warm clothes, love, and come for some hot stew."

Carey's mother stood by the fire with the line deepening between her eyebrows. She stirred the large pot as the flames lapped beneath it. It would be vegetables from their garden, mostly potatoes, and this was the day of the week they slaughtered a chicken, so there would be meat to chew.

Carey changed and then came to the wooden table by the fire and ate her supper quietly, thinking all the while about her new doll cups. After supper she made a dash for the box she'd left in a corner of their barn, grabbed a shovel, and went into the corner of the barn to bury her treasure. She knew about sea treasures. She'd heard about the lantern swinging from a donkey's neck as he stood on the cliff, luring boats to their doom through the fog, fooling the ships into thinking it was another ship at sea. The ship would sail toward the light, then crash onto the rocks, their sunken treasures soon to be plundered by the townsfolk.

When Carey came back into the house, she walked over and stood by her mother, whose hand reached to Carey's forehead and pulled her wet hair aside.

"I'm glad you didn't get pulled in by the undercurrent. It was powerful today, love, according to Mr. Southerby."

Carey didn't like Mr. Southerby; but worse than him was his son, Hawthorn, who teased her. She would never share her secret with him. The Southerbys lived on the farm next to theirs, and the older sons were thought to be the ones who'd placed the light on the donkey that made the last ship flounder and sink. They had gone to claim their bounty long before the rest of the townsfolk had even heard about the sinking. That was five years before, but everybody knew, even the children. In fact, everybody in the village knew this had been going on for hundreds of years. Carey stopped to wonder if she were as horrible a thief as they were? No, she decided. She had not hung the lantern on the donkey's neck to lure the sailors to their doom. She had only found the cups years later, and she didn't know for sure where they had come from.

The next morning, very early, when her father had finished milking Gertie, Carey crept away from her house, circled quietly around her father and the haystack, and sidled into the barn and back into her corner.

She cleared away the straw, dug up the box, and opened it; she gave her dolls a long speech about how they should watch over their new treasures. Carey went over to the side of the barn where a line of tools were hanging, and with the small trowel, walked back and began to dig a deeper hole. This treasure would always have a safe hiding place now, especially when that nasty Hawthorn Southerby from next door came around bothering and teasing her. He'd steal them, she knew. There wasn't anything good about him, her mother always said, but he was the only child for miles, so Carey tolerated him.

Carey heard clinking on the other side of the barn and pushed her box into its new hiding place, hastily covering it with the fresh-dug earth, then sprinkling it over with straw. There: hidden and safe. Usually Hawthorn came onto their property without even a polite hello. She listened. What was he doing outside now? The clinking stopped and he walked away, coughing.

The next day again, Hawthorn was again behind the barn, hitting two rocks together. At eleven years old he was fascinated with power and magic, but especially fire. The year before he'd set fire to her hair. Carey avoided him and went to the barn to check on her treasure. She dug it up and lined her cups up in a row. Her dolls had spent the night in the barn keeping watch. She fed them a little of Gertie's milk for their reward.

Clink, clink, she heard from the back of the barn. Carey lay her dolls down, buried her cups in their box, and covered them with earth and then hay. She ran outside just in time to see that awful Hawthorn lighting the straw with his sparks and the flames lapping up the side of the barn. She ran toward him, screaming as she saw him trying to stamp out the fire, the black smoke fierce in her nostrils, her scalp burning hot; then her scream dried up, her parched throat and lungs sticking closed.

"Hawthorn, run! Get water! Run!" she yelled hoarsely.

The summer heat had dried the barn, and the fire ate at it like a dragon. The black smoke seemed to surround the whole barn, and within minutes the barn was in flames, the hay feeding the fire. Her father ran into the barn to let out the neighing, large-eyed horses. Carey opened the outside gate of the pen next to the barn for the pigs to escape. She got away then and watched as Hawthorn's parents ran over, yelling and pouring water. Carey's hands were blackened as she hugged a baby pig, who squealed like a human. She coughed as the smoke circled above, and heard another baby pig crying; this one had run the wrong way inside the burning barn. She jumped up and ran to the barn to save him.

Carey stumbled over the running pig onto her face, the hot earth against it. "Roll away," she said to herself. The fire lapped against the inside of the barn, singeing her hair. Carey rolled away from the flames, hitting at her hair. Hawthorn ran to her and dropped his coat onto

Carey's head, pulled her arms and body another few feet away from the blaze, and then ran away, coughing violently. Carey tucked her head into the jacket as she rolled a few feet further away.

"Wrong way, wrong way!" yelled Hawthorn.

Carey felt dizzy, began to roll back toward the fire, coughing and choking, hearing the loud crackle of the fire.

"No!" yelled her father, as he ran hard toward her, his eyes bulging, his mouth wide, water splashing from the bucket in his hand.

Carey pulled her face free from the coat. The fire crackled and, with a loud boom, burst into a huge, roaring, orange storm that immediately consumed Carey and the whole blackened barn.

# THE MYSTERIOUS
# PHONE CALL

**The phone call** the next evening came as a surprise. No one knew Catherine was staying overnight at Christopher and Maureen's. Yet, there it was: someone asking distinctly for "Mrs. Evans."

Christopher held the phone toward Catherine's hand and shrugged slightly. "It's for you, Mrs. Evans. Didn't say who it was."

Catherine held the phone to her ear and listened as she rubbed the bandage over her swollen ankle. Maureen stood by with her hand on her hip. Catherine didn't say a word. She hung up the phone and carried on reading *The Daily Mail* and sipping her second cup of tea.

"Beggin' your pardon, Mrs. Evans, but would it be rude to ask who that was on the blower?" Christopher bowed slightly and smiled like they had obviously taught him at the top hotel he used to work at: eyes lowered, not too broad, not too interested; very respectful. Maureen leaned in to listen.

"Well, Christopher, there was a man's voice on the end of that line. He was talking to somebody else, not me. He said, 'She's got them.' I'm sure that's what he said. Do you think he knows we dug up the silver cups? How would he know unless we'd been followed?" She was not really interested in Christopher's answers, and kept speaking. "Well, I'm not afraid, Christopher. I'm getting too old to be afraid to die." She paused again for a long moment. Christopher's eyes were glued to her face.

"Christopher," she said, her pointer finger raised for his attention. "Yes, Mrs. Evans," he said, bowing slightly.

"This is the murderer we're after."

Christopher's mouth dropped open. Catherine lifted her head and adjusted her glasses, which had slid down her nose. She saw that her right hand man hadn't quite the courage required of him. But in all her wisdom, she decided to ignore it. "I think we're hot on the trail. Thank you, Christopher."

"I didn't do nothing. Wot? Dug an 'ole two feet 'round in the wet earth under a deck, that's all. Wasn't even raining much, was it? I'd do it again in a minute. I'm no 'ero, ma'am." Christopher bowed his head and stepped backward. Perhaps he didn't plan on any wilder heroics, but Catherine couldn't promise him it wouldn't get worse.

"Christopher, hand me my handbag, please." He walked over to the table, picked up her handbag, and placed it on her lap. "Now, let me see. I do believe it's payday." She rummaged in her soft, woven bag to find a leather wallet. She took out a hundred pounds. "Well done, Christopher. You are a hero to me." Christopher hesitated politely, then took the notes in his fingers and stuffed them into his pocket, with a shrug backward and a small, sheepish grin.

"Thanks, Mrs. E. Very generous of you. Thanks ever so."

Catherine lay a hundred pounds in front of Maureen, who swept the notes up into her bosom with a gleeful look in her eyes. "Ta very much," she smiled.

Just then the phone rang again. Christopher and Maureen bobbed their heads forward toward Catherine. Christopher handed Catherine the black phone. "Hello?" began Catherine. "Hello?" she said again.

"Hello," said a man's voice.

Catherine's mouth dropped open as she made a face at Maureen and Christopher. There was a long silence. Maureen and Christopher leaned forward, straining to catch a word.

"Hello?" Catherine said again. There was a clicking sound. "Well, of all the nerve."

"At least he spoke. What did he sound like?" Maureen asked.

"He sounded English: a low voice; rude, hanging up on me like that!"

"Maybe he'll call again?" Christopher suggested.

"No point in lounging about. We could wait a week," Maureen grumbled.

The phone rang. Maureen and Christopher pointed at Catherine, who lifted the receiver. "Stop this rude behavior," she said. "State your business. I know what you're doing," Catherine said. Then, after a moment, she held the receiver out to Christopher. "That rude man hung up again."

"Blimey, maybe you're really closer than you fink, Mrs. Evans. Maybe you're sittin' right on top of a pile of gold and only he knows it!"

"No," Catherine said. "He doesn't care about a pile of gold. He doesn't want me to find out he's the murderer."

"Could be," Maureen chimed in.

"Oh, it doesn't scare me one bit. It probably gives me the courage I've been lacking up till now. He's a coward. Let him phone us."

"He could barge in on us and steal the cups!" Christopher laughed.

"Let him try. My umbrella has no qualms about where it pokes an intruder!"

The phone rang. They let it ring ten times. Catherine took the receiver from Christopher's outstretched hand.

"If you're trying to frighten me, you haven't got a chance. You're nothing but a coward," she said and slammed the phone down.

"What did he say?" Christopher asked.

"Nothing. He must have been surprised. No, he didn't say one word. But he heard a few!" They all laughed.

"We've got the cups, and this caller is after either me or the cups, or both," Catherine concluded.

Christopher shuffled around clearing the table and dusting away the crumbs. A squirrel hopped onto the horse chestnut tree just outside the window. The red-and-white check curtains shivered energetically. Catherine sat up straight and listened. "It's strange, but I feel like David's standing by the windows and saying, 'Be careful.'"

# Something
# Incriminating

**"Well, Maureen,"** Catherine mumbled, waking up later in the day from a very short nap in the armchair. "Tell me how your research is going?"

"Well, Mrs. Evans," Maureen began, laying a pile of papers on the table. "I come up wif a startling bit of news about the silver and them 'oroscopes. There was cups made back in Italy in the 1770s or maybe earlier, made for churches and rich people too. Some people liked horoscopes a lot then, same as today. They had huge globes with the stars against the outlines of the constellations. The Catholic Church liked to engrave them globes 'round the edges. Yours has an 'orse with a man's chest and head, shooting a bow and arrow. It's Sagittarius. So, the question is, is this important in our search?" Maureen shifted her breasts higher and smiled broadly.

"Well done, Maureen," Catherine smiled. "That will date the cups. Sounds like they are worth a fortune, whatever was carved on them."

Christopher came home, closed the front door noisily, and opened the kitchen door.

"Hello, love," Maureen bellowed. "Would you like a cuppa tea?"

"Yes, thanks, Mum," he answered. "Mrs. Evans, I've just been snooping through the silver stores at the Portobello Road and came up with this book on silver cups. Lookie 'ere. 'Ere's one almost the exact design as the one we found in the dirt."

All three leaned over the pages as Christopher held the old book in front of Catherine and pointed. Catherine adjusted her glasses.

"The cups are Italian, it says here," she said. "Looks like an identical one." The three looked at one another in silence.

"Could be quite valuable, I'd say," Maureen said, decidedly.

"Where shall I hide them?" Catherine wondered aloud.

"You can hide them here for the moment. It's safe 'round here. Nobody has anything worth stealing!" Christopher said.

They wrapped them up again and closed the box. Christopher pointed to the top of the kitchen cupboard and got a chair. Catherine nodded, and Christopher pushed them to the back of the shelf.

"Now," Catherine said, turning toward Maureen. "What else have you found out at the library?"

"Well, come look here what I found on the microfiche: bloody small print, pardon the expression. Finally had to put me specs on," Maureen said, cleaning her large, round glasses with her handkerchief.

Catherine and Christopher stood on either side of Maureen at the table and stared at the papers.

"Brought a copy. Here, love. Take a gander."

A clipped stack of copied papers lay in front of her on the table. Catherine pushed her teacup and saucer to the right, grabbed the stack with both hands, and moved it into her vision. The pages sparkled under the ceiling light as she settled her glasses on her nose.

"What's this?" she said, pointing.

"That's all about Ruth Ellis, like you told me."

Catherine flipped the pages, remembering that photograph of a mad-looking Ruth Ellis, who had been hanged just over a year before the gavel came down for Catherine for life in prison, instead of hanging.

"That's Ruth Ellis, indeed," Catherine murmured.

She turned the pages about her own trial, the sad photographs of her as she was led away from the courthouse amid the jeering English crowds. There was an earlier photograph of her with David's arm around her, from the beginning of their married days. David's face never aged. He was stuck in his youth forever. And the young woman next to him,

Catherine herself, with the large hat and the open, laughing mouth, had grown over the years into a line-faced, older woman who hardly opened her mouth to laugh much anymore.

Catherine smiled quietly. She picked up more papers and lay them on a stack to her left. She stopped at the article that said, *"Alleged murderer found innocent. DNA at the scene does not match the DNA of the accused."* She pulled the paper closer and read slowly. She was getting warmer. But there wasn't much explanation of DNA itself, so she put it on the other pile and glanced at the next page. This article said all that was needed was a swab from the mouth, a hair from the head, a toothbrush, something personal. After all these years, what would be left of the crime scene that would turn her case around?

"Seems to me I've got to have something from the scene of the crime to start with," Catherine said. She turned the pages in a kind of trance. Her mind was numb against the pain of that horrible moment she found David on the kitchen floor.

She couldn't remember much of that day; she'd been in such a state of shock, and had felt repulsed by David's blood on her hands, and a speck or two on her loafers—the ones she'd worn on the day they took her to jail, and the day she left.

# 1968: Freedom

**The day** they let her out of Holloway Prison off Camden Road in London was eternally etched in her brain. It was the last time she would take off that shredded uniform and the last time she would put on her old, out-of-style, dark-blue flower-print dress they'd kept for twelve years. Those ugly brown prison shoes would go to some other unfortunate prisoner. Her feet had hardly fit back into the now-tough leather loafers she had worn the day they took her to prison. The clouds and the blue sky in the distance shattered the bars that day. She had kicked her old shoes across the floor and laughed as the mean guard puffed up her chest and glared at her one last time.

That day filled her vision like a large screen in a movie. She clearly remembered the squeaking of the wide front door as she walked back into freedom. The mist surrounding the church's steeple across Camden Road only allowed the top to poke through. Where was the pastor with a kind welcoming word? Where was anybody?

Catherine had stepped forward into the silent arms of freedom. Her handkerchief was crushed in her grasp. Her purse contained enough money to get to Kentish Town and a one-way ticket to Vermont that had been sent to her by David's mother in Brattleboro.

Nobody had reached out a warm hand to lead her away from twelve years of jail. She walked away from the door as it closed noisily behind her. She turned for a moment and walked backward along the driveway to observe the ancient building that looked like a castle that had been her home. When she turned around, her steps hesitant, the taste of freedom alarmed her. Nobody told her to walk forward to the bus stop; she figured it out alone. Nobody said look right at the oncoming, one-way traffic. She backed up onto the curb as a mob of cars and trucks barreled toward her, then disappeared, leaving a quiet gap. Nobody said, "Go now, run!" She just did it. Her pace was quickening. She lunged across the street, hugging her case, up the curb and over to the fork in the road where they had said her bus stop was. A throng of traffic noisily shot past her. Nobody said, "Go, now!" But a free voice from inside: her very own; not a guard's voice, said, "Cross now!"

A red, double-decker bus sped down the road ahead, and beyond another bus pulled up Camden Road, heading toward Camden Town. She studied the new coins they had given her, heavy, large, their size nothing to do with their stated value. So much had changed in twelve years; new money, even. How much had they said bus fare was now?

At the red "request" sign, she raised her hand to alight. The bus stopped. She climbed aboard, put her case down, and held out a handful of leaden coins. The driver selected rather a lot of change and issued her a receipt. Nobody on the bus searched her with their eyes, or seemed to suspect her of any wrongdoing. Nobody knew she had just stepped back into life. She made her way back with her case as the bus trundled along. In seven minutes she pressed the bell and stood for her change to Kentish Town. Camden Town seemed to be five times as crowded as the last time she saw it. People dashed by her in both directions. They bumped her and didn't even say sorry.

The feeling of time speeding up overtook her. The rhythm of her life crumbled and nothing recognizable fell into its place. She wound her way across fast cars on new one-way streets and stood in a long bus queue. But when the bus headed toward Kentish Town arrived, people pushed in from the sides: women with prams, young people very well-dressed, very colorful. Where were the dark navy blue raincoats? People even wore yellow coats! The air seemed cleaner. The sky was bluer; the clouds were white, not gray.

"Kentish Town," she said, as the next driver again picked out coins from her outstretched palm.

On the way, Catherine noticed that at least the Woolworth's Store was still there on Kentish Town High Road. The other shops had slick, bright-red signs. London had moved on from the aftermath of the war. Women hardly wore headscarves anymore. Catherine made her way across Kentish Town High Road, past the Light Railway and over to Leighton Road, and the old corner pub, the Assembly Rooms, and their old flat next door.

Catherine stood outside and looked up to the second-floor flat that used to be her mother's. She knew her mother had died, but she needed to look at the building once more. There was no more *home* there, and no more *mother*. But just standing there gave her a kind of peace she hadn't known for a long time. The whole building had a new coat of off-white paint. Behind her a train whistled by on the other side of the brick wall. Catherine noticed that the people walking by there didn't wear dark wool coats anymore, but rather high heels and colorful handbags; they walked with less of a dreary, struggled pace, and more of a quick, purposeful stride.

"Hello, Mrs. Evans," said a familiar voice.

# KINDNESS

**Catherine turned** to see a very hunched old man with chalky cheeks and bright eyes smiling at her. Who knew her name? She hesitated as she studied this person.

"The Brighton house...you bought me house," the old man hinted.

Here he stood, doubled over, as old as any man she had ever seen.

"Mr. Bernie Ward," she said, amazed that this name was still somewhere under her skull.

"Come in and have a cup of tea," he said. He opened the door of the building next to her mother's old flat, and she stepped into the past. She turned right into the sitting room, and he came in and turned on the gas wall heater. "Now, you just make yourself at home, Mrs. Evans, and I'll be right back with a hot teapot for you."

Catherine didn't realize how tired she was, what effort it had taken to become free again. Her head ached with bright new colors, the need she had felt to avoid being run over, the pace of the hordes of people crashing around her. Before she sat, she put the back of her legs to the gas fire until it made a red impression of a crisscrossed design on her bare legs. Then she sat down. The train whistled from across the road over the brown brick wall, and some cars roared by the narrow road between the house, the wall, and the railway tracks. Then it was so quiet she could hear Mr.

Ward talking to himself in the kitchen. She smelled warm toast. Her mouth watered for real jam.

The tray preceded him as he slowly turned into the sitting room and set it down on the coffee table next to her: toasted scones; melted butter and apricot jam; a knitted tea cozy keeping the teapot hot.

"Shall I be mother?" Mr. Ward offered, as he sat down in the easy chair next to her and poured two cups of tea, leaving the tea cozy on the teapot.

"How kind," Catherine nodded, fingering for her handkerchief, and feeling her small case by her leg. It seemed to her that nobody had been kind to her for twelve years. Here it was again after so long: kindness—just for the sake of pleasant company. Freedom was taking a hold of her and producing a tentative smile that had been lost in a fog of fear and anger for years. Her eyes felt different: not just the tears she tried to hold back, but her hidden soul that she exposed to this old man who seemed to care enough to invite her into his home for a simple cup of tea.

As she lifted the cup to her lips, she spotted a painting above the mantelpiece. It was a larger version of their beach house print. She felt a pain squeezing her throat. The handkerchief was on her eyes, over her nose and mouth, and back to her eyes.

"Never mind, love; never mind," Bernie Ward said quietly.

After looking down and fussing with the teapot, Mr. Ward continued. "I knew your mum that last year. I knocked on her door to introduce meself. She was poorly, and I brought her tea every day. She missed you so. She was too weak to visit you, as you know. I did me best to help her. I used to visit her gravesite in the Highgate Cemetery now and again."

"I hope I can visit her grave before I leave for Vermont tomorrow."

"I will be obliged to help you out."

"Mr. Ward. I can't thank you enough," Catherine said. "It was truly the most painful thing I ever went through, being locked up and not able to help Mother. We wrote, or at least, I wrote until she died. I kept writing until someone told me she had died. I remember my chest caving in on itself." Catherine stopped while she caught her breath and felt a fluttering in her heart. "Yes, I shall visit her grave in the morning. Could you draw me a map? It is such a big, rambling cemetery."

Mr. Ward, pen already in hand, drew the entrance to the cemetery and then lines rounding corners of graves. He handed it to her and she put it into her handbag.

As the tea settled her stomach, Catherine shifted herself to stand up. Her feet felt pinched by the stiff leather of her old loafers. She felt Mr. Ward must be risking his reputation with the neighbors. They all knew. As a convicted murderer, Catherine needed to go to Vermont and start a new life. The date on her ticket was for late the following afternoon.

"David's mother has given me the ticket to Vermont. I shall go live at her house and sort out my life. Look at this letter she sent me."

Catherine took an old piece of paper out of her case, stood up, and handed it to Mr. Ward.

"Dearest Catherine," he read aloud. "I know you didn't kill David. I think his death and your imprisonment have shortened my life considerably. I know you won't want to live in England when they let you out, so I am willing my house in Brattleboro to you. You can make a home there. It's not a bad little town. Strange varieties of people, but they will like you. People here live in the present. They look to the future. They don't judge you by your past. They'll want to know what you are doing now. So, pick up the pieces and enjoy your new life. Take up hobbies, get to know people. Don't be lonely. It says in your horoscope you'll be content here! I am not long for this life, my dear. I have a small amount of savings, and I am leaving most of it to you so you can start your new life. By the way, I always knew David couldn't actually marry you, but to me, you were always his wife. It said so in the horoscopes. God Bless You, Mom."

"I'm so pleased for you, Mrs. Evans," he said, handing her back the letter.

Catherine took the letter, stood up straight, and held out her hand as if to say goodbye. "Well, I must be going."

"No! No! You must spend the night here," Mr. Ward said. "Now, just sit yourself back down and make yourself at home. I'll go make up your room."

"Oh, Mr. Ward, I can't thank you enough. I would dearly love to accept your invitation, but..."

Catherine realized she had no plans, apart from flying out of England; no idea where she would sleep this last night.

Mr. Ward rested his hand on her arm and gently nudged her back into her chair.

"You just have more tea, and please, I would truly love for you to be a guest in me home. Your mum spoke of you, and now that she's gone, I feel like I'd like to stand in her shoes and treat you as me own. One night won't be any bother, you know. I won't hear another word."

Catherine sat back down and flashed Mr. Ward a beautiful smile. It felt like a solid iron gate had lifted and a gust of friendliness blew around them, missing for so long from Catherine's life.

"You've talked me into it, dear Mr. Ward. But please allow me to make up the room."

"Nothing to be done. It's all made up. It were just a figure of speech. I love having overnight company. All me friends are gone. Such a pleasure to share me home with an old friend."

Before Catherine could reply, Mr. Ward scuttled out the door with his tiny steps and thick jumper hanging over his bony shoulders.

# A New Life

**The next day** they hugged goodbye. Mr. Ward laid twenty pounds in Catherine's hand. "Highgate Cemetery, mate," he said to the taxi driver, and Catherine was too overwhelmed and grateful to protest.

She knew she would never see old Bernie Ward again, but as long as she might live, she would never forget his kindness. She turned to wave out of the back window and watched Leighton Road recede and be enclosed by pedestrians and buses, honking cars, bicyclists, people in the queue for the next buses. As the people of London hurried about their day, paying bills, drinking at the corner pubs, searching for work, going to the park with their children in strollers, Catherine sped away to visit her mother for the last time.

The gravesite was modest. "Here lies one who was loved," someone had engraved on the stone. Catherine stood over the grave as the wind blew the leaves. A cold chill crept up her coat sleeves. She was ready to go, but longed for the past, for David, for the England she used to know that had disappeared into a mist that was now only memory. It was time to go back to the land of her father and David's mother.

As the plane lifted she looked out at the green football fields, the rows of houses, and the Queen's residence. Catherine slept most of the way on the plane.

Vermont in the fall welcomed Catherine home. Bright orange and yellow leaves fluttered above her as she walked briskly up High Street, into the bookstore, the hardware store, the café. Brattleboro was a tidy old town with its assortment of characters, from skiers to hippies. There were small political protests, homegrown theatrical and musical productions, writers' groups, discussion groups, folksingers' gatherings.

Catherine had found, however, that she needed a sense of privacy there, unlike London; she had a stubborn fear of the gossip possible in a small Vermont town.

No one there ever knew of her sad past in London. Here she was no celebrity, just another woman shopping at the co-op, going to the old cinema, reading newspapers at the new library. It was too late to think of having children. She was too old to have babies. Somehow, although she had gone on several dates, no man had come along in Vermont and swept her off her feet.

The Unitarian church welcomed her, and she gradually made friends. Routines of life and seasons took hold of her. The important daily chores of shopping, cooking, washing, and ironing melted her into the life of each day. Her garden thrived, probably because David's mother, before she had gone briefly to the "extended living" residence, had churned the soil with the best fertilizer. The carpenter mended the porch and fixed the electricity. Her inheritance from David's mother allowed her not to have to work too much, so she took up watercolors, and tried to write and draw children's books. On the clear, cool evenings each time she gazed up at the stars she memorized one more.

Somewhere always rumbling through her mind was the injustice she felt for the treatment she had endured and her sense of outrage that she had been blamed with hardly any proof or research into the murder.

Detective stories took on a new meaning for her. The jail became a magnet, and she frequently visited people in the local prison. They all claimed they were innocent. After a while she could truly hear which ones were not guilty and which ones were liars. She volunteered for the homeless.

Yet London often called to her with a longing that meshed with the final walks she had taken with her mother.

# CONNECTIONS

**Maureen telephoned** Catherine at the hotel. "Hello, love. You won't believe this, but we have to send anything we want tested to Davis, California. They do all the animal things apparently."

"What animal things?"

"Your cat: You said you had a cat. If you can believe this, the fur of that old dead cat could still be on your shoes. Not likely on your handkerchief."

"Of course I had a cat! What difference would it make if they found cat fur on my shoes?"

"Yes, I asked them that. If we can find the shoes of a suspect, like maybe them black shoes on that mystery man, they could be old and still have some cat fur on them."

"It seems ridiculous to send them to California. After all, DNA was discovered right near the site of King's College. I read a plaque there that said so. *Crick, Watson, and Wilkins, Nobel Prize*, I remember."

"Just animal DNA. They do it best in the world there."

"Ridiculous. However, in the interest of science, I'll wrap my old loafers up and we can send them out by DHL. I want them back immediately after they are finished. You never know what information they might contain that we could use right here in London." There was a long silence. "Just a minute," Catherine said. "Do you remember that cat I told you about at the beach house? It looked just like our old cat. They could be related. We need to send Christopher's shoes, too. Run out and buy him another pair, and we can send his old ones off to see if they might have cat hairs on them that relate the two cats to each other."

Within the hour, Christopher, in his new shoes, came and collected her loafers from her, and wrapped them and sent them together with his special delivery to California, where they promised to return them within six weeks.

The next day was Saturday, and though roast beef was the usual fare for Sundays at Maureen's house, she changed Sunday's menu to Saturday. The kitchen smelled of well-cooked roast, and Maureen busied herself like a person who knew all the steps to a dance. Christopher set the table with a knife, fork, and large dessert spoon in each place.

"Christopher, please put the roast on the table, there's a dear," Maureen said.

"Yes, Mum," Christopher answered, and put on potholder gloves that fit him perfectly.

They all sat down together to a midday roast. The little wall gas heater was on in the sitting room.

"He was a nice chap when we was first married," Maureen said to Catherine, like she was continuing a conversation she had never stopped. "Didn't drink more than a couple of pints of an evening. But that night Christopher's older brother was killed in a motorcycle accident, it all changed. He'd stay at the pub till closin' time. Didn't care if I 'ad to wake up at five in the morning to go to work. It just got worse. If I complained one little bit, he was swinging his hand through the air at me. I mostly ducked, and he was so drunk it slowed him up, but every so often he'd knock me up the side of me head and me neck would be off its hinges for weeks."

"Oh, dear!" Catherine said.

"It went on for years like that. It's a wonder I lasted that long. Seemed to get worse, little bit at a time, usually around football season—him and his mates all yelling and cheering at the wireless and knocking over beers half drunk. I couldn't help grumbling at him, and one night he started swinging at me with a bloody hammer, he did. Me 'ead already hurt sumfink awful, and when he was coming down on me head with that hammer, I was lunging from underneath with a kitchen knife, right into his heart, wasn't I? He 'it me 'ard round the earhole. 'Ere, I still have a scar, and I fell unconscious.

"When I opened me eyes, there was little Christopher crying over me. Blimey, when I saw all that blood, and 'im lying there stiff as a poker, I knew I was in big trouble. The lump by me ear was bleeding. I did it in self-defense, so I got off the noose. Got fifteen years, out in twelve for good behavior."

"What a very sad story. Terrible," Catherine said.

"I don't drink much," Christopher chimed in, "not after what I seen that day. 'Ow could I? Me mates hardly want to know me. A game of football, yeah, but the pub afterward, naw, I just come 'ome to Mum and watch the telly and let them get on wif it." He gestured at their small television set with the easy chair in front of it, pointed right at it within easy reach of the knobs.

"Maureen, if I may ask, did you love him?" Catherine asked.

"Well, I thought I did at first. But you can't love someone who bashes you up, now, can you? It isn't natural. I felt sorry for him, but after more of that violence, I made him sleep on the settee. I come to 'ate him. You loved your 'usband, didn't ya?"

Catherine looked through the sheer lacy curtains, and picked up her fork. The roast beef was well cooked, and the gravy was thick on the mashed potatoes. The green peas were large and puffy.

"Me? Oh, how I loved my husband!" Catherine said. "He was God's greatest creation: hardly a cross word with me; always a gentleman, even long after we married. That was just who he was; such a dear man. I thought I was the luckiest girl in the world. But you can't predict the future, I learned. You can never see that sort of thing coming."

Catherine looked sad, put her fork into her mouth, and ate a small bite of potatoes. "No changing it now, is there? You get what life dishes out, and you can't go back and do something else. It's permanent, and it's what you've got for your memories." She put the three bites into her small mouth, one by one, chewing each one for a long time.

They all sawed and chewed for a while.

"We're going to find that murderer for you, Mrs. Evans," Christopher said with his mouth still full, "if it's the last fing we do! We're going to see justice done, right, Mum?"

"Well, I really appreciate your efforts, more than you will ever know." Catherine stopped to move a piece of meat daintily from her front tooth. "I think we're on the right trail. Maureen, how is your research going with the astrology in 1956? Do you remember there was all that trouble with the Suez Canal in 1956?"

"'Course I do!" Maureen said. "Eden and them lot. I did a little research on that year. Got me notes, I do. The librarian is 'elping me, fank God! Well, it isn't easy, mind you." Maureen added some potatoes and peas and shoveled them into her mouth.

"To find out who is ultimately responsible for this murder," Catherine determined, "we have to look in several places. He was in England in the fall of 1956, anyway. There's the silver cup connection. There's the DNA connection. There's the horoscope connection; could be astronomy, too. That needs more research."

Christopher, who had finished eating rather quickly, was scribbling a few words down and circling them and connecting them with lines.

# 1939: CHARLES
# AND HAWTHORN

**One day** when Charles was in his mid-forties, he fairly leapt out of bed before dawn and set out his tools, his saws, hammers, files, levers, and nails. At last, after years of putting a little by for his new barn, he was ready to build. He worked two hours before his neighbor, Hawthorn, came by to help lift wood and chat with him through the day. They were a contented team, never left their farms except to meet a friend from London at the railroad station who might fancy a relief from the fast-paced city living and a little time to put his feet up and breathe in the sea air.

Charles' parents had bought the farm after the barn burned down and the little girl had succumbed to the smoke. It was cheap; now Charles owned it. Carey's parents just had to leave it, and they had sailed to America, he'd heard. They had bought cattle and became farmers in Montana.

Along with the farm, Charles and his parents inherited their neighbor, Hawthorn: five years Charles' junior. Hawthorn was always lazy, and now that he considered himself moving towards some kind of retirement, he spent his time reminiscing. Charles watched how Hawthorn had aged. Hawthorn had graying hair, sore hips, and even the beginnings of a hunched back. It was as if Hawthorn held a sad secret inside that spread into his bones and heart and bent him over with a sigh every time he remembered it.

It was a misty morning, but the summer sun promised to win the battle by the time Hawthorn ambled along. He rolled a cigarette, offered Charles one, as usual, and as usual, Charles reminded Hawthorn that he'd never smoked. Charles whistled as he sawed and measured. Hawthorn stared out along the sea, his weak eyes always searching for a meandering ship. The authorities had banned lanterns on donkeys and ships seldom met their end there now. Plundering for treasures had become a legend; the stories never ceased and were passed on from father to child as if they'd happened yesterday.

Charles handed Hawthorn a shovel and said, "Time to prepare the earth." Hawthorn flicked the tiny butt between his fingers onto the ground.

"I told you never to do that," Charles said, like he did every morning they met there. Hawthorn looked guilty and promised, again, he'd remember. The digging began in earnest as the sun moved higher into the sky and the mist disappeared for the day.

Charles dug his holes for the rock foundation while Hawthorn lingered, chatting, smoking, humming a sea shanty and raising the pick now and again. As Charles hacked around the area where Carey's dolls had lain, Hawthorn slyly watched, never knowing about her buried treasure; but with each shovelful of dirt Charles lifted, Hawthorn felt a pain in his chest for the girl he had inadvertently killed when but a cheeky lad, so full of himself. It wasn't that he'd changed much, but he couldn't shake the agony that accompanied his guilt. He'd never told a soul, not his father, nor mother, and certainly not Charles.

It just made Hawthorn wince to get near it. The dolls had burned with his friend. He remembered Carey as his friend. But perhaps he'd been mean to her. His memory took a blank turn at the time of her death. She'd died in a terrible fire, but he couldn't remember more. Had he been there, too? He hated that one corner anyway; hated it with all his heart.

Charles dug there. "What's this, then?" Charles said, as his shovel lodged against something hard. He'd hit a rock; no, it was not a rock. He uncovered a dark metal box. He fell on his knees and brushed away the soil, revealing a blackened metal box.

"Here, Hawthorn! Look here! Something's buried here." He pushed the soil aside until the edges of the box showed, then he took his shovel and dug until he found its bottom, and he levered it up. Hawthorn came over and helped Charles release it at last from the clinging soil.

Hawthorn wondered right away if this dirty box had belonged to Carey. Peter pried it open and saw the twelve cups, tarnished black, not looking like they were worth much. He thought he'd sell them to the old man who came by infrequently now. Sometimes Charles had chatted with him, heard tales about his great, great grandfather, who had gathered treasures and had taught his son and this old man, his grandson, how to collect the sea treasures and sell them at the train depot to a sleazy bunch of men for hardly anything.

Charles was very pleased when he met the old man with the very old cart and sold him those old cups in their box for a hundred pounds, to be paid over time. With that much money coming in he could just about finish his new barn.

Charles filled in the hole with stones and made it the cornerstone of the barn. His dirty hand had passed the box to even dirtier hands, but the box then fell into clean, stubby fingers and began its journey to London on the Cornwall to London train.

# TIGHTENING CIRCLES

**"Where** does the astrology come in, Mrs. Evans?" Maureen asked. The sun flickered into the kitchen window as the horse chestnut tree outside swayed in the breeze.

"You know, Maureen, I don't really know, but there were signs of the Zodiac on those cups. Why would that be so important that my husband would be murdered for those cups?"

Maureen put a stack of copies of the newspapers from 1956 alongside Catherine's plate. Maureen had magnified them to large print before she brought them home from the library, so that Catherine could easily examine them.

"Why would my husband be killed? He was an innocent man, a budding journalist with a side career teaching English to foreign students. You know, I wonder if we couldn't get his attendance sheets for that Tuesday evening English class he always taught at the Northwestern Polytechnic?" Catherine muttered to herself.

"We Brits keep everything 'ere in England for 'undreds of years," Christopher said. "There's a chance they could be still in some dusty old filing cabinet along with papers from the 1850s. Who knows? Back in some corner of the old building he worked at. Where was that, Mrs. E.?"

Christopher stood, gazing over Catherine's shoulder at the copies of the newspapers.

"It was in Kentish Town back then, about a mile from our flat," she answered sleepily. Her head fell gently forward. She looked up abruptly then and said, "Tell people you love them at every opportunity." She stared at Christopher, whose mouth was hanging open. He scribbled and shaded around his circles, leaving them white and the shading around them dark.

"Yes, Mrs. E. I love you! I do–don't know why. You feels like an auntie to me: some kind of relation. Funny, that." Christopher blushed and looked away from Catherine's eyes.

"Wot about me, then, Christopher? You never told me that," Maureen said, her face slightly pinched.

"Ah, Mum, you know it. I don't need to say it, do I?" he asked, moving over to her chair and resting his hand on her shoulder.

"Well, son, 'course I know you love me. 'Course I do. But a wee bit of jealousy comes over me of Mrs. Evans, that's all," she said, smiling and patting his warm hand. He went back and sat down and began to scribble again.

"Doesn't hurt to say it, though, now Christopher, does it?" Catherine said.

"At the risk of seeming ridiculous, I'll say I love you, Mum. I do, you know I do. It embarrasses me to say it out loud. Unmanly. Don't tell me mates!" Christopher's squiggles became more dramatic.

"All men say it to somebody, their wives, their mothers, their fathers on their deathbeds," Catherine said.

"Not in this country, Mrs. Evans. Some men would rather die than confess to a warm feeling. They'd be afraid people might think them queer or gay or whatever you Americans say." Christopher held up his paper in front of Maureen and Catherine.

Catherine read out each circle: "Horoscopes, astronomy, 1956, Suez Canal, Hungary, ESL, journalism, silver cups, attendance sheets."

They all sat silent. Catherine was trying to make connections, but nothing was immediately apparent.

"Christopher, would you please bring out the cups?" Catherine nodded to Christopher. He went into the kitchen and pulled down a cardboard box labeled Typhoo Tea from the top shelf and carried it into the kitchen. He placed it on the table and began taking the six cups out and setting them in a row.

"'Ere, look at this one," he said. "It's that one with half a man, half a horse, and a bow and arrow engraved on it."

"What else have you found out about DNA, Maureen?" Catherine lifted the dish towel from its rack.

"Not a lot, I'm afraid. I'm sorting through astrology and Italian history. Found a lovely large photograph of one of them globes from the fifteenth century in Italy, full of the signs, it was. Strange how they knew all about astrology back then. Makes you wonder, it does."

Maureen rinsed a glass and set it on the drainer. Catherine began drying the glasses. Maureen opened her mouth to protest, but Catherine put up her palm.

"I still think we ought to know more about DNA. After all, that's what got me out of my rocking chair."

Maureen added two more sparkling glasses to the drainer then turned with her hands on her hips. "Well, apart from the handkerchief, what have we got to match things up?"

Catherine's mind shot back to the horrible bloody scene: the knife; the blood; the groceries she had spilled on the floor. "Maybe they saved the knife as evidence? Shouldn't we give somebody a call and find out?" Catherine suggested.

"I'll look it up at the library. It's a chance. I don't know how long they keep evidence: probably hundreds of years." Maureen wiped the surfaces and brushed the crumbs from the tablecloth.

Catherine winced to think of that kitchen knife. Who had plunged it into David's chest that day? It would be someone not at work; someone who knew David wasn't at work that day. Who could take off work at will? It could have been someone working for himself; not chained to a desk. Who had they known then like that? Catherine couldn't remember a soul who wasn't hard at work. There was a lot to do to clean up from the war. Everybody had a job. Maybe it was someone unemployed? Maybe a resentful person David had done research on for an article? No, DNA was not the only possible answer. The front door had been open when she got home. Maybe the murderer ran out in a hurry. Maybe he saw her coming?

Catherine heard Maureen's loud voice, interrupting her memory. "Think now, Catherine. There's got to be something incriminating," Maureen said.

"Maybe my old shoes," Catherine suggested. "Or maybe David's handkerchief." She felt like she was going around in circles, but they were tightening.

# THE MYSTERIOUS MAN

**Catherine** started drying the silverware, her mind back at her own sink, David washing, while she was drying. She had always dried the glasses first; then the silverware. Catherine's eyes landed on the knife she was drying. She settled her glasses on her nose and felt a familiarity with that knife that took her back years. She held it up and began to study its shape.

"We had a knife like this at our beach house," she said.

Maureen stood very still and watched Catherine turn the knife over and over.

"This is the identical knife David's murderer used. Have you had this since the fifties? It was common then, I think."

"Yes, me mum gave it to us for a wedding present. Not a lot to choose from in them days. Pretty common round 'ere."

Catherine studied the knife, simply used to cut the Sunday roast, no doubt. It wasn't a Sunday, that day David died. No roast for days to come. No meat at all. It was still scarce. Sundays were special. Catherine sat down and held the knife, staring at it intensely.

"Now, there, give me that knife. See what you done, thinking too much about all this. Come now. Why not go for a little stroll along our street. I've got a bit of shopping to do. You could join me. Take your mind off all this for a bit."

Catherine let Maureen gently remove the knife from her hand and put it back in the drainer. She could do with some fresh air. Maybe she had made a mistake. She pulled out David's handkerchief and dabbed her eyes. She stuffed it up her sleeve and stood up.

"Yes, a little walk would do me good," she said, forcing a polite smile.

The glitter of the sunlight on the knife in the drain shot through her body like it was the killer's knife. She pulled on her coat and scurried toward the door with Maureen just behind her.

The butcher shop was only a block down the street. The edges of the road were still brick, but the center had been paved over. Maureen and Catherine joined arms, and made their way on this sunny but chilly day toward the shops. It was good to be in London, where neighbors nodded hello but didn't inquire too closely. Catherine checked the curb carefully and let Maureen take the lead. The road was about twenty feet across, easily crossed if one walked rapidly. Maureen put her head down and moved hastily. Catherine kept a sharp eye out and walked as quickly as she could, letting her bad hip sting. When Catherine had stepped back up the curb on the other side of the street she saw the butcher shop just ahead. Beyond it she saw a familiar figure standing with a newspaper held widely across his face. She thought she recognized his black shoes. She nudged Maureen. "That's him!"

"Wot? Who?" Maureen looked at Catherine. "That man reading the paper," Catherine said.

Maureen looked up. "Can't see nobody reading a paper, me love."

Catherine lifted her eyes from the pavement. He was gone. This time she was sure it was the same person. He was old, but he had a way of disappearing like a young deer in a forest.

"Well, I'm definitely being followed," she said.

"If you say so. Who knows you're here?" Maureen asked. "Someone who doesn't want you or me to know him, exactly, yet stands there for us to notice him."

"That's frightening," Catherine said.

When Catherine lay down to sleep that night, she couldn't keep the picture of that man out of her head. Who cared if she found out who the real murderer was? Would she be murdered for the same reasons David was murdered? She did not fancy death by stabbing.

# A TRIP TO THE VICTORIA
# AND ALBERT MUSEUM

**Catherine brought** the cups back to the hotel for the night. She pulled the cups and lined them up in a row to study their astrological engravings.

Later, as Catherine snuggled down under her covers, she remembered how England had hardly felt like a place to study astronomy. The skies were always covered with clouds, and it was too cold to stand under the stars. Catherine remembered how, after prison, she continued her study of astronomy in Connecticut. It was a hobby she pursued alone, and her knowledge grew such that she was given the chance to periodically lecture to the local Brattleboro Senior Center and was asked later to lecture in the New Hampshire Senior Centers, too. She had been irritated at herself for infrequently checking her horoscope in the paper when she and David were together. She knew it was perfect nonsense, but it seemed to be an innocent enough habit that she secretly continued because it reminded her of David.

In the morning, a gentle knock at her door brought her breakfast: cold toast in a rack, one egg, over easy, jam and butter, and a pot of tea.

As she ate breakfast, she thought about how astrology had been David's secret passion. His mother had raised him to believe in his identity as a Leo. He had brushed it off to Catherine, but every so often out it would come: "I have to be very careful about money this month and not sign contracts." He had said that two months before they bought their house, but she knew from that gentle pause he made when the old man made his offer, that David was calculating that the month was new, and it was okay to sign contracts. Catherine disliked this powerful influence his mother's astrological devilry had on him, but she could see it was like a religion, or an addiction, and that he was not giving it up any more than he would give up his mother. Catherine, though a Sagittarius, had a moon in Virgo–a perfectionist according to astrology. He had taken her birth date into consideration, he told her, before he had asked her to be his life partner.

Now, as she stared at the Sagittarius centaur and Latin inscription around the silver cup, she felt that he had treasured these cups for reasons beyond their monetary value. She read aloud each name: "Sagittarius, Pisces, Aries, Cancer, Leo, Libra."

Why were the other six months left out? Why did he only have these months? Maybe the others had disappeared over the centuries or been melted down?

She caressed the cups as if they were David's cheek, tucked them lovingly back into their new tissue paper, and closed the box. One day she would shine them back to sparkling. For now, they were dark and dreary-looking and needed intense rubbing with some delicate and special ingredient. Catherine wondered at their value. She would send Maureen on another search. Perhaps she could do some kind of research herself.

Catherine gazed out at the blue sky and the fluffy white clouds sailing across this great British island. She decided that this was a good time to pay a visit to the Victoria and Albert Museum, and telephoned Christopher, who was working for two hours at the front desk for his friend, Arne, downstairs at the Churchill Bed and Breakfast.

"Can you come with me on a trip to the Victoria and Albert Museum?" she asked him.

"No problems," Christopher said. "Shall we leave at eleven to catch the sunny weather?" The shadows were long in the mornings and afternoons, and the wind brought dark clouds into the English gardens just after teatime, Christopher had said. An earlier start would be perfect.

Christopher had a taxi waiting as Catherine stepped out into the sunshine. The trees across the road in Hyde Park were fluttering with the last of their orange and red leaves. He offered his hand as she stepped into the tall black taxi. Christopher climbed in after her and sat in the diagonal corner on the pull-down seat.

Catherine and Christopher walked around the cases at the museum, noting the silver spoons, cups, and pitchers. A lot of the cups were nineteenth-century and had handles or were too flat for a comparison. Most of the silver seemed to have been made into crosses. There were very few cups. These were English pieces, not Italian, but a trip to Italy was out of the question.

"Look here," Christopher said. "This one looks almost like yours!" He pointed to a silver cup with engravings of the astrological sign of Taurus.

"I beg your pardon," Catherine said to a bored-looking guard. "About how much would you say that cup, for instance, might be worth?"

"I'm afraid I don't know, ma'am, but the curator is standing over there," he said in a hushed tone. "I am sure he would be happy to help you."

Catherine tapped her umbrella like a cane and walked over to the curator. "Excuse me, sir, but may I ask you a question?"

"It would be my pleasure," said the man, his hair brushed deeply from his side part to cover the baldness on the top of his head.

"I am interested in the value of a cup in that case," she said, gesturing to the case where Christopher was standing.

Six children sat cross-legged on the floor sketching a silver pitcher in a nearby case. The curator walked over to the other case with Catherine and she pointed out the cup. "That's about early nineteenth-century. Would you like it in dollars?"

"That would be interesting," she answered.

"In dollars? I'd say possibly about $10,000, give or take…"

Catherine stared at the cup. Ten thousand dollars! That was hardly worth killing over. But twelve times ten thousand dollars might be.

"I wonder if I may ask one more question?" she said. He nodded gallantly.

"If that cup were made in Italy in, say, 1770, or earlier, say 1550, how much would it be worth?"

The curator put his hand under his chin. "They hardly made any cups of silver then, but if there were cups with astrological engravings, and particularly if all twelve cups had the twelve astrological signs, the complete set might be worth forty million pounds. But you really should get an appraisal idea at Sotheby's."

A winter chill surrounded her legs; she sneezed. "Pardon me. Thank you very much." She turned to Christopher. "I'm feeling cold. Let's take a taxi back to the Churchill."

Christopher saluted her and walked briskly outside to hail a taxi, then scuttled back and escorted her to it. That would be over sixty million dollars. Catherine decided she needed to go to Christopher and Maureen's for another overnight. It might be time to hide those cups in a safer place! Catherine and Christopher took the cups from her room at the hotel, put them in a bag, and bundled into the waiting taxi back to the East End.

# THE LETTER:
## DIGGING UP THE PAST

**Sitting down** to breakfast the next morning, Maureen studied a letter from the pile of letters that were dropped daily into her mail slot in the front door.

"Blimey," Maureen said. "You've got a letter right here at me own house. Who else knows you're staying here the weekend?" She handed Catherine the envelope with her name typed on the front: *Mrs. David Evans.* She hadn't used that name since she left prison. She used Mrs. Catherine Evans, like all the women were starting to do in the late-sixties in Vermont. A clammy coldness entered her being that her hot cup of tea could not alter. That feeling that someone might be watching her had been replaced by the surety that she was being followed. She took her knife and slit open the long side of the envelope. Her fingers grasped a page of white typing paper, and she pulled it out and unfolded it. Maureen leaned in closer. Christopher stopped sweeping. The birds outside seemed to sing louder. Catherine adjusted her glasses and read the typewritten message aloud:

*"Mrs. Evans, Don't dig up the past unless you are willing to share it."*

It was not signed.

She thought of Christopher with the shovel digging up the cups. Share her cups? No. Digging up her past must have meant her research into the murder. But *"share it"*? She sniffed the envelope. It was as strong as a real rose under her nose. "Old Spice," she mumbled. "It's a man," she told Christopher. "David wore Old Spice, a smell that meant true love to me then. Now, it only makes me afraid. Should I be afraid? What can he do to me? Kill me? He already did that for all those years I was in jail."

Catherine looked at Maureen and Christopher. "Are you afraid? He wouldn't harm you, would he?"

Christopher and Maureen looked at each other for a long moment.

"We're not afraid, Mrs. Evans," Maureen said.

"We'll be your extra eyes, Mrs. Evans. Don't worry. I'm not afraid," Christopher said.

Where had these angels come from? Were all people so nice or was Catherine just particularly fortunate to have chosen the Churchill Bed and Breakfast next to the pub where she had met Christopher?

"You are great friends to me," she said to them. "I'm a person who doesn't give up once I make up my mind. But to have helping hands by my side makes me feel that little extra bravery that my weary body needs to push on and solve this mystery."

She reached one hand to Maureen and the other to Christopher, and she squeezed their hands as hard as she could.

"What is the next step, then?" Maureen asked.

"For the time being, we'll have to rely on the microfiche. But I want to get to real things, like dirt and decks and silver cups. And we need to get hold of some DNA expert to lead us in the right direction. How does that sound?" Catherine asked, leaning forward to hear what Maureen might say.

"Well," Maureen said, setting her cup down politely, "I'd say that we go back to me library what's built right over the old bombed-out one." Maureen nodded at Christopher.

"Yes, Mum. Lovely library it is, too. Now me, I'm not what you call a reader like. But whoever designed that place makes you want to stop in it and relax in one of them sofas and pick up a book or a magazine. 'Ere, mum. I'll do that," Christopher said, relieving Maureen of the cups and saucers in her hands.

"Oh, Christopher, you are such a dear. I am blessed with a lovely, considerate son, I am." A delicate smile crept over her face.

Christopher switched on the television. The newscaster was just finishing a sentence. "...the missing silver cups." All three faces twisted in unison toward the screen.

"And now on to sports," he continued.

"Why not go to the library now?" Catherine suggested. The three rustled toward the front door, helping one another put on their coats.

Christopher walked briskly out into the street toward Brick Lane to hail a taxi.

"We could walk," Catherine said, her hip being unusually cooperative. "But look here, a taxi arrives like a magic carpet!"

The library was tall and had large, modern glass windows. There was a gently sloping ramp next to the stairs. They chose to enter that way.

The librarian took them to the microfiche section and explained to Christopher that he could find out about DNA from newspaper articles she showed him.

He found paragraph after paragraph of information. Maureen drew two straight-backed chairs to either side of Christopher and she and Catherine sat down, leaning forward. After a few minutes they both sat back.

After an attentive lull, Christopher exclaimed, "Here!" Catherine shot up and Maureen jumped forward.

"Here's an address for DNA testing: seems to be connected with the police. Shall we call them?"

"Never mind that," Catherine said. "Where are they? Can't we visit them?"

"We could. Look, here's the number. Write it down, Mum."

"Let's go home now and call that number," Catherine said.

They hailed a taxi immediately for the short ride home. Catherine immediately called the number and set up an appointment to meet the DNA expert, a Mr. Townsend.

Catherine had a warm feeling: the handkerchief; the shoes; the cups; they could all hold the key. And now a DNA expert would tie it all together.

# SOMETHING FAMILIAR

**Catherine returned** to the hotel. A little time to herself to sort out her feelings was on the top of her agenda. After a while, she thought to her herself, "A spot of tea in a tea shop would be perfect at this afternoon hour." She went back outside into the street and hailed a taxi, which took her over to Oxford Street.

At an outdoor newspaper stand, a small white-haired old man stood waiting for customers. *The Daily Mirror* was displayed next to *The Daily Mail* and *The Daily Express*. Below, *The Guardian* and *The Times* displayed the news in calm, British middle-class fashion. *The Sun* blared out the latest about Diana and Charles on the other side of stand. Catherine fumbled in her change bag containing the heavy British coins. A pound used to be a valuable note. Now it was a weighty coin, easily tossed among the other coins, whisked away for hardly a dish of ice cream. The newspapers shouted at her, *"Buy me!"* Catherine trusted her intuition and she followed this voice inside her, though swearing at the same time that she was not superstitious.

She placed the coins into the old man's hand and exchanged them for *The Daily Mail*. David had always dropped at least five daily papers onto the kitchen table when he arrived home from work. He had always said a journalist should know what his competition was writing about.

Catherine felt the paper with its strange comfort of times past, even its size, easy to open in a crowded train or bus or underground.

She spotted a narrow tea shop along Oxford Street full of single people reading the afternoon news over a scone and a pot of tea, and tucked her paper under her arm, moving with the crowd along two narrow shops. She went inside and sat at a small table next to the window. The waitress, her brown curly hair tied in a high ponytail, helped Catherine settle in.

"I'll have a pot of tea and toast, please," Catherine said.

"Right you are, love," said the waitress, scurrying down to the back window and ordering from the kitchen.

Catherine put the newspaper in front of her and let her eyes scan past the blaring headlines that David had taught her to ignore. "Turn the page," he had said, "and search for the smallest article you can see. There's the real news." She ignored the colorful photos of Diana and other royalty, scanned all the small headlines, and searched for the most important news in the paper. And there it was: the paragraph that had put the coins into the newspaper seller's palm.

MISSING SILVER CUPS STILL A MYSTERY, read the small headline. She read on. *"A police report stated that an unidentified man has allegedly said that he heard that the silver cups had surfaced and were in the hands of a person who possibly had no rights to them."* Catherine's eyes widened. She rubbed them and started the paragraph again, reading each word aloud. *"...had no rights to them."* Who was this man who thought she had no rights to them? Of course she had all rights to them! Why didn't this mysterious person identify himself?

She looked up and scanned the other people in the tea shop. A young man with long hair puffed on his cigarette. A young woman applied her faint lipstick and brushed back her poofy hair.

Catherine knew someone could be following her right now. Perhaps that unsigned letter writer was lurking around. Sometimes, lately she had an uncomfortable feeling that she was not alone. Of course, it looked like someone knew about her cups, so she could now imagine why that someone might be following her. A white-haired man in the back sat reading his paper, but he was there when Catherine came in, so he was not following her. She looked out the window at the crowds milling past, carving space between their flashing eyes. A middle-aged man leaned by the lamppost with a small newspaper shielding his face. There was something familiar about him. She thought she might just get up and try to get a look at his hidden face through the better vantage of the door.

The waitress brought her some hot water for the teapot, but Catherine excused herself, saying she would be right back, and walked to the door and opened it. But by the time she managed to walk over to the door, the man was gone. She looked up and down the crowded sidewalk, but he was nowhere to be seen. Catherine closed the door and went back to her table, feeling sure that man was watching her. He reminded her in some way of that Mr. Smith from jail, who sat there at visiting time all those years. How strange. She would never know his face by now.

Catherine tried to remember the face she had mostly avoided looking at for twelve years. There was no voice attached to it. He had put his fingers to his lips whenever she started to speak. Those were his rules. So she grew to know his face in stolen glances. He had a sad countenance, or was it thoughtful? How could he sit there for twenty minutes and never talk? He had a full head of hair and a moustache and a small goatee. Sometimes he closed his eyes for the whole time. Sometimes his eyes penetrated her very being, forcing her to glance at the clock or her lap or her shoulder. After years, their silence had bonded them, though neither glanced much at the other. It was almost a routine, and it happily broke the daily prison drudge, so Catherine had even looked forward to his visits.

Catherine sipped her hot tea while her mind wandered off into the past and she remembered how he had sat across from her every three months or so for twelve years. He would never talk. That was who he was to her: just a silent man, who hardly looked at her, just sat.

There was definitely something familiar about that man outside the café. Wasn't he wearing black shoes, possibly with little holes? She didn't see many people wearing those shoes these days. Well, all those old men were dead. She sat down and put her chin in her hand and stared out the window. As people passed she found herself scanning their shoes: pink shoes, high boots, heeled shoes, brown lace-ups, black and white sneakers, loafers. She sat for a full ten minutes but never saw those black shoes on anybody, not even the elderly man shuffling by, peeking in the rubbish bin.

How could that man have moved away so quickly? He was probably hiding very nearby. Catherine paid the bill, gathered her purse, and decided to hunt for him around the café. He was probably lurking, waiting for her.

A cold breeze made her grip her coat closed at her throat as she scanned the street. To her right, she saw the man briefly before he vanished into the crowd near a narrow side street. She walked over to the street and turned onto it, keeping her eyes on all the darkened corners. A shadow arcing across the old buildings angled and bent. The sun, playing at the edge of the rooftops, still shot hard shapes conveying movement, commanding fear. Catherine knew she should hail a passing taxi, but a perverse desire to solve the mystery of this man glued her hand solidly to her side. She thought she heard his panting, his footsteps.

As she turned the corner, a taxi sped in her direction down the narrow road, and her hand automatically flew up into the air and waved as her breath quickened.

The taxi screeched to a halt. "Hello, love. Mind your step," said the driver, his thick glasses hovering at the tip of his nose.

Catherine's head twisted slightly and saw the shadow holding still. Slowly lowering herself into the plush seat, she said, "Please drive away quickly." The shadow moved again and disappeared. Catherine pulled out her compact and checked the rear view from the taxi. A man in a black suit and with an umbrella stood in the distance, one hand against his heart. He didn't seem to be hiding. He seemed to want to be seen. He replaced his hat just as the taxi turned the corner.

"'Scuse me, ma'am, but where was it you wanted to go?" asked the driver.

"Circle back to where you picked me up. I'm following someone," she heard herself saying. He turned several corners, and the familiar walls of that street came into view. The shadow had gone. The sun had shrunk over the edge of the world. The stretch between sunset and night was a long yawn. If there was a man lurking nearby, Catherine couldn't see him.

"Is that the fellow you're looking for?" asked the driver, pointing to a figure in the darkness near a footpath and a brick wall.

Catherine adjusted her glasses and saw the figure disappear down a footpath, much too narrow for the taxi to follow. It wasn't fear that lingered all over her body now; it was more like the breath taken after holding it for a long minute.

"The Churchill Bed and Breakfast, please," she said. "I'm afraid...I'm afraid we've lost him."

"We could wait here a bit, if you'd like," said the taxi driver.

"No, no. I've had enough. Let's go," she said, stretching her neck around for one final look.

Catherine called Maureen from her bed of clean sheets. Steam shimmered from her teacup. "He's been following me. Just after I left a café on Oxford Street, he was there. It was like he was playing cat and mouse with me, trying to scare me. Silly man!" Catherine said.

"Do you want to tell the police?" Maureen asked.

"Not yet. We need more information first." Catherine wished she knew what information she needed, but there was a gap that needed filling, and she wasn't sure it would be filled by that man. She didn't like the police at all after all those years in prison and she didn't want them interfering. They'd tell her to go home and leave well enough alone. Her tea was cooling and she drank it down, feeling only slightly calmed by it.

# 1939: The Young Thief

**Harry could just see** the tiny brown ponies and white sheep in the green meadows as the train sped along, its smoke belching black against the white clouds. But the rumble of the iron against the track made young Harry sleepy. The ride from Cornwall to Paddington Station, London was endless. He slept atop the barrel crates that held the strange findings whose destination was far from the rocky coast at the very tip of southwestern England, the last land before the huge Atlantic and the long voyage to America.

Young Harry's only job was to accompany the crates and deliver them at the station to a husky man, who would be smoking a cigar. From there he was to return on the train back to Cornwall without stopping in London. Young Harry didn't like his orders: Every few months he'd be right there in London, yet he had to return without spending one night. Harry was now fifteen, not a boy, but a lad with brains and foresight beyond his age. It was time they stopped calling him "young Harry," he often thought.

When Harry finally awoke, the train was halfway there. He recognized the stations as they went by. He knew he needed to act swiftly between stations. His small knife worked to loosen the barrel most easily opened. He pulled the wooden top off and reached in. He'd only need to nick one item to sell and he could stay in London for a fortnight. At the top was a metal box that Harry slipped out and onto the floor. It wasn't too heavy, but perhaps heavy enough to contain something to sell. He closed the lid and tapped it back into place, then rolled the metal box into his coat.

It was a fine day, only hinting of rain. By the time the train stopped at the next station, the deed was done. With the money he'd been advanced, he could make his way to Portobello Road. Maybe then he might see how to start up his own business there.

The city called to Harry from a deep place. His grandfather had come from the East End, sailed away, and landed on the shores of Cornwall years before and stayed. He told young Harry, who'd sat upon his knee as a child, that the city was a dangerous place, but still exciting. One day he'd take him there. But his grandpa died of a stroke, and young Harry was left only with dreams. It was now, this moment, as he held his wrapped treasure, that not only his dream, but Grandpa's dream, was coming true.

The train arrived at the huge, covered station, moving alongside many trains on parallel tracks, passengers piling out and hurrying along toward their important destinations.

"Right, then, lad," said the man with the cigar. He counted eight crates, then paid Harry the balance owing. "It's all here. Good lad," he said, patting Harry on the back. "Your train back is on the next platform," he added, handing him his ticket.

"Thank you, sir," Harry said, disappearing through the throngs, his treasure tightly held. He stuffed his ticket and money into his pocket and began his new venture. Maybe it would be forever, not just a fortnight.

Paddington Station was gigantic. He looked above at the huge arched ceiling over the lines of trains and tracks. People bumped him in their hurry as he looked at the rows of platforms and the smoke belching from the trains. The sound of voices shouting, yelling instructions and good-byes, some in strange languages, overwhelmed the boy's head, so used to the pastoral sound of the clip-clop of one horse's hooves, the rolling waves, the seagulls above. Harry stood quite central in the mass of human-ity, his mouth agape, and wondered how he was going to get to Portobello Road. He studied the paths taken by the passengers. He tried to read the signs. It was an explosion of information, and he felt a tightening in his throat. There, over his shoulder, a blast came from a train that would soon be leaving for Cornwall. He stepped toward it, like it was a lifeline.

"'Scuse me, sir," he said to a man in a uniform. "How often does the train go to Cornwall?"

"Dunno, mate. I should say, once or twice a week, likely. I only sweeps up here, me lad. Where are you wanting to go, then?" He pushed a paper on the ground into his dustpan and lifted it into his wooden wheelbarrow.

"I want to go to Portobello Road, thank you, sir."

"Bus right outside, over there through them doors. Can you read?"

"'Course I can!" Harry said with a certain combination of pride and indignation.

"Well, then, look for the numbers. Probably come by every three hours."

"Right, sir. I do thank you," said Harry, loping off in the direction of the exit.

Upon entering the light of the afternoon, Harry was met with the noise of horses trotting every which way. How was he to find this strange place, this stop? The smell of horse manure was familiar, but overpowering in a way it had not been in Cornwall. Harry again looked back to the platform. He could just make it onto the train for Cornwall. He could run. He could leap on even as it left the station.

"Where are you going, little lad?" a woman's voice sang into his ear. "You look a bit lost."

"Beggin' yer pardon, ma'am, I be looking for the Portobello Road bus," he said, bowing slightly at the elegantly dressed lady.

"Not to worry," she said lightly. "It's right along there." She pointed to a group of people standing in a jumbled queue.

"Thank you, ma'am; most appreciated," Harry said as nicely as he could and walked over to the line, his package still tucked into his coat.

The lady turned back to him then and asked if he wouldn't mind the walk? "No, I wouldn't mind. In fact, I'd rather walk, thank you," he answered.

"Good. Here, then, my young lad. First, turn right at Praed Street there, then right again at Eastbourne Terrace. Got that? Good. Follow Bishop's

Bridge Road; then turn right at Westbourne Grove for a good ten minutes, or less for a young lad like you, and you'll run into Portobello Road. Can't miss it."

"Ta very much," he said, then Harry shuffled about for a minute, his package still tucked inside his coat, and asked her to repeat it three more times, hardly stopping for her last words as he dashed toward Portobello Road, hoping only that his memory might hold fast this once.

# THE MOVE

**The Churchill** Bed and Breakfast was getting expensive, so Catherine decided to move. Her extravagance was becoming an embarrassment to her. She made inquiries at the desk and was told of a small flat in the law buildings right by the Houses of Parliament looking out over the River Thames. The Thames remained the grand container of history, with new galleries springing up, but the Globe was being refurbished, St. Paul's Cathedral was still royally rising across the river, where the famous architect Christopher Wren could watch his ideas form into stone, arches, and colored windows in a clearstory that pained a visitor's neck leaning back to see the height of the top of the dome.

Christopher arrived the next morning as planned and helped get Catherine and her luggage into a taxi. He jumped into the taxi, and they sped off toward the Houses of Parliament and the wide River Thames. After several turns, they found themselves outside an exquisite old building, not far from many buildings that looked like antiquarian government offices.

The front desk was situated inside the door, straight ahead and just high enough to lean on, and behind it sat a clerk who greeted them pleasantly, ready to help in a quiet, unobtrusive manner.

The foyer was large but cozy, with paintings, plants, and mirrors and a large, red, circular Persian carpet in the center. A well-dressed woman was sitting in an ornate Victorian armchair reading *The Times*. A gentleman in a black tailored suit and a soft, silk blue tie stood talking to a woman in high heels and a dark blue suit and white frilly blouse. Catherine and Christopher were escorted up to her room by a quiet, unassuming man who opened the door for them, handed Catherine the key, bowed slightly, and left.

"Right you are, then, Mrs. Evans," Christopher said as he put her case down in the room and set her small bag of biscuits, tea bags, sugar, and milk on the table.

Catherine looked around the large room. The furniture in her new sub-let was dark brown, practical, small; utilitarian. There was an easy chair, a desk and two straight-backed wooden chairs, and a lamp with a green glass lampshade on it. The curtains on either side of the very tall, wide windows were weighty burgundy velvet. There was another smaller lamp with a frilly, flowery lampshade on a tiny table, and a rectangular Persian carpet on the floor. Two wooden, high-backed chairs were placed near another, larger round table, which snuggled next to a window that might have been six feet high from the bottom ledge to the top. Not only could she see the Thames, she could watch the people in the little park below, with its oval path circling around the green grass in the center, and the bushes and trees at the edges, all enclosed by a black, wrought-iron fence and four gates. She wouldn't be bored here. There was a feeling of sparseness in her room that made an otherwise Victorian feeling of heaviness into a light and airy place.

"Christopher: May I ask, where is the bed?"

Christopher cleared this throat, stepped over to the wall, opened two folding doors sideways, and pulled down a double bed.

"There you go, Mrs. Evans: from sitting room to bedroom in a flick of the wrist."

"How lovely. I think I'll save my wrists and leave it down for now."

Now it was time for a nice quiet cup of tea and a long look through her large window at the green grass below, and the glorious Thames nearby. She put the kettle on in the closet-sized kitchen and stared out of the large window.

"Sit down, Christopher. A quick cup of tea is in order." Christopher sat down on the other chair by the little table.

Beyond wrought-iron gates, the wide rushing Thames carried colorful tourist boats and barges. Catherine sat down by the window for a minute and she and Christopher quietly watched people walking on both sides of the river, mothers and fathers pushing carriages, people carrying banners, men coming from the law offices, or the Houses of Parliament, policemen on horseback. Catherine could see the end of the bridge over which the trains crossed the River Thames, and the black taxis and buses busily moving toward their destinations. Every quarter of the hour, Catherine knew, whether it was pouring rain or bristling sun, Big Ben's clock tower bell would ring out the time, and on the hour the sound of its bell would ring up and down the Thames. Catherine wouldn't have to look at her watch now.

Her hand smacked her chest as she saw a man in a dark suit and black, suspicious-looking shoes sitting on a bench in the garden two flights below, reading the paper.

"Look, there, Christopher!"

Catherine adjusted her glasses and squinted. At least it looked like the man that had been following her. She looked around the park and laughed as she saw dozens of individual men dressed in dark suits, with black shoes and hats, carrying newspapers: all lawyers; clones. No, that wasn't that man: they were all "that man."

"Christopher, tea will have to wait. We've got to go down to that park."

Christopher helped her on with her coat. Catherine turned off the gas under the kettle, grabbed her umbrella, and set her face, stern enough to impress any man in black shoes. Christopher offered his arm, and they made their way to the elevator and down to the enclosed grassy area.

They found an empty bench and sat down, the pigeons fluttering aside. Their cooing comforted Catherine. For five minutes they sat in silence. The day was warm for autumn. Catherine's eyes were glued to every man who approached and especially every man who held a newspaper and had black shoes.

"It's a lost cause here, Mrs. Evans. They all look…" Christopher's eyes apparently stuck on the man about fifty yards away, at the other edge of the grass, who had just sat down on a bench and was holding up *The Times*. "He's bloomin' peeking over his newspaper at us." But Catherine had her eyes steadily following another man walking toward the clock tower of Big Ben.

"That's him," she said, pointing to the escaping culprit.

"No, there, on the bench, with the paper," Christopher confided in a loud whisper.

Catherine turned her attention to the man on the bench. When she turned back, the man walking toward the clock tower had gone out of the gate and disappeared from her view.

"Follow him, Christopher. Quickly! I'll watch that one. Go!" Catherine, thoroughly confused about these black-suited creatures, now had a sense that not one, but at least two, must be watching her and following her. Who could they be? Was it her imagination? How could that man with the brogues know where she was? It was all too strange.

Christopher leapt up and rushed out of the garden, while Catherine settled in to keep her eyes set on the man with the newspaper. His shoes were black, partly in shadow. Catherine looked at her own black shoes. She hated lace-ups, but her weak arches demanded them most of the time. He stood up. Catherine sat up straight, shoulders back, ready for the meeting, at last. He looked both ways and walked directly toward her.

# CONFUSION

**"It was him,"** yelled Christopher, coming from the direction of Big Ben. "He got away, though," he panted. The man approaching Catherine abruptly turned around and briskly walked away.

"Who's that, then, disappearing around the back gate?" she asked. Christopher looked at the man in the distance.

"No, that's not him." Christopher looked at Catherine's face and then at the vacancy left by the man at the back gate.

"It's him," she spluttered.

"Oh, blimey," Christopher said and took off after the man.

Catherine sat back and wondered aloud, "Could there be two of them?" That would certainly account for his ability to be almost everywhere she was. But who was the second man? She must be mistaken. One of them was her mystery man. That was all. She felt dizzy watching the men in dark suits cross in front of her.

"Sorry," Christopher panted. "He got away. They'll be back. They always are."

"They? I think I need a cup of tea."

These men following her seemed to be connected. They were definitely watching her. Why? What did they care about an American lady in England? Well, an ex-con, true enough. Catherine searched her brain. David was dead. She had served her term. Maybe they didn't trust her back in England, but they couldn't prevent her from traveling. Maybe at the Churchill Bed and Breakfast they could more easily spy on her. Now, in this flat, her comings and goings would leave her freer but more unprotected. She studied Christopher's profile as she linked arms with him and they walked away from the bench. Christopher turned his face and looked at her. Black birds twittered in the trees. A barge foghorn sounded on the Thames. A couple passed them, speaking in Russian or Polish. Another couple passed, speaking in French.

Catherine felt tired, ready for a long nap. The idea that she was now being watched by two men in black frightened her. This was becoming a lot more complicated than her original idea, which had now become quite obscured in her mind.

"Mrs. Evans, me love, it would appear you have company that may not be just your mystery follower," Christopher said, pulling her arm tight against his side.

"Have you ever seen those men before?" Catherine asked.

"No," Christopher answered with some hesitation. "Half a mo', I think I might have. Can't say exactly where, but the one I was following looked familiar. I thought it was because of that mystery man who looked like that. But now there are two of them, I could be mistaken."

Catherine had come to trust Christopher. If she couldn't trust Christopher and Maureen, she couldn't trust anybody. She might as well just pack up and go home. She certainly couldn't go on alone. Christopher was a strong shoulder to rest her psychic troubles on, a sounding board, a gentle soul who listened and talked to her like she was a good person. She looked at his profile again as Big Ben chimed two.

They stopped for a rest at the edge of the park. Catherine nodded toward a bench. They walked over to it and sat down. Catherine needed to think.

"We'll go up in a minute, but a little more fresh air will help me get there," she said. At the edge of some distant bushes Catherine saw a man in a dark suit hovering behind a hedge. A lady with a poodle on a leash walked in front of her. Catherine turned to Christopher, whose eyes were glued to that man's figure like a cat ready to pounce on a little bird. Catherine looked back. Now the man was striding across the lawn in the opposite direction.

"That's the same man!" Catherine exclaimed. "Shall I go after him?"

"No. Wait a minute. Let's just sit and watch him for a moment."

"Give me the word, ma'am, and I'll be running after him."

The man turned and held a small camera to his eyes; he seemed to be taking their photo.

"That settles it. We are their target. Are you willing to carry on with me, Christopher? This is becoming rather difficult; could be dangerous."

"Mrs. Evans, I would not be able to leave you now. You may be in danger. What do you think these men want with you?"

"If I knew that, I'd feel better. Now I'm on my own in my new flat. I might feel safer at the Churchill Bed and Breakfast after all. Maybe I should move back?"

Christopher stopped, quite still, his eyes glazing over for a moment.

"I know where I saw him. He was that bloomin' well-dressed man at the Churchill Bed and Breakfast, hovering about like, ever since the day you arrived."

"Is that right? Maybe I'm safer *not* being there for now."

"You could come live with us: me and me mum. We have that spare room; a bit cold, but we could install an electric heater."

Catherine surveyed the blue sky with puffy clouds sailing overhead.

"I could pay for the heating bill and add some in for rent."

"Right then," Christopher said.

To their left the second man peered from behind another hedge, and Catherine could see he was definitely taking their picture.

"All right. Let's get my suitcase and go: right now!"

They started to make their way back to Catherine's flat. "Maybe those men are from Scotland Yard," Catherine said, panting. "That article I read in *The Daily Mail* where it said I had no rights to the silver cups: Maybe they're after me again for killing David. They can't do that, can they?"

"'Course not, Mrs. Evans."

They walked through the large front door of the building and got into the lift. Christopher pulled Catherine along in unusual haste. Once in her room, he lifted her suitcase from the small closet and walked to the door.

Catherine peered out of the window for a moment from behind the drapes. Then she looked around for anything she might have forgotten. Christopher escorted Catherine out of the room and back into the lift.

When they reached the curb, Christopher yelled, "Taxi!" his finger pointing upward, his arm slightly raised in a gentlemanly manner. Out of the corner of her eye Catherine caught a man in black down the street taking her picture again. Christopher gently shoved Catherine into the taxi, jumped in, and slammed the door. "The East End, mate," Christopher said. "And please make it fast, so we won't be followed."

"Right you are, mate," said the taxi driver, as they sped off leaving two astonished-looking men lingering on the pavement behind them.

"Are we being followed, Christopher?" Catherine asked, settling back into the comfortable seat and closing her eyes.

"Two men are running after us, but I think we surprised them."

The taxi left the men behind as it screeched around the corner. Catherine took out her handkerchief from her handbag and dabbed her eyes.

"Christopher, I feel a little like giving up and going home; it's too much."

"Begging your pardon, Mrs. Evans; we're going to find the murderer," Christopher said. "You must realize that we're getting very close."

Christopher was her strength now. Perhaps she would carry on for a while longer. Her hip hurt more. Rushing in and out of her new flat couldn't have helped.

Before she knew it, they pulled up to Christopher's brick house. Catherine paid the driver and Christopher helped her alight. As he opened the front door, Maureen was walking down the hallway toward them.

"Hello, then, Catherine—suitcase and all. Come for a nice long visit, I hope? Don't you worry none. There's plenty of room for you here."

"If you wouldn't mind, I'd like to stay for a few days," Catherine said. She began to unbutton her coat. A few days away might give her perspective. At least, it would give her time to reconsider her situation.

"Stay a year, me love, no worries," Maureen said, helping Catherine with her suitcase and coat.

Catherine only wanted a nap. She would figure out her next move after a nice, peaceful daydream.

# The Man and
# His Newspaper

**"I've been out** early buying up all the newspapers I could find," Maureen said the next morning. "Let's check the horoscopes then." She lifted the stack of all the papers containing horoscopes and handed *The Daily Mirror* to Catherine. She opened *The Daily Mail* and flung *The Sun* over to Christopher.

"Here!" Christopher said. "Look what the horoscope says. It says for Mrs. Evans, *'You will find what you've been seeking today.'* That's for you, Mrs. Evans, ma'am." Christopher laughed. "Here's mine then: *'Keep close watch on your business affairs.'*"

"Lookie here," Maureen said, holding the paper up to the light. *"An old friend will turn up in your life.'"*

Christopher, Maureen, and Catherine laughed together and traded newspapers.

Later on, Catherine felt an urge to go out into the world–a little shopping at the corner market, perhaps a cup of tea at the tea shop after Maureen went to the butcher for their dinner.

Catherine, umbrella in hand, stepped out into the street. Maureen followed her down the two steps, linked arms with her, and they both turned left. Catherine stood tall for a moment, looked both ways, then surveyed the narrow brick road. On the opposite side of the road was an old six-foot brick wall. Down the street to the left were the shops.

There was little traffic at this hour. The world had arrived where it had to be.

As they made their way down the street, Catherine saw a man reading a newspaper, leaning against a pole at the end of the street where it met with Brick Lane. There was something familiar about him, but just then Catherine's total concentration was on where exactly to put her foot. Each brick was smooth and had a life of its own, a depth and angle of its own, its own chips and cracks and its own way of hitting the sole of a shoe. Catherine's ankle was still weak, and she feared another twist. When she looked again, the gentleman had left. They moved along slowly toward the shops, passing the green grocer's, the tobacco shop, the newspaper stand, a butcher's shop, a shoe shop, a hairdresser, and a bookshop. They finally got to the café and went in. Catherine stepped straight to the table by the window. What was a café without the people outside walking by for Catherine and Maureen's entertainment? They ordered a pot of tea and scones with marmalade. As Catherine looked up from rifling around in her purse, the same familiar-looking man was walking across the street.

After their tea, Catherine paid and they walked down the street, turning into the butcher's shop. They both leaned close to the red meat displayed behind the glass.

"I'll have that nice, juicy roast there," Maureen said.

She paid, and the butcher dropped the wrapped roast into her cloth carrier bag. Catherine looked through the window. The man was there again, his newspaper hiding his face.

"Now, this is ridiculous. We must wave him over," Catherine said as she opened the door and the bell jangled. She put her arm through Maureen's, and they squeezed together through the doorway.

"There he goes, disappearing again," Maureen said, shifting her breasts higher and turning toward home. "What a silly man. Doesn't scare me none." The clouds were moving slowly across the blue sky, and the sun was making a dash low in the southern sky from east to west. The shadows could almost be seen moving and extending.

By the time they stepped into the brick street and back up the opposite curb, the man had positioned himself in the distance, too far to be identified, near enough to be noticed.

"I think he wants me to give all this up," Catherine mumbled.

"We're just starting to solve this lark," Maureen answered. "Not a good time to stop, I'd say. In fact, I'm having a jolly good time, and I'm not letting some bounder spoil our fun." A bobby strode past the corner swinging his baton, and the distant man turned and disappeared around the corner.

"Let's think about DNA then, my dear," Maureen said.

Catherine and Maureen stepped up to the front door. Catherine stopped. "I brought the hairbrush they sent me in that basket. That'll have David's hair in it. I never threw any of that away. I just couldn't– all these years. Well, we have plenty of DNA for David, but how are we going to find the DNA of the killer?"

"The knife, of course," Maureen said.

"Yes, but we don't have the knife. Anyway, all they found were my own fingerprints on it."

"What about them silver cups? Maybe they have fingerprints on them besides David's?" Maureen suggested.

"They probably have DNA going back hundreds of years. How can we match up the ones from the fifties, the nineteen-fifties, that is?"

Maureen fidgeted in her handbag and pulled out the front door key, then put it back in her handbag and opened the unlocked door.

"Do you think there's a place we could go to get the DNA off those cups?" Catherine asked her.

"That's my next job. But, blimey, I can't think where to look."

"Must be labs in London now that do that sort of thing," mused Catherine. "I read in the paper about them just a few weeks ago: scientists of some sort. We could ask the librarian, couldn't we? We could go to the University of London and ask a professor."

"Blimey," Maureen said again. "We might as well look in the phone directory; check all those ideas. It's a start, now, isn't it?"

Catherine stepped inside first and Maureen followed, and they hung up their coats in the hallway right next to the front door.

Maureen led the way down the hallway to the warm kitchen at the back of the house. Catherine fell asleep as soon as she sat down in the armchair.

It seemed only a few minutes later she heard Maureen rustling through the pages of the phone directory. "I've found a place, right here." With a little more rustling and mumbling, then some sounds of glee, Catherine thought she heard Maureen say, "Thank you ever so, goodbye."

"What's that you say?" Catherine said, wiping her eyes.

"Bring them cups. I've got a smashing gentleman, some bio-researcher, who says he'll help us tomorrow morning. Not far from the Law Courts. Says he's the only one in England who can help us."

"Wonderful. I'll pack them together and we can leave at ten," Catherine said.

The next morning, Christopher arrived at her bedroom door in his corduroy trousers and sports jacket. After breakfast, he hugged the bag of silver cups with one arm and offered Catherine his other arm.

"How fortunate I am," Catherine said. "You are such a fine man, Christopher. I don't know how I would have managed all this without your steady presence."

While they waited for Maureen in the taxi, Catherine opened the bag. "I don't think it matters if we touch them now as we've already clobbered them with our DNA back at the hole you dug in the dirt." She handed him the half-horse, half-man Sagittarius cup and studied the Libra cup, noting its exquisitely carved balances as she turned it slowly around in her palm. "Just think, DNA from hundreds of years," she said, as the taxi made its way along. "Quite exciting, isn't it?" They switched cups, and she felt along the gracefully designed man-horse prancing along the curve of the silver, not noticing that the taxi had not budged.

"Hello," said the taxi driver, looking at Catherine through his rearview mirror. "You got some lovely cups there."

"Old ones an' all," Christopher said.

"Mind if I have a gander?" he asked.

"Not at all," Catherine said. She lifted Sagittarius up and displayed it to him.

"Blimey, must be them horoscopes. Here, you got the bull on one?" he asked. "That's me own sign."

Catherine knew she didn't have a cup with a bull on it. "Taurus," Christopher said.

"I don't have a cup with a bull on it."

"Must be one somewhere," he mused. "Do you have them other matching cups at home, then?"

"No, just these six here," Catherine said.

"If you had them other six matching cups, what a fortune you might have. A whole bleedin' horoscope set! Like them stars in the paper," said the taxi driver. "Blimey! I remember a man who knew all about silver. Lived in the East End, he did. I drove him to the Portobello Road and back many a time. I reckon he could help you out. He would know people at Portobello Road, an' all, who might know where them other six cups might be. He wore a mustache, as I remember."

Catherine and Christopher's eyes widened considerably. "You don't happen to remember where you were when you picked him up or dropped him off?"

"Not too far from here if I remember anything."

Catherine was stunned. Someone might know who had the rest of the set. Someone might want her six to make the whole set. Did that some-one have black shoes with holes in them?

Maureen came out of the door and Christopher waved her toward the taxi. She looked into the taxi's passenger window.

"Oh, hello, Archie. It's you, is it?" She turned to Catherine. "He's always bantering with the Irish blokes at our local pub. Christopher, you remember him from our pub, don't you?"

"Sorry, mate," Christopher said to the driver. "It's not my pub. I don't have a pub. Mum, this man remembers a customer who might know something about silver; goes to the Portobello Road and knows people what knows about silver."

"You don't say. Blimey!" Maureen said. "Where is he?"

"I can drive you all to the road I let him off at, if I can remember it," Archie offered.

Maureen climbed in and plumped herself down next to Catherine, who held the bag tightly against her chest.

The cab circled along the lanes and down the blocks, making them dizzy. "Is that where you live then?" Archie asked Maureen.

"Cheeky! 'Course it is. You knew that. What about the bio-researcher?" Maureen asked, turning to Catherine.

"He'll have to wait," Catherine asserted. The taxi sped on. "Matching cups?" she muttered.

# THE TAXI RIDE

**The taxi** stopped to back up and let another car pass through a narrow lane, shot forward around some tight corners, dodging black thick-wheeled bicycles, a cart laden with vegetables pulled by a horse with blinders, red telephone kiosks, zebra crossings, scuttling pedestrians everywhere, and pubs with names like Peddlers Lane, Hackney Pub, The Brick Layer. Archie displayed his intimate knowledge of every crack in the road, avoiding potholes, shaving along the roads close enough to frighten the pedestrians but not enough to actually hit them. Every bump was dodged with a slight twist of his wrist. It was as if he'd driven this route blind for thirty-five years.

Catherine closed her eyes after she saw a man shaking his fist at their taxi. The ride seemed interminable. Christopher leaned forward, listening to Archie's tales about World War II and the buildings that used to be there. Maureen sat quietly looking out the other window. "Brick Lane," she read aloud, from the sign above the street on a wall of a building. As the taxi turned the corner to the right, she again read aloud from a sign on the corner of another brick building, "Woodseer Street."

"Here we are, then," Archie said, halfway down the block. Catherine opened her eyes. Christopher unlatched the large, heavy black taxi door and stepped onto the sidewalk, offering his hand to Maureen and then to Catherine. Catherine shifted her shoulder bag, handed her umbrella to Maureen, and stepped down carefully, her eyes studying the smooth brick road.

"Shall I wait for you?" Archie asked, fingering his long mustache. "No, ta," Christopher said.

"Yes, please!" Maureen and Catherine said clearly at the same moment.

"Right then, I'll stop right here then. Take as long as you like. I'd like to hear the rest of this horoscope story." Archie turned off the engine and pulled his newspaper over the steering wheel, lit a cigarette, and turned up the radio.

Catherine peered at the green door in front of them. The walls came right out to the sidewalk, which was only wide enough for two people walking together at a squeeze. Maureen and Christopher craned their necks backward, up along the brown bricks and the three stories with two large windows per floor above them.

"What I'd like to do," Catherine said, as the other two turned toward her determined face, "is to knock at this very door. It's as much out of my own laziness as it is out of my ignorance about what we should be doing here. How does that sound?"

"Sounds right enough," Maureen said.

"I'm for it," Christopher said.

All three stepped forward one full step, and Christopher knocked firmly on the green door. The radio voice in the taxi behind them was announcing the news in the Queen's English.

Christopher knocked harder.

"I'm coming. Hold yer bleedin' 'orses," said a woman's voice from inside the door.

They heard a clank and jiggle on the other side of the door. It opened, and a woman perhaps in her late fifties, complete with flowery apron, toothless mouth, and thin white hair, pulled back in her bun said, "Well, a fine howdy-ya-do! Maureen, what you doing 'ere?"

Catherine glanced at Maureen's face, noting her startled look, her dropping jaw.

"Who might you be, then?" asked the woman in the flowery apron, eagle-eyeing Christopher.

"I'm Maureen's son, as a matter of fact," Christopher answered.

"Well, 'oo's this then?" she asked, nodding at Catherine. She squinted and leaned forward, studying Catherine's features. "Don't tell me. It's that American what killed her husband!"

"I did not kill my husband," Catherine said, recognizing Gracie from Holloway Prison and pulling herself up as tall as she could. "How many times did I tell you that?"

"Seems you always said you killed him, an' all," Gracie countered. "Well, never mind; whatever you say." Gracie opened the door flat against the wall. "Come in and have a cuppa tea, then." She led them past a small side table and down a dark, narrow flower-wallpapered hallway. All along the walls were old framed pen and ink drawings. She led them past a small table and into the kitchen, where the kettle was quietly whistling.

"Me boiling kettle keeps me company, eh?" she said, grabbing the gurgling kettle and filling it up at the sink. "Sit down, make yourselves at home."

They each pulled out a chair from the rectangular table and sat down.

"Right, Christopher. This is an old friend of ours, Gracie."

"From Holloway," Catherine added.

"Hello, then," Christopher said.

"When did they let you out?" Maureen asked Gracie. "I thought you were in for life?"

"Hello, Christopher," Gracie said, nodding in his direction. "I got out a year after you did, Mo; good behavior and crowded prisons make for freedom." She chuckled and hacked a smoker's cough as she pulled out her cigarettes and matchbook from her apron pocket.

"Allow me," Christopher said, and took the kettle and started to make a pot of tea like he lived there.

Gracie pulled out a chair, sat down, and lit her cigarette. "Isn't it amazing, all three of us again together, bloomin' amazing, it is."

"Quite a coincidence, you living here," Maureen said. "He's a good lad," she added, leaning toward Gracie.

"Spittin' image of 'is dad," Gracie said.

Christopher looked up and stopped moving. "You knew me dad, then, did you?"

"'Course I did; knew your mum since she was ten."

Christopher turned his back and grasped the steaming kettle, pouring more water into the teapot as the three women settled themselves over their teacups. Catherine remembered Gracie's story all these years later. Gracie's husband was that one who drank too much and drove Gracie to hit him over the head with an iron frying pan, killing him instantly. She got as long a term as Catherine.

"But," Christopher interjected, setting the kettle back on the stove, "how did you know me dad?"

"Oh, he was a drinking mate of me late husband, Ernie, God rest his soul."

"Ernie–that name: in *The Daily Mail* when I was a little boy. Was you the one...?"

"'Course I was. He deserved it, God rest his soul. Coming at me with that knife!"

Catherine cringed as she imagined the scene, reminded of someone going at David with a knife. She remembered how young Gracie used to say, "God rest his soul," but then she would laugh hysterically and slap her knee.

"Mum, did they both go to the Nag's Head, then?"

"I suppose so. Your dad never liked me to go there, so I never met Ernie; only heard about him in Holloway from Gracie here. I did see him in the distance a few times."

Now Gracie started laughing, rather like a horse: those buck teeth, a little green at the tops, still curtsying as her upper lip raised to meet the creases around her flat nostrils.

"Well, then," she said, simmering down to a sip of tea. "What brings you to visit me here?"

Catherine was too embarrassed to tell the truth, so just as she opened her mouth with a white lie planned, Maureen said, "Oh, we never knew you lived here, did we, Christopher? It's just that Catherine didn't feel like walking..." Maureen shot Catherine a glance. Catherine looked down.

"What I mean is, this is where our taxi driver, Archie, dropped us off," Maureen spluttered. "Oh, blimey, he's still out there waiting!"

Christopher continued, "...because of the man with the silver cups."

Gracie looked like a startled statue. "You mean..." she said.

"The one with the bull on it," Christopher said.

"The taxi driver?" Gracie asked.

"No, them silver cups," Christopher said.

"Twenty-five years ago," Catherine added.

"I know why he dropped you here, then," Gracie said. All three faces leaned forward, mouths dropping like wilted flowers.

"'Course, that man used to live 'ere, long ways ago," she said.

"Do you remember," Catherine asked, wondering about the man with the newspaper, "if he wore black shoes with holes in them for design, and laces?"

"Well, I remember them black shoes. Yes." She sipped her tea and stared at Catherine over the teacup's lip. "'Ow do you know about them black shoes, then?"

A budgie twittered in her blue cage. The cups clattered against the saucers. Christopher stopped his endless helpful dance around the ladies.

"I just guessed about the black shoes," Catherine said. "It's just that a gentleman keeps turning up in my life here in London—a stranger—and he has those black shoes; brogues they call them, I remember now."

"What's his name, then?" Maureen asked, rubbing her hands together.

Catherine, Maureen, and Christopher froze as they waited for Gracie to speak.

"Blimey. Must be going dottie," Gracie said. "I can't remember. He didn't live here all that long. I had ten people live in his room since then, at least."

They all picked up their teacups and sipped. "Think!" Maureen commanded.

"I can't! It's no use. It's not coming. But I do remember them shoes," Gracie said.

Christopher poured more tea and opened the tea biscuit tin and added a handful to the cup in the center of Gracie's kitchen table.

"What a lovely son you've got, Maureen," she said. "Not like his dad; doesn't drink a drop."

"Now he's even lovelier. Not that I have anything against a pint or two."

"'Course," Maureen said.

"Wait. It's coming: Smith. It was Mr. Smith."

# THE PHOTOGRAPH

**Christopher,** Maureen, and Catherine sat back and sighed. "Smith," Christopher chuckled. "Good name. Easy to spell. Easy to check in the telephone directory."

"Did he tell you his Christian name, then?" Maureen asked.

"Oh, no. I always wondered about him, maybe lying about his real name. But there are real people called Smith. I couldn't pry really: paid his rent on the dot; lived here only six months; had a wife, it seems."

"Go on," Catherine said.

"That's it: kept to hisself; private; quiet. That sort. Never drank or went out to the pub, not that I could see."

Christopher cleared the table. Catherine pulled out her handkerchief for a tiny, polite blow. Maureen stared at the photos on the wall. Gracie stood up and pulled her apron over her head.

"Is that you, all young, like?" Maureen asked, pointing to a photo.

"You knew me then–right after that silly smiling face broke the camera. I keep it up there to remind me there was a time 'before': I lost me youth and good looks right about then."

Catherine remembered Gracie with her slightly turned-up nose and dark eyebrows, her shiny black hair and her full lips. Yes, it was a long time ago.

"You don't know where he moved to, do you?" Catherine asked.

"Well, yes. He moved to Belsize Park, up near Hampstead Heath: him and his wife," Gracie said, now standing with her wiggling pointer finger in the bird's cage. "I think she was in 'ospital while he lived here. I suspect she got well so he found a bigger place. Don't know really. Said he liked to run on Hampstead Heath: rain or shine." The bird hopped onto her finger and Gracie leaned in for a mutual kiss. "He's old now, my Freddie. Can't last much longer. Look at them feathers, all frayed round the edges."

Rustling and mumbling, they made their way down the hallway toward the front door and donned their coats. Christopher opened the door, and as they began to file out Catherine glanced at the doily on the small round table by the umbrella stand. A framed black-and-white photograph, slightly browning, enticed Catherine to lean down and adjust her glasses. She reached to pick the frame up when Gracie lifted it gently but swiftly from her hands and pulled it to her side.

Maureen put her hands on her hips.

"All right, Gracie. Up to your old tricks. Let's have a gander." Maureen's hand was shoved palm up toward Gracie's stomach.

Gracie looked down at the white, gnarled fingers.

"You don't scare me none, Maureen. Them days is over. It's me own photograph, that's all. Put your bleedin' hand away, if you don't mind."

The two women stood glaring at each other, jaws protruding, chests heaving.

Meanwhile, Catherine cocked her head and studied the photograph sideways. There was a standing pair of lovers: young Gracie and a man, both smiling at each other, his arm around her tightly, his shoes black, perhaps with little holes in them.

"Hold still, I can't see his shoes," Catherine said. Gracie spun around.

"You little sneak, Catherine. Always were prying. Quiet like a prowling cat, you were." Gracie stepped back two steps. "Right, then, you snoopy lot, it's 'im and me. He was a married man." She shoved the photo at Maureen's palm, and Christopher and Catherine crowded around Maureen's hands, now holding the photo up to the light.

"Open up that door so we can see him, Christopher," Catherine said.

The light brightened up the photograph like the first chapter of a new novel.

Catherine stood up straight. "That might be the man."

"It's me own secret. His name is Smith, if you'd like to know. He's a lovely man, and he loved his wife all the while." Gracie smoothed down her apron.

Maureen passed the photo to Catherine, who held it up and stared at it, trying to make out the details of his face. Between her bad eyesight and the small size of the photograph, she couldn't be quite certain.

"I'd need a magnifying glass to be sure," she said.

Christopher pulled out his keys. "Here you go, me love. I always have this little one for emergencies."

Catherine moved the magnifying glass over the man's face as the keys jingled alongside it like a distant jailer. The man smiling back had a happy look. The man who had sat with her all those years at visiting time had a sad look.

"It's the one," she said.

"Which one?" Gracie asked.

"This man came and sat with me for many years every few months and never said a word. He sat with Maureen once, right, Maureen? Then Maureen left and he switched to me."

"He had a wife who died—God rest her soul," Gracie said. "Not then, but later; had multiple sclerosis. I never knew her, 'course, but Mr. Smith always told me the latest. He so loved her, but, well, relations had all dried up years before, and a man has his needs," she said, glancing at Christopher, "beggin' yer pardon, me darling."

Catherine stared at the back of the photo, Christopher looked down at the carpet, and Maureen surveyed the framed drawings on the wall.

"Where does he live now?" Catherine asked finally.

"Don't know. Lost touch years ago, we did. Such a pity. Lovely man."

"But he's the one following us around. Look at those shoes in this photo," Catherine said, holding it again up to the light.

"No doubt about them shoes," Christopher said. There was a silence.

"Nothing more to say, then," Maureen said. "Our taxi's waiting there." She nodded toward the front door down the hall and the black cab hopefully still waiting outside. They stepped out the door, one by one. Gracie snatched the photograph from Catherine.

"Well, nice to know you lot are still out causing trouble," she said in a friendly way. "Drop by again, then."

"Goodbye, Gracie," Maureen said. "We may well drop by again, so hide the evidence!" She and Catherine chortled into their double chins.

It had been an exhausting afternoon for Catherine, and all she wanted was a nice hot bath.

# THE CHASE

**Christopher held out** his hand for Catherine as she very slowly pulled herself up into the large back seat of the taxi. Then he shoved Maureen in, lunged in after her, and slammed the door.

"Who's got them silver cups then?" Archie asked, stubbing out his cigarette and turning off the radio.

"Oh, goodness," Maureen said. "We forgot all about them!"

"But we found out about the man," Christopher said, facing backward on the pull-down seat and leaning sideways toward the open window section between the front and back seats. "He lived right in that house. You remembered well."

"Well, them doors and bricks all look the same, but I do have a great memory for places, they say," Archie said. "Makes a good taxi driver, they say." Archie started the engine and pulled ahead over the bricks along the narrow road, by the brick walls along the bridge over the railroad tracks, with the sidewalk only a foot wide in some places.

Maureen was rustling through her handbag, and Christopher was talking about football with the taxi driver. Catherine noticed a familiar-looking man turning the corner ahead. As they drove by she turned her head as far as she could manage, then she turned her whole body to look out the back window.

"That's him again! Turn the taxi around!" Catherine commanded.

Archie was a miracle worker: With no room for the taxi to budge, somehow with bits forward and bits backward, he managed to turn and go back.

"Left, left here! There he goes!" Catherine yelled, suddenly not feeling the least bit tired.

The taxi swung and bumped over the bricks, and they all grabbed the inside handles as they were jostled over the rough road surface.

"Black shoes!" she yelled, pointing with her free hand.

A man came out from one of the houses ahead. He wore an overcoat and carried an umbrella and a newspaper. As they sped past him Catherine looked at his shoes: black. That's all she could make out. Did men all wear these black shoes this side of London? She looked at the shoes of other men walking on the other side of the street. Working men's shoes: not black and shiny.

Catherine was getting confused. Maybe that wasn't the man, after all.

The taxi swung around another corner just in time for them to see the heel of a black shoe disappearing through a door: a green door.

"Here we are, then. Back to your friend's house," Archie said. "Well, what do you know!" Catherine exclaimed.

"That old liar," Maureen said.

"Shall I follow 'im?" Christopher asked, reaching for the door handle and opening the door slightly.

The taxi screeched to a halt on the other side of the narrow road.

Everybody looked at Catherine who was shaking her head.

"No, son, me love," Maureen said. "I think we have all the information we need. We'll do a bit of spying tomorrow, now we know where he resides. That Gracie! Always was such a liar!"

"Home, Archie," Catherine said, tapping on the window with her umbrella.

Catherine felt a sudden need for those dreams that led her to a land where problems dissolved into answers. Who were these people? It made no sense: even now, Mr. Smith was obviously still in Gracie's life, if not her bed.

The minute she got into her cold bed at Maureen's, Catherine snuggled down, hugging the stone hot water bottle, closing her eyes and feeling a vague longing to be back in Vermont.

# 1939: THE KING'S ARMS

**A few months** afterward, young Harry yawned and stretched and crawled out from under his very own barrow at Portobello Road. Little by little, he had begun to make money: the first really good money he had made in his whole short life. He remembered that old man who'd bought the tarnished metal box that Harry had stolen from the barrel on the train. He remembered how he traded the box with the old man for his barrow and everything in it. Harry, with his new, gray working man's cap tipping forward on his head, remembered how the old man–John was his name–had limped away clutching the box.

Old John had bargained so quickly that young Harry thought the old man was about to fall over and die right on the spot: His eyes were yellow; his beard long and gray; his nose was large and red; and his clothes were tattered.

But in the exchange, there was a gleam in John's old eye that had been lying in wait since he, himself, was a lad and began the trade with his father, who had taught John to watch over the years for a priceless treasure, and when he saw it, to get away from the seller as quickly as a cat being chased by a dog. John couldn't walk quickly now. His father would have laughed to see his own son limping away, huddled around his new treasure, while the young lad who got his barrow rubbed his hands, not knowing what he'd given away for his new business.

Young Harry made enough money that first day to eat a bun for dinner. He didn't know what "enterprising" meant, but he had a feeling that he had an energy, now that his true independence had begun, that rivaled anything he'd felt on the train journeys to and from London.

Old John had passed the King's Arms, then turned, saying to himself, "I deserve a pint before I sell this box. That boy will never know what he sold me. Besides, I done it fair and square."

John's father would be chewing down his dirty fingernails now if he were alive: He would be yelling, "No, lad, don't stop in there, not today, not so early; not before you done your business and sold your treasure!" But the father would have had to look on at his son, who had, it must be admitted, the same longing for the drink in his veins that his father had had.

At last the old man was free! Free to have a little celebratory drink right in the middle of the day, whilst his mates called out to potential customers and tried to sell enough to feed the wife and children. He had no wife to worry him, no dog, no children. He ordered his pint at the bar and looked around, clasping his box on his lap. Nobody John knew was in the pub. He'd never seen it so quiet. Only the bartender yawned as he slid his pint toward him and said, "Morning, mate."

Oddly, none of that seemed to matter to John. The pint sliding in front of him, spilling its foam over the edges, full, like he finally felt; full and free at last. He drank it down, spilling it along his mustache, slammed the empty glass down. He turned to leave, but the taste was fresh on his throat–perhaps one more would do the trick. After all, this was a day to celebrate. His labors were finally over. "And again," he said to the bartender, Stan, who knew the old man well, and had placed his second pint in front of him before he'd finished asking for it.

John felt a lovely calm as he knocked back his second pint; he didn't notice that he had not even ordered the third and fourth pints. They were placed in front of him as usual. Stan knew his habits. By the time John had had six pints, Stan was busy with others who'd finally arrived for their steak and kidney pie, and John grasped his box and staggered out into the cobblestone street. He looked both ways and momentarily yearned to go back to his barrow and call out to the people passing to buy his small treasures, but instead he clutched his box and staggered off toward the pawn shop. His head was spinning as he chuckled to himself. He took one more glance back toward his old barrow and turned the corner.

Around the corner a stocky young man rushed at John, saying, "I'll have that."

"No, you don't!" spluttered John, reeling backward, twisting his ankle and falling, sending his treasure some yards away into the street.

The young man rushed past him, swept up the box, and sped away while John groaned at the pain in his ankle and his lazy eyes tried to follow the man in the distance with his box, his future; his life.

The young man sped down the road and around the corner, down the basement steps in front of a building, into the door and down the long, dark hallway toward his mother, Helen, who sat slumped down, depressed and sad in their dreary one-room flat.

"Cuppa tea, Ronnie, me love?" she asked, nursing her own cup of tea, now almost cold.

Panting, Ronnie laid his treasure on the table and plunged himself into the tattered, deep, comfy old chair.

"Mum, bloody cold in 'ere. I'll turn on the fire." He leaned forward and laid his fingers on the gas tap.

"No, darlin', take your tea, it'll warm you. We can't afford gas now. Here's your cardigan."

The tea warmed Ronnie's insides. This Depression was endless. How long could they live on tea, bread, and lard, and a little sugar now and again? Ronnie looked at his treasure.

"What's that you've got there, Ronnie?" Helen asked.

"Aw, Mum. I dunno as yet. Nicked it off an old bloke staggering out of the King's Arms: drinking too early; serves him right."

Just then there was a knock at the door. "Who's that then?' Helen asked.

"Dunno," Ronnie answered, not budging, but sipping his steaming tea.

His mother, with her bowed legs, tottered down the hallway. "Who is it, then?" Helen yelled at the closed door.

"It's me–John," said the voice.

She opened the door, but didn't recognize the drunken old man at first.

"Hello, then," she said, remembering her husband's friend from Portobello Road. "Come on in. Have a cuppa tea, then."

John staggered along the hall, bouncing off the damp walls until he reached the kitchen. Ronnie looked up and then jumped up, tossing his cup to the floor. He grabbed the box and darted around the old man until he came face to face with his mother.

"What's going on, son? Where're you going with that box?"

"It's my box," old John slurred.

"Is it then?" she said to Ronnie.

"Aw, Mum. I didn't know you knew him." He turned and laid the box back onto the table.

"Here you are, then, mate, whoever you are."

"He's one of your dad's mates from the King's Arms. It's John. You remember him from when you was five?"

"Not really. Sorry. Have some tea, then, mate. And take your box. Sorry about that. It's only we're bloody starving here since our dad passed, aren't we, Mum?"

"That's true an' all," she answered, wiping her hands on her faded flowery apron.

"When I sober up, I'll go pawn this and bring some real meat, chops, maybe, and we'll celebrate, then. How's that?" John said.

Ronnie stood by the door, shifting from one foot to the other.

"Hey, old man. What say I go with you, make sure they don't skin you alive?"

"If you promise not to run off with me treasure, 'course you can come."

"He won't run off. He's a good lad, just bloody hungry. Come back with pork chops, potatoes, and Brussels sprouts and we'll all have a nice little party!"

After tea, the two men made their way to the pawnbrokers and came home with enough cash to buy dinner for three for a year!

# THE CASE OF GRACIE

**"Gracie,** this is Catherine," Catherine said, holding the phone close to her ear. She was sitting at the kitchen table, with Maureen and Christopher hardly breathing nearby.

"Hello, wot a lark seeing you two all old an' that. 'Course, I look the same to you, likely, eh?"

Catherine remembered the two faces of Gracie: young, open, cheeky, and the old, sly, entrenched, lying sneer. "You look just the same to me, Gracie. Same big eyes, same smile, only white hair is a shock from your jet-black head I knew. Look, Gracie, I've called to find out about Mr. Smith."

"Go on," Gracie said. The sound of a radio diminished. "We need to know more about Mr. Smith."

"I told you all I know. How can I tell you more, if there isn't more to say?"

"Gracie, you've got to try. Did he ever tell you about his childhood or where he was born and went to school?" Catherine asked.

"Naw: never said nothing. He liked antiques, is all. I liked 'em an' all, so we had that in common. Mine were the cheaper variety. He liked the genuine antiques, he did."

Catherine wondered how to pull more information out of Gracie.

"Gracie, we saw Mr. Smith going into your door after we left that day. Couldn't you set up a meeting with him and me, and you, if you'd like?" Catherine suggested.

"Oh, no! That would never do. I wouldn't want him knowing I ever said a word. He'd get all upset, being his private self."

"We could drop by," Catherine tried.

"Please, love. I'd rather you didn't. It would throw a spanner in the works between us that just wouldn't do."

"What else can you tell me, Gracie?" Catherine asked.

There was a little guttural sound at the other end of the line. "I've told you all I know."

"Gracie, how did you come to know him?"

"Can't say as I remember."

"Seems strange," Catherine said. "If he's the one who sat next to me all those years and never said a word...do you remember if he ever told you about me?"

"No, can't say as he did."

"Gracie, what did you and he have in common?"

A smothered giggle filtered into Catherine's ear, sounding like Gracie did in jail all those years before. "Don't be daft. You know what we had in common. Cheeky devil."

Catherine felt little red capillaries coming alive along her face. "You must have talked about something."

"That's no time to chat, me love!"

"But didn't you ever have a cup of tea together, sit and talk? You know."

"Suppose we must have. Small talk, that's all. He'd tell me about how his wife was faltering and that."

Catherine was feeling mounting impatience with this bundle of lies. "You are such a liar; always were. Now come clean, Gracie. I'm not getting any younger, and I've come back to find out who killed David. I didn't do it."

"So you've said."

"I did *not* do it, Gracie. Do you think Mr. Smith had anything to do with it?" Catherine glanced at the light flickering from the traffic and the unusual sunlight of the morning.

"Got to go, love," Gracie said.

"Right, then, Gracie. You know my number at the Churchill Bed and Breakfast if you want to talk."

"I thought you was staying...I mean... Right, then. Ta-ta!" she said, and Catherine heard her hang up the phone.

Catherine felt she was getting close, very close to the answer to this mystery. It was clear she was too close for Gracie's comfort. It was time to corner this Mr. Smith. The way he followed her around, it wouldn't be that difficult. What was Gracie hiding? She, Christopher, and Maureen sat in the kitchen trying to work out how to set the trap.

Catherine told Christopher and Maureen that she had decided to return to the Churchill Bed and Breakfast for a while. Gracie might phone her there, but Catherine wanted a little time to herself to think and sort through all the possibilities.

# CATHERINE'S CUPS

**Back at the hotel**, Catherine turned from her side to her back and then onto her stomach in the large double bed. The sounds of Saturday night London traffic interfered with her attempt to shut out the world. The wings of sleep would not come, though her jaw extended with musical yawns while stretching her arms and pointing her toes: exercises that she repeated, hoping she would fool her mind into a dreamy state. She could hear the soft voices in the hallway, but she couldn't understand them and didn't care to. Her body hung heavily anchored to the mattress, unable to move anymore, and eventually she slid into a delightful slumber where dreams mixed with reality and neither could be made sense of later.

The heel of his black shoe disappeared into the green door that slammed in her face. A laughing man clasping six silver cups echoed into a small hole evaporating into space. Gracie held her umbrella open and lowered it to the center of Catherine's dream, blocking the vanishing vision, and all that was left were the scattered sparkling reflections of the sun against the cups–Catherine's cups.

Catherine woke up and sat straight up. "My cups!" she said, flinging the blankets off her body, turning sharply, waiting for the resettling of her bones and spine, then pushing her body up with her palms against the bed and aiming toward the bathroom.

Since reading *The Daily Mail* article that she had spotted at the bottom of the page about the silver cups, Catherine had wondered about the exact value of *her* cups. (Of course, they were *her* cups!) Up to now, they were a loving extension of David and the man she had loved and lost, tangible evidence of a life before prison; a life of love. But she had to acknowledge that they were also evidence of a blemish on their romantic love, proof of his secretive nature, something to examine with her bad eyesight that quietly demonstrated that her David was not exactly the honest man she had made him out to be in her mind. But she realized that she had probably turned a blind eye to his faults, not unlike how she now knew she had turned a blind eye to her own self. How could she imagine David would not marry a woman that was carrying his child?

Catherine knew David was a realist and not a romantic. And yet Catherine, though a romantic, prided herself on her solid, feet-firmly-planted-on-the-ground, facts-first kind of personality. She preferred seeing David as a man without flaws, rather than the actual man he really was, dealing with the conflict he must have anguished over, in swearing to the real Mrs. Evans that he would never tell Catherine about his baby, while Catherine was given to presume his honesty. And yet, Catherine preferred the lie; at least she now remembered not wanting to think about it all. She preferred to be cozy with David and dream of their future family, albeit without a marriage license. It was not only their secret, Catherine knew, but an era's secret. So many people lived "in sin," while married to others who had also moved on after the war and had found other partners. Marriage was for the young, when permanence was a dream. Divorce was too complicated, along with the need to survive.

It seemed she was discovering a lot about the past without any DNA evidence. Something about the old-fashioned ways was more appealing to her now, and she decided to save it for last-straw evidence, and only if she needed it. Meanwhile, she came back into the bedroom and sat on her bed, lifted her legs, covered them with the blankets, and began to count the ways she knew more about the murder.

Mr. Smith was alive and high on the list of suspects. However, why would he want to kill David? Had he been flirting with Gracie on alternate visits to the jail? How did Gracie get into his life and how did he get into her bed? Was Gracie the murderer? Was she a support in his endeavor?

Gracie had been sly as a prisoner. If you needed something smuggled in, Gracie was the connection, always a businesswoman; always talked about her business, selling wares on Saturdays at the street market. What was it she sold? Old cutlery, wasn't it; dishes with famous engravings of the potters on the back. Catherine remembered how Gracie talked back in jail. It bored her: Gracie and all her junk.

Catherine never thought of herself as interested in antiques. She was a reader: Books were her first love. David would come home with the evidence of his strolls through the streets of the East End on a Saturday morning: doilies, plates, cutlery, all tasteful, perhaps even valuable; all treasures for David. Catherine's treasure was the house and the sea, the armchair and lamps. David's treasures were smaller, decorating the walls, filling the shelves, and adding the feminine touch Catherine took no interest in. It was a perfect match: David with his antiques and Catherine with her love of their home.

The telephone rang. Catherine's eyes shot open. Her half-clothed arm crashed onto the phone.

"Hello?" she said. There was only silence. "I know it's you," she said. No one hung up. No dial tone interrupted. She heard her own breathing. Should she hang up? She shifted onto her elbow. "Hello?" she said. This time she was wide-awake. Click; then she heard the dial tone. He was there, like a firefly; gone, like a dead soul.

She sat up. Just as she reached for the light switch, the phone rang again. She let it ring as her hand hovered over it. It stopped. She twisted the knob, and the light flooded her bed. She waited. The clock said two a.m. Maybe it was a call from Vermont? Maybe it wasn't that man. Why was there this silence? She felt too old for these games. She switched off the light. Darkness was interrupted by wisps of streetlights through the crack in the drapes. She snuggled down and waited.

The phone rang again, but only once. Catherine turned over. Her eyelids were not heavy now: her eyes were wide open, following the light at the edge of the thick drapes.

Catherine saw the dawn through the window, the clearing of the clouds, the light creeping upon the edge of London as she remembered David's mother, her kind letters; her understanding of Catherine and David's love for each other.

How could she untangle this mystery? It surely was that man, Mr. Smith.

# MORE EVIDENCE

**Catherine** knew there was more to know about Gracie and Mr. Smith. There was nothing to do but go meet her face to face and see her cringe as she told her lies.

Christopher and Maureen met Catherine at the hotel in a taxi she told them to hire at their house. The new taxi driver said his name was Charlie, and wore a working man's peaked cap and a thick mustache, while his cigarette dangled on his lower lip. He said he was a local man from the East End, and seemed to know both Gracie and Mr. Smith.

"That man, Mr. Smith: he's been calling round 'er place for donkey's years," Charlie said. "I picks him up and drives him there regular. Me mates at the pub know him, an' all. He's a right lark. Always carrying antiques he's bought from Portobello Road or Petticoat Lane."

Catherine couldn't help prying more. "Do you know much about his girlfriend, Gracie, then?"

"Oh, yes, she's another right one. I tried to take her for a drink when she first got out of the clinker, but soon enough ol' Mr. Smith came along and that was the end of that. Lovely woman, really. Course, she's a right liar, an' all, but got a sense of humor, so that's all right then. No 'arm done."

"What sort of things do they bring home from Portobello Road?" Catherine asked as the taxi swerved into Gracie's road.

"All sorts: furniture, pictures, silver–whatever they fancy. Here we are then, and don't mention you met me, right?"

"No problem," Catherine said, handing him some pound coins.

"Not bloody likely," Maureen said.

"Ta-ta, mate," Christopher said.

Maureen banged unceremoniously on Gracie's door. After a bit, Gracie came to the door and opened it. Her face looked as if someone had hit her in the stomach.

"Well, thought I'd seen the last of you for a while." She stood and stared at them for a bit, then said, "Might as well come in and have a cuppa, an' all."

They filed into the hallway and stood there, nobody talking. Then Gracie said, "Well, hang up your coats, then, and come on into the kitchen."

In the kitchen Catherine noticed two settings of dishes still unwashed from the morning. Mr. Smith couldn't be far. She sniffed that scent like a cat in the darkness closing in on a cornered mouse. The kitchen table was too large for the kitchen. Catherine imagined how Gracie had spotted it at the market. It probably had stains and scratches all over the top, which she had lovingly sanded away. She probably knew it was too large for her kitchen. Getting it through the doors must have been, at the least, a comedy. Gracie had to draw in her belly to scoot around it sideways.

A large table was a necessity in England, where the cold outside held people inside sitting around it, warming their red fingers on their hot cups of tea. Apart from the pubs, which held people together out of the cold, the kitchen table was the point of conversation. Newspapers were open and piled high from the week. The rest of the house might be tidy or collect dust, but the kitchen table was a picture of movement and life. Catherine liked, more than anything else, to be invited to a "nice hot cuppa tea." It was a moment of mutual sharing, relaxing: time to just acknowledge the larger family that necessitated the gift of a cup of tea and a place to settle one's bones. It was an invitation to talk, to matter; to say what otherwise might be kept silent and festering. Gracie poured their tea, then sat down and brushed some crumbs off the table surface and into her palm.

"I read me horoscope this morning," Gracie said as she shuffled through the paper. "You won't believe what it said."

Catherine, Christopher, and Maureen fussed with their cups and biscuits.

"Well, it said..." she came to the page. "Here it is, then. It says: *Pisces: You and your Aquarian friend are slipping. Hold your secrets inside. Prying eyes will unnerve you.*"

Gracie looked up at her listeners. "Blimey, it's like they even knew Mr. Smith's horoscope!"

"Are you a Pisces, then," Maureen asked, with a look of indifference.

"'Course I am. Always was," Gracie laughed. "Don't know as I believe in all this, but that Mr. Smith reads his horoscope regular. Never misses a day. It was like a religion to him. I just goes along. Don't really believe it mostly. Just some bleeder scratching out a living at the office, laughing at us all who takes it serious."

"I read me own horoscope every day," Maureen said, "and I tell Christopher his, just in case. No more beating about the bush, Gracie. We want to know anything you know about this Mr. Smith. We know he's been here. Look at them dishes: most likely his. No more lying. What is going on with him and you, then?"

Gracie stood up, wiped her hands on her apron, and walked over and leaned against the sink. She heaved her breasts upward, looked at the broom a moment, and then sighed. "All right, you lot. I've known him a long while, but he won't tell me anything at all about his interest in you. He's close to hisself, he is; just spends the night here now and again for you-know-what, that's all. Never tells me anything, I swear."

"When did you two meet up, then?" Maureen asked.

"Right. It was at the jail. I got out four years before his wife died. I actually met him on the day I was leaving; he was coming to visit you, Catherine. He only asked me if I knew of any place to stay when he came up to London, so I gave him me address, didn't I? Simple as that. One thing led to another. Been like that a long while now."

"We think he has something serious on his mind about Catherine," Christopher asked. "What is it?"

"I don't know nothing. He keeps to hisself, that's all I know," Gracie said. "Anyway, he's gone now; back to the country."

Catherine sipped her tea and let her eyes search the room for clues.

There seemed to be nothing that would indicate anything out of the ordinary was going on in that house. She felt tired and discouraged.

Then she spotted a pair of glasses lying on the Dutch cupboard. She peered at them when Gracie was putting more water into the tea kettle. They were identical to the pair she had found in the earth under Mrs. Angela Evans' beach house.

# DNA

**The DNA office** was next to the postwar building of King's College on the Strand, not far from Fleet Street on one end and Waterloo Bridge on the other. The taxi pulled up around the small, ancient church of St. Mary's that stood in an island on the road, and dropped them off while a car honked behind them. The spire from the church glowed with the rain. The street was plugged with swarming taxis and buses. Catherine and Maureen made their way gingerly out of the taxi and onto the road next to Christopher.

"Look!" Maureen said, pointing to a plaque on the wall of the building. "It says DNA was discovered right here at King's College. Blimey!"

Christopher, Maureen, and Catherine, all under Catherine's umbrella, read the sign together, which said DNA was discovered there in King's College, then ambled into the building and sat waiting in the outer office as the umbrella dripped onto the Persian carpet.

They waited for twenty minutes after their appointed time of three o'clock until at last, a small man appeared with red cheeks, a handlebar mustache, bowler hat, and a large, black, wet umbrella.

"Dreadful traffic. Terribly sorry. Won't be a moment," he spluttered as he swept past their bedraggled little group of three, who had almost fallen asleep waiting on the couch and chair. After a few minutes he peeked through his office door.

"Come in. Please come in and sit down." He gestured at three antique chairs. The office reminded Catherine of a dentist's waiting room, only larger, with a huge window overlooking the rooftops and beyond them, the River Thames. There were magazines on the coffee table, all scientific, it seemed. There were charts on the walls with large illustrations about DNA that looked a bit like some modern, primary-colored art or tinker toys for children.

"As you must know, I am Mr. Townsend, at your service," he said, bowing slightly, and coming right to the point, he added, "Now, how I can help you?" He stroked his mustache in a hypnotic way. His shiny bald head was halved by four inch-long, white curly tufts around his ears and the back of his neck. He looked like he was rehearsing for the part of an old man.

"We are trying to find out..." Catherine began. She realized she had not quite pictured this scene or what she would say. Should she reveal her past or keep things unsaid, skirt around the truth, keep to the science? "Well, could you tell us how DNA might be helpful to find out about something that happened thirty years ago?"

"I must tell you that the most amazing people come to me," he said, his smile indicating a slight boredom, "with astonishing reasons to find out if DNA can be used: people looking for their relatives, ancestors, possible fathers, even people who had changed identities. Certainly, whatever happened in the past can be opened up using DNA in new ways never imagined before. If you could be more accurate about what you might need it for, that would be rather helpful."

"This lady 'ere," Maureen started. "She's been framed."

"Not framed, Mum. Mr. Townsend, sir: just condemned for something she didn't do."

"Wants to set things to rights for her family, like, before, you know..." Maureen added.

Mr. Townsend shifted his gaze from Christopher and Maureen, who sat to his left, over to Catherine, who sat to his right on the other side of his huge, antique desk.

"You see," Catherine began.

"It weren't 'er fault an' all," Christopher said. "They didn't have this DNA in them days, just fingerprints...." He looked up at Catherine. "Sorry," he said.

"And her fingerprints was on the knife, of course," Maureen added, leaning forward, confidentially. "She'd just cut up the apples for the pie, an' all." Mr. Townsend looked at Catherine. Or rather, he peered at her for a long while.

"Madam," he said. "I seem to remember your face from somewhere. Now that you sit before me and tell me these things, you begin to bring back memories of the Old Bailey."

Catherine cleared her throat, sat straight up, and answered, "I was the first woman accused of first degree murder and not hanged for it in England."

"Yes," he said, pulling his mustache thoughtfully, "I never forget a face."

"Yes, but I didn't kill him," she heard herself say, quite tired now of the echo it had made through the years of her life.

"Well, then, that may be what you're here to find out," he indicated. "That is, indeed, why we are here."

"Ruth Ellis, whom you may well have heard of, had just been hanged just over a year before. You were quite a celebrity then."

"If you call being hit in the face with tomatoes a celebrity!"

"Well, yes, but I meant historically. I think I would like to work with you. You say you are quite innocent?"

"'Course she's innocent!" Maureen said, indignantly. "Look at them eyes!"

"Seems to me I recognize you as well," he said, nodding at Maureen.

Maureen turned purple. "Lookie here," she spluttered, "I done me time. He deserved it, the bleedin' drunk, pardon me French." She dusted off her lap. "Even if he was your father," she added, patting Christopher on the shoulder.

"How did you recognize me mum, then?" Christopher asked Mr. Townsend.

"You might say I have a photographic memory. But as a lad I was very interested in law and visited the Old Bailey every chance I could. So you see, I've seen both of you before, when I was quite young. I promise, however," he added, nodding at Catherine, "I didn't throw the tomato. In fact, I always thought they didn't have enough proof to put you in jail. That is one of the reasons I went into this field, now that I think of it. I follow all those stories, even today. It's an easy walk to the Law Courts from here."

Catherine was so pleased to hear him say that he thought she wasn't proven guilty, she sat up even straighter and imagined giving this Englishman a hug or at least a simple embrace; but then again, it was a long way up out of that chair, and his heavily waxed mustache, which looked so comical, covered too much of his cheeks.

"We will need physical evidence from that era. Do you have any suspicions about the real murderer?"

Catherine stood up and walked to the window. Mr. Townsend stood up as well. The rain had stopped, and the sky was turning blue, peppered with white clouds. She turned. "I never had any idea who could have wanted to kill David, but I have been followed all over London on this trip, and I've gotten strange phone calls and letters from an unknown person." She hesitated, then added, "You see, Mr. Townsend, there is also the question of the silver cups created by the famous Cellini."

# THE EXPERT

**"The silver cups?** Who is this man Cellini?" he asked bluntly, as he stood poised in thought. "Ah, yes, I think I read something about that in the paper. Are you the one who has the silver cups?" He took a step toward Catherine. "Do you have them now?"

Catherine didn't know this man at all. For all she knew he might be working with the mystery man.

"They're well-hidden," she answered, stepping backward. "Cellini was a great silversmith from Italy back in the 16th century. You've heard of him?"

"Yes, yes, of course," he said, walking around his desk and sitting down. "If you don't mind, I'll need to see them all. Also, may I inquire about what other information might you have that puts this mystery man at the scene of the crime, as they say?"

Catherine sat down. "I've got an old pair of glasses I found when we were digging out the cups at the beach house where they were buried. They're David's. I remember them well. I saw an identical pair at the house of a woman who rented a room to this mystery man, whose name, apparently, is Smith."

"Smith, you say. Hmm," Mr. Townsend mumbled. "Anything else?"

"I've got my handkerchief," she said, pulling it from her sleeve. "It used to be David's. It was in his coat pocket it the day he died."

"We can test that. Anything else?"

"We've got a hairbrush with David's hair in it. We've sent my loafers off to Davis for DNA testing. We had a cat. Might still be our cat's hairs on their soles."

"Excellent," he said, pulling at his mustache. "Well done!"

They left Mr. Townsend's office, and Catherine opened her umbrella as she, Maureen, and Christopher stood under it at the edge of the curb. Patches of blue opened and closed as the wind whisked the clouds along. Christopher waved down an approaching taxi.

Back at Maureen's house Catherine shook out her umbrella until the last drop came off. Christopher relieved her of it and put it into a tall Chinese umbrella stand.

"Tea?" he suggested, inevitably. They bundled down the hallway, past the old photos, the plates, the small, framed paintings of copies of Constable and Turner. It would appear that Maureen and Christopher had fine taste in art: Catherine imagined that perhaps the Turner, with its crashing seascape and ship lost in the storm, reflected the active and enthusiastic Maureen, while Constable's quiet river scene with the cows and trees mirrored Christopher's steady hand and constancy toward Catherine.

"We didn't mention the horoscopes," Catherine said, more to herself than the others.

"They're nothing to do with DNA," Maureen said, "but he seems to know a lot, and we ought to tell him anything we know in case it throws a light on whatever we might not know about."

"I'll phone him after tea and set up another appointment," Catherine said, biting into her scone. The feeling of fatigue passed over Catherine. She thought about the horoscopes and David's love of them, his mother's insistence on following the predictions. Then she had a hunch that an investigation into the astrology of those days in 1956 should take precedence in Maureen's research. Maybe Maureen could figure out a way to copy every day from every paper for three months before David's demise. Perhaps a thread of logic to his movements could be followed.

"We've got to get them cups down to Mr. Townsend," Christopher said.

"Imagine! Not only the DNA on the cups, but the fingerprints from ages ago," Maureen said.

"I don't think fingerprints stay on like them DNA prints, not for centuries, like," Christopher said. "They would have been polished off years before David got them."

Christopher stood on a chair and reached back to the top of the cupboard and drew out the cups. Catherine watched him peel the new tissue paper from them and turn them in his palm.

They all peered at the signs engraved on their sides. It was the missing signs that Catherine wondered about.

"Maureen, please, can you find the horoscopes, and study only the six signs which are *not* on these cups? The ones we have here are: Leo, Sagittarius, Aries, Libra, Cancer, and Virgo. Then the missing ones will be...Aquarius, Pisces, Scorpio, Gemini, Capricorn, and Taurus." Christopher scribbled these down.

"Don't you think that if the murderer has those cups, he may have selected one of them with his own sign on it? If that's true, that will cut your work in half. Now, why not look for instructions about doing something on the day David was killed; or the day before? You know, like, 'Now is the time to act.' Then maybe we'll know what sign the murderer is."

"Gracie said Mr. Smith followed the signs," Catherine said.

"But if we found out his sign, we could follow it right up to the day of the murder and even afterward," Christopher said thoughtfully as he wrapped the cups up and put them in a stack, one inside of the other, then brought out an old cloth bag. Maureen grasped it and held it open as Christopher fed the cups into it, leaving the box aside.

Catherine was closing in on the truth, but she still needed more clues. "Mr. Smith liked astrology," she mumbled to herself. "Isn't that what Gracie said? He read his horoscope every day?"

# THE EPHEMERIS

**Maureen came home** the next afternoon and breathlessly laid out her discoveries to Catherine, who had arrived home not twenty minutes before.

"I found out the murderer's sign. Well, what I mean is, what might be his sign," Maureen said as Christopher and Catherine leaned forward. Maureen placed several files in front of her and shoved her teacup and saucer to the center of the table. She opened one file and pulled out a pamphlet she called an astrologer's "ephemeris," smoothed it down in front of her, then turned it around for Catherine and Christopher to see.

"The murderer, by me own deductions," Maureen proclaimed, "has got to be an Aquarian." Her expression indicated an absolutely final deduction that Christopher and Catherine would never dare to doubt.

"Right," Christopher said. "How's that, then, Mum?"

"Well, it's simple: David was a Leo, right, Catherine?" She nodded at Catherine.

"Right, indeed," Catherine said, willing to see what Maureen had concocted.

"Well, he died on November 3, 1956." She breathed in deeply and smiled mysteriously. "Did you know," she went on, pointing at some lines in the ephemeris, "that on November 3rd and 4th, 1956, see here,"

211

she pointed at the page, "the sun was in Scorpio?" Her face lit up with glee as she pounced on the word, "Scorpio!"

Catherine and Christopher hung in mid-air, waiting for the punch line. Perhaps it had already been said? Christopher put his index finger on the line in the ephemeris and squinted as he tried to decipher the figures in front of him. The rules of astrology were a blur for Catherine; a fading memory of David's mother flowing through his mouth at the most surprising moments of his indecision.

"Scorpio?" Catherine asked, fearing the look of temporary insanity on Maureen's lighted face.

"Scorpio, yes!" Maureen said, raising her eyebrows, moving her finger along the ephemeris. "Scorpio is *death!*" Her eyebrows burned downward, and the lines between them deepened. "Scorpio is really bad for Leos and Aquarians." She stood up, proclaiming, "Aquarian's suns and Leo's suns square Scorpio's sun on November 3rd and 4th, 1956. A lady pointed that out to me in the library, and that makes Mr. Smith, or the murderer, an Aquarian! Right?" she said, brushing her palms, like it was foolproof information. "This," she added, "is a double dose of death for them two signs."

"So," Catherine asked, "if Mr. Smith is an Aquarian, he's the murderer?"

"Exactly! Brilliant, Mrs. Evans!" Maureen said, hands on her ample hips.

"Mum," Christopher said softly. "Would this hold up in court?"

Maureen put her left pointer finger alongside her nose and her left thumb underneath her chin. Her body seemed to shrivel before them. "I expect not," she said, her triumph sputtering like soap bubbles in the bathtub.

"Anyway," Christopher said, "no harm asking that liar Gracie when Mr. Smith's birthday is. It could point right to him, I'd say."

Catherine volunteered to phone Gracie again. Although she was grateful for all of Maureen's work, she felt they were on another meaningless road that danced them down the lane, away from the facts, DNA, and tangible evidence. But she had vowed to find anything that might somehow lead them to the murderer. She turned inward and quiet for a few moments.

"I've got it!" Catherine exclaimed, as she hit the table.

Maureen stopped closing the ephemeris. Christopher's hand hovered over his notes.

"Don't you see?" Catherine said. "It might hold up in court—not because the judge believes in astrology, but because the murderer would have planned the murder using *his knowledge* of astrology and he would believe it was the best moment to pounce, according to the signs!" Catherine's face broke into such a wide smile that her front teeth sparkled like the stars in the sky.

"So," Maureen said, "you think the murderer picked that very day knowing his sign and David's sign?"

"Yes, and, more to the point," Catherine added, "the sun was in Scorpio on that day, exactly like it says there." She pointed to the ephemeris that Maureen now held to her breast. "And he planned it all and knew David's sign."

Who knew David's sign? Catherine wondered to herself. She knew it. Would this Mr. Smith know it? How would he know it? Why would he know it? Did Maureen know it from those years sitting with him in the visiting room? She didn't even know Mr. Smith back then. It couldn't be Gracie. Who knew David's birthday? Of course, it was printed in the newspapers on the day he died. But if the murderer planned it, he had to know David's horoscope before that date.

# THE SILVER SPOONS

**"Right, then,"** Christopher said the next afternoon. "Let's hop a taxi back to Mr. Townsend's."

The early afternoon tea had added energy to Catherine's veins. With renewed spirits, she put on her coat, settled her hat, and went into the fresh air and light drizzle as Christopher held the opened umbrella over her. He grasped the box of cups, now wrapped in a sack, in his left arm like it was a baby, and after seeing Catherine down a few steps, he awkwardly waved down a taxi with her umbrella.

As the taxi pulled up to Mr. Townsend's old building near the small church, Christopher held the sack of cups in one arm, as Catherine readied herself for the climb out of the comfortable taxi. She glanced up.

"Don't get out!" Catherine said as she pointed at the taxi ahead, where a gentleman holding a package identical in volume to Christopher's sack was getting into another taxi. Catherine wasn't sure, but he looked like Mr. Smith. She had never seen him this close in the street, but those shoes were black and there was a familiarity about him that sent chills down her spine, like she was a dog struck by a dangerous scent in the air.

The taxi ahead pulled into the flow of the traffic. Catherine and Christopher sat together in silence for a moment.

"You want to get out 'ere, then?" the driver asked.

"Oh, sorry, of course. Could you hold here a moment while we talk?"

"It'll cost ya," the driver said.

"That's quite all right," Catherine said. "Christopher, did I imagine it, or was that Mr. Smith?"

"He looked ever so familiar, he did, and what was that package he was carrying? That's what I'd like to know."

"And," Catherine added, "was he coming out of Mr. Townsend's building?"

"And," Christopher said, "out of Mr. Townsend's office?"

Catherine turned and looked at Christopher squarely. "Can we trust Mr. Townsend?"

"We can go in and confront him," Christopher said. "No 'arm in asking. We could be quite mistaken." Catherine nodded to him. "Right, then," Christopher said, opening the door.

Catherine handed the driver the money, tipped him well enough, and reached for Christopher's hand before she even looked back up from her purse.

They sat in the waiting room, Catherine's glazed eyes surveying the black-and-white prints of historical sailboats; Christopher holding the package of the cups like someone might come and snatch them.

"Do come in," said a slightly breathless Mr. Townsend, opening his door.

Catherine studied his face as she passed him at the doorway. He was stroking that long mustache like he was making a plan. His smile looked crooked. His eyes seemed narrower. His body bowed slightly with an angularity Catherine found suspiciously obsequious.

Again Catherine surveyed his plush office and settled onto the antique chair across from the desk. Christopher sat next to her. Mr. Townsend held out his hands toward the package as he walked past Christopher.

"Let's have a look, then, shall we?" he said. Christopher didn't budge. He stared at Catherine. "Not just yet, Mr. Townsend," Catherine said.

Mr. Townsend withdrew his hands and put them behind his back as he strode around his large desk and sat down, elbows on the desk, hands folded under his chin.

"Well, now," he said with a sly-looking smile, "we can't go much further without looking at the cups, can we now?"

"I have to ask you about your last client before we proceed further," Catherine said.

"Certainly, but confidentiality first, of course," he answered.

"Mr. Townsend, we saw Mr. Smith coming out of your building. It says in the horoscopes that it was a good day for business for Aquarians."

"He's an Aquarius, right?" Christopher asked.

"I don't think it's relevant or any of your business really," he said, pointedly looking at Christopher, "if you don't mind my saying so." Catherine raised her eyebrows and nodded knowingly at Christopher.

"Who was he, then?" Christopher blurted out.

"He's an old client of mine; strong interest in antiques, like me. He comes in now and again to verify values and eras; things like that." Mr. Townsend leaned back with a self-satisfied look, and then leaned forward, looking into Catherine's face. "Is there a problem, Mrs. Evans?"

"We're not sure. We're working with you on a level of strictest confidentiality here," she said, "but we think you might have a conflict of interest." It sounded pleasant and thoughtful, but not threatening. She'd let him reveal more.

"How could that be?" he inquired, leaning back and staring at the ceiling.

"What was in the package he was carrying into his taxi, then?" Christopher asked.

"I don't know. Now you mention it, it was about the size of that one you are carrying, wasn't it?"

Was this man lying? Why would Mr. Smith drag that package across London if not to show its contents to an expert?

"Didn't he open it?" Catherine asked.

"This is really out of order, if you don't mind my saying so," Mr. Townsend said, looking hurt and indignant. "I have a bond of confidentiality with him, of course, the same as with you."

"We need to know if he was carrying cups like ours," Christopher said. "...because if so, we can't do business with you. You understand, I'm sure," Catherine said.

"Ah, I see," he said. "He was here on quite another matter. He never opened his package, or mentioned it, except to say he'd just been to the silver experts nearby." His lower left eye twitched and his smile seemed to turn downward on the right side. "Our discussion was of a legal nature, not about antiques, as it happens."

Catherine fussed with her purse. Legal? What could that mean?

Christopher shifted in his chair.

"Still, it might be a conflict of interest," Catherine said. "We think he is the man that's been following me around ever since I arrived in London."

"Oh, I see," he said. "Are you certain?"

"Not absolutely, but fairly certain," Catherine said.

"I can send you to another forensics expert, if you'd like." Catherine liked the sound of this possibility. It seemed like Mr. Townsend had no reason to want to talk to them about Mr. Smith. But still, it felt eerily uncomfortable.

"If you don't mind, I think we need to have a private talk," she said.

"Please, stay here. I'll just get a tray of tea for us all, and be back in five minutes. How does that sound to you?"

"I think five minutes will do nicely," Catherine said. Mr. Townsend left the room, shutting the door quietly.

"Well, Christopher? What shall we do now? He could send us to another expert who might be involved with him anyway. Probably all we need to know is if any DNA is on these cups that is also on the shoes or handkerchief or glasses. I think we can trust him that far."

"I dunno, Mrs. Evans, ma'am," Christopher whispered. "He seems a bit sleazy to me. But I will leave it to your better judgment, I will." He hugged the sack to his heart.

"I am running out of energy for all this," Catherine mumbled. "I think we are going to have to trust him. I just wonder what that legal matter would be. Let's see if we can pry it out of him."

Mr. Townsend arrived royally and held the door open for his secretary, who put down the tray, complete with a Dutch designer antique teapot, matching teacups and saucers, and engraved silver teaspoons.

"We have decided to go with you, Mr. Townsend," Catherine said. "Two lumps, please," she added.

Mr. Townsend smiled as he put the cup and saucer in front of her and offered her the sugar cup. No cubic lumps, but two nice teaspoons of sugar would be perfectly fine. After she poured the second spoonful into the cup, Catherine noticed the engraving on the bowl of the spoon. "It says here: 'Scorpio,' and it has a little engraving of a scorpion. How intriguing!"

"Ah! Yes. I bought those many years ago. I have twelve spoons like that, each one a sign of the horoscope. Lovely, don't you think?"

"Very. It is strange to say, Mr. Townsend," Catherine said, "but the cups we have also have six of the signs of the zodiac on them."

"How very interesting! Mrs. Evans, I do wish you would let me see at least one. We can go so much further from there."

Christopher hugged the sack of cups with one hand as he stirred his tea with the other. Catherine nodded at him. He put his spoon down after a quick examination of the design on it, and began opening the sack.

"Stop!" Catherine said. The coincidence of the spoons and zodiac signs was too much for her. "I do believe I need to think more about this before we go on."

They left their tea and bundled out of the office, complete with the sack of cups and no information on the DNA.

# THE HOROSCOPES

**Catherine sat** in a daze as the taxi whisked them away into the throng of the crowd of people, buses, and taxis. She didn't know what to do now. Mr. Townsend's apparent love of astrology engravings on silver was suspicious, and his connection with Mr. Smith was just too coincidental. Why couldn't things be simple, uncomplicated; obvious, even? Why did London seem so small? Everybody seemed to know everybody. People bumped elbows with neighbors in pubs, buses, movies, schools, and yes, jails. She looked over at Christopher, who sat immobile, watching the traffic through the window.

"Right, Christopher. Back to square one. That Mr. Townsend would have been the perfect person to help us with these cups."

"Which is why," Christopher interrupted, "Mr. Smith found him, I reckon."

"Exactly," Catherine said, opening her purse and taking out her handkerchief.

Christopher hugged the package of cups. Catherine studied the initials on her handkerchief.

"We need to talk to Maureen," she said. "I'm sure she's dug up more information. That will lead us to our next solution."

When they arrived home, Christopher stood on a chair and placed the silver cups on the highest shelf in the cupboard above the sink.

"I've been gathering that astrology information, like you wanted," Maureen said. Catherine waited, hoping for something positive. The disappointment over Mr. Townsend was burning into her aching bones.

Maureen spread out pages of copies of astrological predictions for three months in 1956 from five major newspapers.

"But first of all, Northwestern Polytechnic, where David taught, is long gone, and they don't know where the old records might be stored."

"Okay. We'll have to move on. It's a pity, though. What else have you got?" Catherine asked hoping for a positive clue.

Christopher picked up one page and read aloud: *"Aquarius: Patience is of the utmost importance.'* Well, that could apply."

"Here's another I liked," Maureen said. "It's Aquarius. It seemed like Mr. Smith would match it. Here you are. *'Your plans will be rewarded. Act immediately.'* That was from *The Daily Mail,* just a day before the murder."

Catherine picked out another page and read aloud: *"'Leo—Be on the alert for swift changes.'* Well," Catherine said, "here's the date again, the day before he was murdered."

Catherine's head sunk into her chest. Why should someone make a plan like that, using their knowledge of astrology to kill a person? It didn't make any sense. She wondered if some person David had been interviewing, maybe even a celebrity, had killed him in revenge for revealing some horrible truth about them. Some of those people had hard lives, grudges, things that might have pushed a fragile person's button; someone who needed a scapegoat in their lives.

"Listen to this one," Christopher said. *"Aquarius: Don't associate with people who may block your path.'* That could mean, make sure you, Mrs. Evans, was out of the house that day."

"Or," Maureen said. "That could mean he should get David out of the way so he could get the cups with no one blocking his bleedin' path."

Catherine read bits from the hundreds of pages Maureen had stacked before them. *"'Sudden events will change the course of your life,'"* she read. It sounded so familiar. She stared out the window. Nothing sudden had ever happened in their village. She folded that page and stuffed it into her purse without a word. She would hold onto it for now. It seemed a memory from the time "before." She filtered through dozens more. She was looking for a definite prediction. These were important, but still they didn't shout out evidence of her theory.

"Here, then," Maureen said, holding the paper up to the light. '*The time is ripe to complete your plan, Aquarius.*' This was two days before David was murdered. If the murderer followed horoscopes, it would be a perfect guide for him."

"Or," Catherine said, "a perfect trap for him of his own making." Maureen and Christopher stared at her. "If he was foolish enough to follow this rubbish, it's his own fault," Catherine added.

"I follow me own stars," Maureen huffed, her hand resting firmly on her hip. "Does that make me foolish, doing what they say?"

"No, of course not," Catherine lied. "But if you are planning a murder and theft, following horoscopes might even add to your own danger. Don't you agree, Christopher?"

"Well, Mrs. E," Christopher stuttered, glancing at his mother, his face red, "perhaps you're right."

There was a moment of silence. Christopher shuffled his feet. Maureen sighed. Catherine studied her fingers. Maureen finally said, "Let me see. If he followed astrology, he could have planned the killing on the best day for him and David using what he knew of where their suns intersected. That's what the bleeder did, right?"

"We don't know," Catherine answered. "That's what we're trying to figure out."

"Oh, yes, of course," Maureen said. "I do get carried away. Truth is: We don't know if Mr. Smith is the real murderer, an' all."

Maureen looked away from Catherine and wiped her hands on her apron. She turned toward the sink. "Hello, darlin'," she said to her budgie.

"Could be him an' all," Christopher said.

"Could be," Catherine echoed.

"Well, who else could it have been?" Maureen turned back to them. "We have no other clues."

"It could have been…" Catherine trailed off. She knew of no one. "It could have been an irate person he'd written about. Some people take offense at what's written about them: me, for example. I didn't do it, but those articles about me saying I killed him. I hated those writers; not that I would have killed them."

"Maybe we should scan David's old articles, say, three months previous to his murder," Maureen suggested. "We could see who he wrote about: some maniac, perhaps."

"Dangerous profession, I'd say," Christopher said.

"I think it's got to be Mr. Smith," Maureen continued. "There are too many clues leading to him. Them other cups what the taxi driver remembered. That's a link-up. Mr. Smith obviously wanted to steal Catherine's cups and make a fortune with the whole set."

"Do you think so?" Catherine asked. Might have been other motives we don't know about. A judge couldn't condemn someone who might have followed the stars, but surely if it could be shown that he avidly followed his stars, it just might lean the judge against him."

"Judges want facts," Christopher said. "They want to see it all in black and white."

"Well, then," Maureen said. "We will just have to find out Mr. Smith's birthday. That's a fact!"

"Did you see," Catherine said, "how Mr. Townsend hedged when we asked if Mr. Smith was an Aquarius?"

"And, do you remember when Gracie read out her horoscope and said she was a Pisces?" Maureen added. "The other sign was Aquarius."

Christopher sat down, pulled out his pen and a sheet of paper. Catherine and Maureen leaned over and watched as Christopher drew a strange drawing with labels saying "Aquarius" at one end and "Leo" at the other, with "November" in the center. Then he crossed it all out. He drew two lines intersecting like an X and put "Aquarius" at one foot, then rested his pointer finger on his lips for a moment, then put "Leo" at the other foot, and wrote "November 3" in the center where they crossed.

Catherine's mind raced; she had questions, and she needed the answers. Who was Mr. Smith? Where did he come from? Where was he raised? How did he know her? Did he know David? If so, for how long?

When Catherine got back to her hotel, the man at the front desk, Arne, handed her a brown envelope just large enough for a manuscript. The man said the person delivering it was called Peter, and he said that she would know him.

Catherine could hardly wait to open it, but calmly made her way to her room, where she opened the manuscript before she even took off her coat.

There in front of her was a short letter from Peter explaining that he had made a copy of David's manuscript, which his mother had kept, and the manuscript was called *The Mystery of Cellini's Silver Cups*.

The first words she read were: *"Twelve silver cups have been missing for over four hundred years. They were only referred to briefly in a shred of Cellini's writings that never made it into his autobiography. The cups disappeared..."*

So here was the story. After a quiet supper, Catherine read it. She read of David's imaginings about a man called Caruso who helped Cellini polish the cups the day they were finally finished and who later died when his ship crashed on the rocks of Cornwall. She read about Carey and other characters in David's strange manuscript. How could he possibly make this up? It was rather interesting, indeed. But it could hardly be true. He always said it was fiction.

The cups became symbolic now, of larger things like beauty and value, art, money, greed, toys, meanings of things that people put on the cups; about people making ships crash on the rocks in Cornwall just to plunder their bounty; about the Depression and the desperation of the poor, stealing from one another; about the way people treat other people, using valuable objects to get in the way of their lives; about love and happiness. Catherine read and read and fell in love with her husband all over again, hearing his voice; this man who loved antiques, but seemed to guess at their larger meanings, of astrology, of art and creativity, and of what people would do to satisfy their greed or their need.

The manuscript was unfinished, of course. Catherine slowly read his final words: *"What would Cellini's revenge be for having his amazing cups stolen from him? The author, the owner of six of them, cannot fathom what his revenge might be. These cups were stolen, hoarded, loved, cherished, admired, hidden, tossed away, sold cheaply, but worst of all, fought over. Cellini's revenge might be that the twelve cups might never be joined together into the twelve astrological signs; and mankind would continue to wonder where the other six had vanished, or..."*

Here the manuscript ended. Catherine sat in silence, trying to put this puzzle together. Slowly, she began to realize that, although David would never know it, his own death, in a way, might have been Cellini's revenge.

# 1939: The Doctor–London

**The picture** Nurse Pritchard had in her mind was a set of toy cups or dishes made of porcelain, perhaps very tiny, decorated with delicate pink flowers and green leaves. Her hand passed along the small objects that the pawnbroker had set out for her. The Depression had carried many a treasure into this pawn shop, but she couldn't spot anything like a toy set. A small cup caught her eye. But it was dull, not a playful object to give a small, sickly girl. She sighed and shifted backward. Maybe she would try another shop. The doctor had sent her here for reasons Nurse Pritchard could hardly fathom.

As she turned and opened her mouth to say good day and thank you, her eyes landed upon a box. It had a worn look almost like it had been under the sea for years and had eroded into this dried-up brown box. She stepped forward and smoothed her hand across its rough surface. It felt magical. She asked to look inside. She opened the box and twelve small, tarnished silver cups met her eyes. She picked one up and rubbed the outside, noticing that there were tiny engravings of figures. Little Christine would love that. Nurse Pritchard bought them, and despite the large amount of money, felt that the child's mother would approve. After all, for the doctor's dying child, money was no object, Depression or no Depression.

When Nurse Pritchard asked Christine if she liked her cups, her little blue eyes brightened as much as the eyes of one so pale and weak could. Her bony hands turned the now glistening silver cup in her palm. Her little mouth corners turned upward for the first time in months. She slowly peered at each cup's side, felt the engravings, and lined them up with the precision of a tidy mind: the offspring of two bright doctors; the face of a child that would never grow old despite all the medical profession tried to do for her.

A small sandbox was brought into the office, and Christine played all day, interspaced by sleeping on a small cot in the corner, where she could try to regain strength enough to play a little more. The sandbox was full of toy soldiers, rubber frogs, pails and shovels, shiny green and black rocks; an old earring glinted at the corner. The room now overflowed with gifts from all the doctor's patients: the old man with arthritis and a cane; the four-year-old girl who also had liver cancer; the woman with the interminable cough; the actress who kissed everybody but had lost her voice; the three children with the flu; and a stream of card-signing patients who only knew Christine by her photograph on the doctor's desk.

The doctor had another child, a boy, but he was away at boarding school. The doctor's husband, a doctor himself, had died of a heart attack two years before. The doctor was glad her husband was not alive to witness their ravished daughter languishing while playing with her twelve silver cups in the sandbox far from children's tea parties, down to a too-rapid decline that no medication would alter.

Nurse Pritchard sat near Christine and read stories: sea stories, stories of children from hundreds of years before, but mostly boy stories. Nurse Pritchard one day pretended to be reading and made up a story about a little girl called Carey in Cornwall who once played with these very same cups and lined them up for her dolls. The story never had an ending, for little Christine became comatose, and even if she could hear it, Nurse Pritchard and Christine's mother, the doctor, would never know.

One day, three years before the end of World War II, as the doctor leaned toward Christine's pale face, she knew she would never put her stethoscope to her daughter's heart again; never kiss her warm cheeks; never see the longing to live in those sad eyes.

Instead she kissed Christine's cold forehead, pulled her eyelids closed, and pulled up the blanket just under her chin.

"Take everything in her sandbox and get rid of it," the doctor said to her nurse. "It will torture me and remind me only of her illness. I never want to see any of it again."

Nurse Pritchard gathered up all of the dead child's toys into a large, burlap sack, tied the top with string, and waited a day until she heard the familiar cry from the street: "Rag and bone! Rag and bone! Any old iron?"

She slipped out of the office door, put her gas mask on, and, carrying the heavy sack, moved to the horse and cart and the dirty, bearded old man sitting high above her.

"Hello, love. Can you swing it on up, then?" he asked her, his gas mask hanging about his neck.

Nurse Pritchard pushed off her gas mask and lifted the bag and tossed it on top of a pile of old metal junk, then watched as the horse and cart pulled ahead at its slow pace.

"Any old iron?" she heard him shout as his horse clip-clopped slowly down the road.

The next Sunday the junk, the toys, the sand even, would be sold "cheap" to the rugged Cornish man, Harry, the one with the barrow on Portobello Road: the one with the story that he always told his mates in their pub about how, as a young lad, he had traveled on the train from Cornwall to London so many times, carrying items rescued from floundering ships, and how, one time, he had exchanged something he'd nicked from the barrel on the train for a whole barrow from an old man called John.

"Here's a bundle for ya," said the bearded, "any-old-iron" man atop his cart. The horse stamped his rear foot and shifted his weight. Other vendors were bustling around yelling about their wares for sale.

Harry came around from his barrow and took the bundle, passed two shillings up to the driver, and set the bundle aside on the ground. He'd check it later; probably a few good things in there. He was bound to make a profit; enough for dinner, at least.

Two teenage boys came by later in the afternoon, as they did every weekend, and rifled through Harry's treasures.

"What's in your bag there on the ground, mate?" asked the younger one with the red hair.

"Dunno," Harry answered, puffing on his cigarette. It would rain soon. It had been a slow day. "You can have the lot cheap," he said, "can't be bothered to lug it home."

The two boys picked through the small toys in the bag.

"What's this, then," whispered the older boy to his red-headed pal, holding a tarnished box is such a way that Harry couldn't see it.

"Open it, then," said the younger boy. They peered into the box.

"They're ours! Now, let's just buy them and get out of here," said the other.

They paid Harry and then stuffed the box they had found into a leather bag.

"You can keep all the rest, mate," said the younger boy to Harry. The two teenagers dashed off down the lane and around the corner, where they stopped to fully inspect their amazing new find.

# MR. RUTHERFORD,
# ASTROLOGER

**Catherine turned** on her right side and closed her eyes. It was past 11:30 at night, but sleep was not in her body. Although the pubs were closed, London still rumbled, distant laughter echoing down the lanes. She knew well the yellow streetlamps that lit up the hairdos, cropped and slanted with the times; the high heels clacking, black straps adorning ankles; cotton frocks of paisley design twirling, but not very bright colors–that would not do, not unless they wanted to shock, to yell, "We don't all have to wear dark blue." But then they were making their Friday night statement, cigarette in hand, which would have faded by Monday morning, by then adorned with all the proper dark colors, and dutifully clamoring toward the office. The young, with an orange glow about their mouths and cigarette smoke blown up with a bottom lip protruding, jerked their heads to swish their hair aside, and pretended not to know you were there. Muffled voices from the street below the Churchill Bed and Breakfast indicated that tipsy people were just returning in taxis to their rooms at the hotel.

All the astrology pointed to Mr. Smith. If he were the person she felt he must be, she could trap him by having him meet her at the Churchill Bed and Breakfast on the exact day his horoscope indicated that it was the right thing for the sign of Aquarius to do. If he came, then he was the murderer, in her mind anyway.

A court battle was not especially to her liking. Twelve or fifteen years would be a joke, if they gave that to him. She needed to find out why he had sat there all those years and also if he had the other six beautiful silver cups. She needed to know Gracie's part in it all. Mr. Smith was a pretty good runner for his age, but he couldn't run more than five to ten more years. She would set a trap; but how?

The next morning she decided to consult an astrologer. She remembered that Gracie had read her horoscope from *The Daily Mail*. Mr. Smith would most likely read it, too, if he was at Gracie's house. She made inquiries and telephoned the astrology columnist for David's old newspaper.

"Hello, Mr. Rutherford. You may remember a journalist called David Evans who was murdered back in 1956?" Catherine began.

"Who's speaking?" Mr. Rutherford asked shortly.

"I will tell you in a minute. I need your help; your knowledge of astrology," she pleaded.

"Who's he to you?" Mr. Rutherford sounded very weary.

"I'm his...wife, Catherine Evans," she said, waiting for him to slam the phone down.

"Ah, Mrs. Evans! Of course I knew David Evans. We shared a pint now and again in the old days. Don't say it, I already know: You didn't do it. It says so in your horoscope, my dear. It was someone else, probably an Aquarian."

Catherine was so stunned she could hardly speak. Here was another person who believed her to be innocent, even if it were just because of astrology. But he also thought the murderer was an Aquarian! She gathered up her renewed energy.

"Mr. Rutherford, I thank you for your confidence. It is comforting to have your opinion at this late stage, when it has felt like the whole world was forever against me. I am back in England hunting down the real murderer. I am going to clear my name before I die, if I can." Her voice broke. "Is it possible to meet you fairly soon?"

She felt like she'd been there for years, and it had only been two months.

"I'm free this afternoon. Can you come to my office? I'm an old man, all hunched over, but they still like what I write, so I go on working."

"I would be delighted to," Catherine said. "Say, two o'clock?"

He gave her the address of his office at *The Daily Mail* and hung up. Should she go alone or ask Christopher to accompany her? With her lightened feeling deep within her soul from being seen as innocent, she decided she would go alone.

Fleet Street always gave Catherine a romantic feeling. St. Paul's Cathedral rose above the buildings at one end. This was David's hunting ground. It was David's life: the place he told Catherine about every night at dinner when they lived in Kentish Town, and on the nights he made it home to Rottingdean in time on the train from London to Brighton. Fleet Street, with its busy life: cars and buses squeezing by the narrow lanes, up the slope, down the other side; old buildings built with the levity of a newspaper that had the power to make or break a politician, win a war, make their architects famous, save an institution, ruin a celebrity, announce wars, celebrate the ends of wars. Tall buildings with classical facades anchored themselves triumphantly next to new buildings that covered the old bombed-out lots.

There was a sense of urgency in the hurry of the dark, gray-suited Londoners: making news, typing it up, sending and receiving it through Western Union, mailing it through the Queen's postal service, with the Crown signifying history, power, loyalty; a war won for the Queen. Some horse-and-cart men slowed down in the bustle around them, yelling, "Rag an' bone! Rag an' bone! Any old iron?"

The taxi sped past David's old pub, the Mucky Duck. Catherine stepped out, paid the driver, giving him a large tip. She turned slowly and gazed up and down the familiar street. Pedestrians bustled across her vision, almost at the point of running. The sturdy old buildings felt like her second home. Every corner, every jutting shadow, was hers. A scruffy man stood before her begging. She dug into her handbag and pulled out a pound coin. She dropped the coin into his hat and looked deeply into his old eyes. He would have been young once, perhaps ambitious.

Catherine breathed deeply and walked deliberately toward *The Daily Mail* building. It looked cleaner. "Sorry," said a woman rushing by, knocking her handbag against Catherine's back.

Catherine stood facing the old building, studying the large entrance as she had never really done before. People pushed in and out of the doors: young, ambitious people. They reminded her of David's energy. She stood there for such a long time that only a loud honking sound behind her jarred her into the present. As she took a step toward the door, she remembered how she had promised herself never to come here again. Yet, here she was. It broke some kind of silence with the past, stepping over the threshold. She moved slowly, her elbows slightly out, her eyes picking up quick movements all around her. Everything seemed brighter and everybody seemed serious, but happy.

"May I help you?" asked the woman at the front desk. She looked so young, so red-lipped. Catherine studied her face. She looked like the receptionist Catherine knew in the fifties. "I have an appointment to see Mr. Rutherford."

# THE PLAN

**There was a large** armchair where she could wait and stare at the ornate lights high above. Wasn't this the same chair she had sat in years ago, once when she was waiting for David after work? She sat down there again and remembered how, in the summer of 1956, she had entered the Mucky Duck, and had seen David at the bar, finishing an interview with a client. She had walked over to them.

"Hello, love," David said, "won't be a minute."

Catherine had smiled and nodded at the other young man, then went to sit at a nearby table. In less than five minutes David was shaking hands and bidding the celebrity goodbye.

"Wasn't that Eleanor Roosevelt's grandson, the one I saw in the papers in August, when she went to meet him and his cousin at the Southampton Docks? It was the Holland-America line, if I remember correctly!" Catherine didn't mind showing David that she kept track of events, even more than her mother did, sometimes.

"It was, indeed," David said, placing a tomato juice in front of Catherine. "That was a young man named Johnny Boettiger, only seventeen, President Roosevelt's grandson. Seems very intelligent and well-read. Plays bridge well. But that crew cut! He must freeze in winter!" They laughed and touched arms in a delicate, subtle fashion, so as not to disturb the conservative sensibilities of the other customers there.

Catherine settled back into the plush chair and watched the busy people dashing back and forth with the news, and was reminded of how David, around the same year, 1956, had come down from his office after she had waited about five minutes. He was bright and jolly and she jumped up from the chair and linked arms with him. They took long strides toward the door, where he bowed and winked as she whisked through before him.

The pub was only down the block and Catherine naturally turned in that direction, but David's strong arm caught hers and twirled her toward the opposite direction.

"I've got a surprise! Come this way, my love," he said. He kissed her cheek and they lightly strode ahead and turned the corner. "It's ours," he said, pointing to an old, black Ford.

"Oh, darling," she said, moving over to it, and hopping onto the front fender. It was cold to the touch. She put her hand on his warm face and he leaned in to kiss her on her cheek. Catherine remembered that kiss, warm, direct, and loving; all the things he was to her in one tender kiss.

"You may go in now," said a voice, shocking Catherine back into the present. She thanked the woman, maybe the granddaughter of the receptionist from the fifties, took her umbrella, and made her way slowly across the shiny marble floor.

"Come in, Mrs. Evans," Mr. Rutherford said, his thinning but still-thick gray eyebrows raised cheerily as Catherine entered the musty room. He graciously showed her in, gesturing for her to sit down on a nice antique high-backed chair opposite his desk. He sat down and put his elbows on the desk, folded his fingers together, and looked directly into her eyes.

He didn't look like an astrologer: He looked like a journalist. His jacket was old and hung badly, and his trousers were too big. Obviously, this man had shrunk, but kept wearing the same old clothes he'd bought in the fifties. He wore a mustache, but not the long variety, just barely visible, with bald patches here and there. His white goatee distinguished him, and made his face even longer than it already was. The large, old antique desk had neat piles of paper stacked all around the edges. There were books lining the floors, and the bookcases reached right to the ceiling; a dusty feeling hung about the room, like nobody had ever cleaned it.

"What can I do for you, Mrs. Evans?" he said, smiling at her in a kind way that made her want to just stare back at him.

"I think I have discovered the real murderer," she answered. "What I need to do, Mr. Rutherford, is to catch him, by having him follow the stars and fall into a trap I would like to set."

"Well, that sounds very exciting," Mr. Rutherford said. "How do you plan to do this?"

"I thought all night about it," Catherine said, glancing around the room. All the books seemed to have something to do with astrology. "I was wondering if you could possibly write a horoscope for Aquarius that says something like: *Tomorrow is the day you must meet your Sagittarius. The signs are changing and moving out of your favor. Do not hesitate if you want to fulfill your desires. You must go to meet her at noon.'* Something like that. Then I will sit in the restaurant next to the Churchill Bed and Breakfast, where I am currently staying, and wait for him to arrive. If he arrives, that will prove to me that he killed my husband."

"Isn't that rather jumping to conclusions?" Mr. Rutherford asked, his white, fluffy eyebrows arched.

"Not really. I was thinking that if you look at the stars in 1956, you can see that the sun in Scorpio squares Aquarius and Leo on November 3rd of that year, or something like that. I don't quite know how you say it properly, but I am sure you know what I mean. David was a Leo. If this person followed astrology, which I suspect he did, he could have planned the murder on that very date, just using the stars as a guide," Catherine said, amused to be telling an astrologer his own business.

"Mrs. Evans, it seems to me you might not be too far off the mark. It seems a reasonable possibility, if you think this person really follows his horoscope. I'll just check that for you, my dear." He reached into a pile of ephemerides that had turned yellow, and studied some pages, mumbling all the while about how he couldn't really quite understand how that would catch the killer. "Could be true," he said. "But you know, love, I can't just make up something out of the blue. It has to indicate it in the horoscopes for that day."

"Mr. Rutherford," Catherine said firmly, "surely you can find a day that indicates honestly that an Aquarian should meet a special person on her own ground and tell the truth?"

Mr. Rutherford rummaged through a new-looking ephemeris pamphlet, mumbling about "ephemeris" this and "astrology" that and "could be true," but then, "how would that work?"

"Just a moment, my dear; this needs thinking about," he said, and went on pointing and mumbling. "Yes," he said, looking quite cheerful, "the day after tomorrow I could honestly write that."

Catherine felt like hugging him, but she was in England and knew the rules of conduct: No physical contact unless absolutely necessary and then stand back as far as possible from the person you would rather be hugging. She smiled broadly, knowing that now that he was willing to do this, it would be the final test.

"Mr. Rutherford. How can I pay you for this?" she asked.

"Tut, tut, old girl. Not a farthing. Just doing my job."

She got up, shook his hand, and wandered out into the hall past the receptionist and onto the street in a contented daze.

# WAITING

**Two days later,** a knock at her door in the hotel found a young bellhop holding a package sent special delivery from Davis, California. Catherine tipped him and laid the package with Christopher's and her shoes in it on the table.

Later on, at lunchtime, Catherine sat alone in the small, elegant restaurant next door to her hotel. She felt a slight fluttering of her heart, like a warning. Her breath became shallower, listening for his footsteps. Her eyes peered around the room like the second hand of a clock. The man might even be looking at her right now. The waiter's footsteps made her sit up and sniff like a dog, as if the waiter were an approaching predator. The clink of silverware on the plates rang loud, like a warning bell. Dishes crashed to the floor just inside the kitchen door; a man was swearing, picking up the pieces, tossing them into a bin.

The waiter, who was clean-cut in appearance, his mustache trimmed to the last detail, smiled at Catherine, then bowed as he served with expertise the potato from the elegant serving dish to her plate. A sprig of parsley was placed neatly along the edge. The chicken on the platter before her was decorated with roasted pineapple chunks and tiny onions, and smelled like the very unusual and special barbecues from her childhood.

Catherine seemed to have so many memories of her younger years these days, but the present was becoming hard to remember. She chuckled to herself as she remembered when she and Christopher had found the silver cups: so easy, as long as you had the directions. Who would have dug there? Nobody; ever. The cups would have been lost for at least hundreds of years. Only she had had the key. But now somebody else wanted those cups.

"Thank you," she said to the redheaded waiter. "Where are you from?"

"I'm from Wales, Mrs. Evans, and you don't have to ask: Yes, I do sing!" he smiled, laying the chicken carefully on her plate and covering it with the pineapple chunks and onions.

"I went to Wales in my youth," she said. "Mountainous country. I drove right up the whole country from the south to the north with my husband: breathtakingly beautiful, those mountains." She eyed the tiny white onions and quietly sniffed the aroma of the delicately cooked chicken.

"Yes, Mrs. Evans. I rode my scooter the whole way myself a few years back: Only one accident," he answered, stepping back with a slight bow.

"Oh, how awful! Sorry to hear that." The smell of the chicken, onions, and roasted potatoes was making her mouth water.

"But here I am, aren't I, now?" he said. "It wasn't bad really, just a skid on the gravel, turning a corner too hard. Only my elbow was bruised. My scooter was lying on my leg, as I remember it, and two little old women, beggin' your pardon, came up to me and asked me would I like a cup of tea? Can you believe that, Mrs. Evans? I said, 'Well, first, could somebody pull this scooter off my leg?' I wiggled out myself. They just stood there and stared at me lying under that scooter. How do you like that? Always a cup of tea to heal anything!" he laughed.

Catherine ate quietly, her eyes flashing from her plate to the door and back. She missed Christopher and Maureen and their cozy kitchen. She knew they were being polite and she felt they had overextended themselves. The Churchill Bed and Breakfast was home now. She missed the daily adventure of it all. At least she had retrieved David's silver cups.

As she waited patiently for Mr. Smith to show himself, she didn't know whether she would be relieved or frightened if he should actually fall for her astrological trap. She felt sure that if he were in his own trap of astrological superstition, he would have to turn up. Nothing could stop him. It was like a religion, and the faithful must follow. She had now plotted his own downfall using astrology to guide him straight to her table. She certainly had no time for astrology otherwise, and never would. Every few minutes she peered around to see if anyone had entered the restaurant. Smells from the kitchen reminded her of dinners past in England, mashed potatoes, lamb chops, onions.

"Excuse me," said a voice coming from behind her. She sat bolt upright. The smell of Old Spice aftershave lotion caught in her nostrils like a ghost from the past. On the floor, as she rotated her head slowly, she saw two black, shiny shoes with little holes. She made a slight sound as her breath pulled inward. She slowly looked up his trousers, and finally she saw his face: a gentleman, pressed, stylish. His mustache was long but trimmed carefully like that of the waiter. Catherine couldn't place him, yet his face she knew like she had dreamed of it every night.

# THE STRANGER

**"I would like** to introduce myself," said the voice of this gentleman. His eyes were green or hazel behind some familiar glasses. His face was lined. His hand was steady.

"My name is Michael Evans," he said, and bowed slightly. "You know me, don't you?"

Again she glanced casually at his polished, familiar shoes, with their laces and little holes.

"Of course I know you," she answered, the Old Spice carrying her swiftly back into the prison visiting room. "How do you know me? I'm a hundred years older."

"I know that you never knew who I was, and I was sworn not to tell you. But you and I are both alive still, and the story is old and dead. May I?" He gestured to the chair across the table. A waiter came up and pulled the chair out after Catherine nodded.

"Wine?" she offered, glancing at his shoes again.

"Zinfandel?" he said to the waiter, who bowed and backed up slightly before he turned away.

"Well, then, who *are* you?" she asked, slightly irritated, peering at his face.

"I am the man who used to visit you in prison."

"I thought you might be," she said, knowing perfectly well that he was that silent man. "But who *are* you?"

"This is going to come as a shock, Mrs. Evans," he answered, "but I am David's half-brother."

Catherine's eyes opened wide as she studied his familiar features. "He never told me he had a brother!" she said, eating a small bite of chicken. She couldn't quite take it in. David had told her everything, or so she thought. Well, no, not about having a son called Peter. "Have some bread. Have you eaten?" Changing the subject might give her a moment to compose herself.

"No, as a matter of fact, I haven't," he said.

"Well, look at that platter. I could never eat all that. Help yourself."

Michael Evans nodded, and a waiter placed a plate before him and began serving. Waiters had ears, it appeared. Michael steadied his glasses and scanned the menu. Catherine looked at him. Those glasses looked like David's, the ones from the dirt hole. She stopped chewing and leaned toward him to inspect them. Michael looked up at her and she leaned back. He was wearing the same glasses as the ones at Gracie's house. He was not only the man from the jail, this Michael Evans, but he looked like Gracie's boarder.

"Yes," Catherine thought, as she chewed her food thoughtfully. "Mr. Smith." A shiver went from her toes right up to the top of her head, and she felt a little dizzy.

"Why are you here now, after all these years? And why didn't you ever speak to me?" she asked, staring at him now, trying to put the two people she knew about into one, and finally tasting the pineapple chunks and onions that melted in her mouth in spite of her guest.

The waiter poured an inch of wine. Michael tasted it, and nodded, looking at Catherine.

"Wine?" he asked her.

"No, I don't drink too much now," she said, frowning.

"Right, then, here's to our meeting again, finally," he said raising his glass to toast her and taking a sip.

"I'm waiting," she said sternly, laying down her knife and fork.

"This is going to be difficult, Mrs. Evans," he said. He picked up the knife and tapped the plate thoughtfully.

"Get on with it. Nothing surprises me anymore," she answered, eyeing the knife.

"We had a fight," he started.

Catherine stopped chewing and looked straight into Michael's eyes. That was it. They had fought, and Michael had stabbed David to death.

"You killed him," she accused. "You're a murderer. Why are you sitting here, telling me this?"

"We started to punch each other..." Michael began, tapping the plate faster.

"David wouldn't do that!" Catherine raised her voice and hunted for her handkerchief.

"I'm afraid he did, and it wasn't the first time, either. We wrestled all the time when we were teenagers, especially at our grandfather's farm."

Catherine's mouth opened slightly as she looked down and remembered when they had driven to David's grandfather's farm. Maybe they *were* half-brothers. She wished he would put that knife down.

"We were in your kitchen and he had the knife in one hand, like this. He swiped at me with his free hand," and here Michael pushed the knife through the air, "and he accidentally tripped. I am sorry to say that he then fell on the knife himself. I never touched the knife, I swear to you. He died and lay there with the knife still sticking into his body. I was shocked and terrified. I could see that he was dead, and I ran out of that house before I could think of what else to do." Michael Evans finally laid the knife on his plate. Catherine sighed, and then the hot anger of years flew from her mouth.

"Oh, no, that's not true. He was murdered; he must have been murdered! I served years in jail for it!" She peered at this man's familiar face, not ready to believe his story. "Why didn't you say anything?" she demanded.

"I am sorry to say that my wife Janet had MS, and my son had Down's syndrome," he said softly. "I had so much on my hands. I felt horrible about what had happened to you. I didn't murder him, as you think, but who would have cared for Janet and our son if I had been accused of murder and had gone to jail?"

Michael offered his handkerchief to Catherine. "I knew I was innocent, but I couldn't risk it. I felt horrible that you had been accused. I felt trapped by my huge responsibilities for my wife and son." After a pause, he added, "They've both died now. I feel free to tell the truth before it's too late."

Catherine dabbed her eyes and blew her nose, and stared at his handkerchief. Through her tears, she couldn't help noticing that it had the initials M.E. on it, in the same script as David's handkerchief.

# MICHAEL'S STORY

**"I'm so shocked**! Why didn't David ever tell me about you?" There was a long pause while Michael took another drink. The waiter came and topped up his glass.

"Because we hated each other; mostly it was because of the silver cups. But apart from that, I think he had convinced our mother to hate me, so she took me out of her will." Catherine, who, it was clear now, had inherited at least Michael's share of his mother's money, could not immediately process all of this information. David had never had a hint of anger or violence about him, as long as she knew him.

"Our fathers were enemies," Michael continued. "It was all over money. I visited David regularly, but we'd get into squabbles over money and try to solve our parents' anger and resentment about the impending inheritance. The David you knew had mellowed, it appears. But when I came back on the scene to get my silver cups, everything re-emerged and we fought like we used to."

Catherine looked up in astonishment. "*Your* silver cups?" she said loudly.

"Yes, of course, *my* silver cups. I found twelve of them in a barrow on Portobello Road and I paid for them, and years later David hid six of them at his house for me. I hid the others at a friend's house. I didn't want our mother to know about them. She was horrible to me about money, so I asked David to keep six of them, just after he first bought the beach house. I loved those cups and had written down their engravings and was studying where they were from: Most likely they were made by Benvenuto Cellini in Italy over four hundred years ago. Have you heard of him?" Michael Evans paused and lowered his voice, and went on as Catherine nodded.

"When I found out they were really valuable, we started fighting over them, and David said he had hidden them somewhere I'd never find them. I came back that day he died, when you were out. I made sure you wouldn't be there. I knew I was a secret from you. I don't know what got into us. You see, it was all the years of anger and hatred and resentment between us and our families that severed our bond."

Catherine was stunned. "What about Gracie?" she said, and handed Michael's handkerchief back to him.

"I met Gracie on the day she left prison when I was coming to visit you," Michael said almost apologetically. "It just happened. She was willing, to be frank. That's all there is to it. I know she told you lies, but she was just trying to protect me until I was ready to come out in the open and talk to you."

"I don't see what all the mystery was about. What was all that legal work you were doing?" she asked.

Michael folded his handkerchief neatly and put it in his suit's breast pocket as he looked furtively around the room.

"I instructed Mr. Townsend not to mention that to anyone," he said, clearing his throat.

"He didn't say anything specific," Catherine said. "I was just wondering if it had anything to do with the silver cups."

"In a way; I was trying to figure out if the cups were legally mine or David's or even yours."

"How is it that we both hired the same man?" she asked, leaning back.

"I found him in the phone book. He was the only person doing that sort of work. I had no idea you were using him as well, until I saw you in the taxi."

"So!" Catherine said, triumphantly. "What did your legal experts say?"

"The cups are mine, in short," he said, smiling softly.

"I'd like to see that in writing. As far as I am concerned, they were David's, and now they're mine."

"You shall," Michael said, his eyes lowered.

"May I ask you one question?" Catherine didn't wait for his answer. "Do you always wear those black shoes?"

"My brogues? Only when I follow you; kind of a superstition I've had all these years."

Catherine realized some people were superstitious; they believed in horoscopes and black shoes. She sat like a numb statue, trying to put the pieces together. The past was now a jumble. She hated Michael. It seemed that he was a kind man to his wife and child, but how dare he leave her in a prison for twelve years when he knew she was innocent?

Catherine looked up to see two men in black suits appear at the door, walking toward her. She hardly had time to think about running away when the nearest one grabbed Michael by the arm.

"Scotland Yard: You are under arrest, Michael Evans," said the man, and put Michael in handcuffs. "Sorry, sir, but them's me orders," he added in a low, confidential tone into Michael's ear. "Sorry to bother you, Mrs. Evans." He nodded to her like he knew her.

Catherine was alarmed. What were they doing with Michael, and how did they know her name? Were these the men following her in the park? They looked different. She jumped up and away. There was a scuffle as chairs fell over.

"Mrs. Evans–Catherine! Please forgive me," Michael said as they pulled him away from her and sat him in a chair across the room. "I own the other six cups. David gave them to me!" Catherine could only stare at this strange scene and try to understand what Michael was saying.

The detectives, using force, removed Michael's shoes and put them in a plastic bag, lifted his glasses off his nose and slipped them into another plastic bag. "Sorry, Mrs. Evans," one of them said, nodding at Catherine, "they want the DNA right away."

Then the men dragged Michael away in his socks, in great haste.

The last thing Catherine heard him say was, "I didn't do it. I didn't kill David. I didn't kill him for my cups!"

"Your cups?" she whispered.

"We'll be back to talk to you later, Mrs. Evans. Not to worry. We know you are an innocent party."

# THE EVENING STANDARD

**Quite stunned,** Catherine sat for a while at the restaurant table. What a fuss: six cups! After all, she had dug them up. She had found them! After a moment of contemplation, she stood up and walked thoughtfully back to her hotel and into the lounge, past the chairs and small green, shaded antique table lamps. She lowered herself down onto a firm easy chair tucked away in a corner, and promptly fell into a dreamy slumber.

In a hushed tone, the manager asked her if she would like some tea. Catherine nodded sleepily, her eyes still closed. An early edition of the afternoon newspaper, *The Evening Standard,* was delicately laid on the table. She sat up, settled her glasses, looked over at the newspaper, and read the headlines: *"The Owner of the Six Missing Silver Cups Has Been Apprehended."* How did they publish that so quickly? Did they have inside information even before Michael was arrested? Knowing what David had told her about the media, she thought so. She kept reading: *"The silver cups, each with a separate engraving of one of the twelve astrological signs, are believed to have been created by Benvenuto Cellini in Italy in the sixteenth century. Their whereabouts has been a matter of speculation for decades throughout Europe and England. Many eminent historians have written about the disappearance of the twelve silver cups made by the Renaissance master, and now Scotland Yard is involved and aware of the fact that six of the twelve have reemerged, and must now seek evidence as to the ownership of the cups in question. It has now been determined that the resurfacing of the other six cups revolves around a murder in England that Scotland Yard had considered a closed case. These other six cups are still missing, but one theory has it that a certain Catherine Evans of Vermont, USA, freed after a twelve-year prison sentence for killing her husband, the famous journalist from* The Daily Mail, *David Evans, in 1956, knows of their whereabouts. The authorities are looking into this at the time of this printing."*

Catherine called Christopher from the phone at the desk. "Hello, Christopher. I must ask you to bring me the six you-know-whats up in the you-know-where to the Churchill immediately. Don't ask any questions and don't answer any if anybody asks. Now, please come right away."

"Yes, Mrs. Evans. I know what you refer to, and I will be right there, no worries."

"I'll have a nice strong cup of coffee, please," Catherine said to the waiter as he was clearing the tea tray away. She noted a man in a black suit standing near the door watching her, reminding her of the one who took her photo in the park. She pretended not to notice him.

Christopher arrived within forty-five minutes carrying a bundle that looked like a shopping bag.

"Evening," he said, nodding to the manager, and proceeded toward Catherine.

"I believe you left your shopping in the taxi. Here you are, ma'am." He handed her the tidy bundle and backed off slightly.

"I must thank you so much for this and for all you have done for me," Catherine said quietly. "I will call you later and tell you everything. You won't believe me, and Maureen won't either; but there you are. Don't worry. Now off you go, and many, many thanks again for all your help."

Christopher backed off with a slight bow, turned, and left.

Catherine signed her room number on the bill, picked up the bundle in her arms, and walked past the man in the black suit and smiled at him. He didn't smile back. Some people: You could never tell what they were thinking, especially in England; like those soldiers outside the Queen's palace with straight faces and red suits and tall, black fur hats. He didn't follow her now. It would be rude, of course.

Catherine proceeded to her room. When she reached her door there were two tall men in black suits standing looking down at her.

"These are my cups, gentlemen. Please stand aside." She grasped the cups under one arm, and after they parted for her, she strode past them. They stood silently as she unlocked her door, walked in, and shut it.

# CELLINI'S REVENGE

**The bundle** of cups rested on the table, just touching her hip. She picked up the phone and rang the operator to connect her with the Italian Embassy. The hotel operator was unusually quick and helpful, but the number to the embassy rang and rang until Catherine had crossed and re-crossed her legs a dozen times.

"This is the Italian Embassy. May I help you?" said an Italian woman's voice.

"Hello?" said Catherine, snapping to attention. "My name is Catherine Evans."

"Please hold the line," replied the woman in a whisper. "Someone will be right with you." Catherine fingered the package from California, which lay next to her cups. When she was connected to the proper party, she said, "I believe I have some silver cups that rightfully belong to the Italian people. Please meet me at the Churchill Bed and Breakfast as soon as possible."

"The gentlemen standing outside your door are the ones you should give the cups to," said an Italian man's voice.

"What? You're already here standing outside my door? Are you sure? Aren't they English? Shall I give *them* the cups?"

"You may give them the cups," said the Italian voice.

Catherine cleared her throat. These were, after all, now her cups.

But they were causing altogether too much trouble in her life. "Even if they're mine?"

"It must seem like the cups are yours, but if they are the genuine Cellini cups, they are legally the property of Italy."

"They aren't mine?" Catherine said, her voice raising almost hysterically.

"They rightfully belong to Italy, where they were made, according to the international laws of antiquity."

"Are you sure? What if they were bought at Portobello Road?"

"I'm sorry–even if you bought them at Portobello Road. It happens a lot, I'm afraid."

"I see." She paused to consider this new piece of the puzzle. "You know," she sighed into the receiver, "I don't like trouble. Do you think I could just pack my suitcase and leave quietly if I give them the cups?"

"Of course," said the confident voice.

"You do?"

"If you would also leave your old loafers behind for further DNA testing by Scotland Yard that would be very helpful. And did you have a cat?"

"My loafers?" she mumbled. "Yes, we had a cat."

"And apparently there is a cat still living in your old house in Rottingdean who looks just like your cat did. It could be its offspring."

Catherine was astonished to hear this information from the Italian Embassy. "Excuse me, but am I still speaking to the Italian Embassy?"

"No, madam; they transferred your call to Scotland Yard."

"Oh, I see. They sent my shoes back to the hotel from Davis just today. I will leave a note saying you may have them. May I now leave quietly?"

"We thank you for your complete cooperation. Of course, you may leave as long as you give these items to the gentlemen waiting outside your door. Thank you very much. Goodbye."

Catherine put the receiver down and stared for a whole minute at the door as her mind raced through her last months: digging up the cups, figuring out the whole thing.

No: They were her cups. She stood up and grabbed them against her breasts, then shoved them under the bed, pushing them further with her shoe. She crossed her arms: David's and her cups. She rested one hand against her back. Outside stood the two gentlemen in dark suits.

Puffing, groaning, and mumbling to herself, she kneeled down to get the box back out. It was too far under the bed. She moaned as she stood up haltingly, walked over to her umbrella, turned, and walked back and got back down on her knees. She hooked the box with the umbrella's gold antique handle and, panting and mumbling, pulled the cups back out from under the bed.

Catherine realized that she was now acting as greedily as Michael. She wondered where that had come from. Was she, in fact, just like all the other greedy people in the world? Catherine realized suddenly that not only was David's death like an expression of Cellini's revenge, but also *she* was Cellini's revenge: her suffering in jail, her name being torn to shreds, her life devastated. She realized that it was all because of David and Michael's greed that their own love and appreciation of the beauty of the kind that Cellini created in his wondrous cups was destroyed.

Catherine remembered the greed of the man in David's novel who stole the cups from the Master himself, who in the end had paid for it with a murderous stab from Cellini's sword. It was, indeed, how *Cellini's revenge had soaked the centuries with blood.* By returning the silver cups created by Cellini, Catherine could enact her own kind of revenge by giving back Cellini's art, not only to Italy and the world, but to history.

Catherine panted as she took out the Leo cup and unwrapped it. As it rested in her palm, she thought she could see David's reflection. She rubbed it against her cheek. It didn't shine. It would remain in her memory a tarnished cup, as David, with his secrets, had become a slightly tarnished memory. It was appropriate. Her devotion remained the same for him; he had his reasons. Perhaps he might have told her about his baby after she had had her own.

There was a knock at her door.

"Just a minute," she said, in a raised voice.

She put the cup back on top of the Sagittarius cup, covered them with tissue, and folded them into the box. They weren't heavy, even all six in the box together. She shifted them over to the corner near the door, stood up tall; her chin raised, her shoulders back, and opened the door.

"Good afternoon, gentlemen. I need to see a lawyer." They bowed toward her in synch.

"I am a lawyer, as you call it," said the young man with piercing eyes, in the Queen's English. He took out his identification papers and displayed his credentials, complete with an embossed stamp from Scotland Yard and Her Majesty the Queen.

Catherine stood there, looking the two men up and down. "All right, then," she said. "I have a bargain to make you: You give me all the photos you took and all the negatives; you never publish them or sell them to the news. In return I'll give you these six silver cups. Can we do this?"

The man with a thick mustache stepped forward and spoke with an Italian accent.

"But of course, Mrs. Evans. Our job is to recover the cups. We do not come to harm you at all. Sir?" he said, turning to the lawyer, taking a camera from his pocket, opening it, and removing the film. The other man reached into his black bag and took out five rolls of film, which he dropped, one by one, into Catherine's outstretched hand.

"Is that all?"

"Absolutely all: upon my word as an Italian."

"If you find any more," she said, sternly eyeing each of them, "I expect you to send them all to me, undeveloped, or destroy any copies you might still have."

"Of course: upon my honor as an Italian."

"Upon my honor as an Englishman," said the lawyer.

"Wait here," she said, and went in and placed the film on the table near the door. Then she reached for the box and, holding it against her breast, she opened the door wide and stood there, offering what felt like her baby to the Italian with the mustache.

"Grazie," he said. "By the way, we read astrology in *The Daily Mail* too. Tante Grazie."

"And the shoes?" said the lawyer.

Catherine went back and swept the package of her old shoes into her arms and delivered them to the Englishman, hoping never to see them or him again.

"Goodbye, then." Catherine backed away and closed the door, like it was a final chapter in her search. She walked over and sat on her bed, not quite satisfied, her head nodding forward, not moving at all.

# CATHERINE'S VISIT

**The DNA** on her shoes might reveal nothing; then again, it might reveal something. The handkerchief didn't appear to have other DNA on it, just hers and David's. So, that wasn't going to help. She remembered the glasses at Gracie's that matched David's; that would put that Gracie where she needed to be, harboring a criminal, and would connect Michael to David. Better yet, Michael's shoes would reveal that he was at the scene of the crime if they compared the DNA of their cat hairs with the cat hairs of the current cat. They might even match the DNA of the cat hairs if there were traces left on her shoes. Anyway, the cups would be returned to the Italians. And, come to think of it, the knife might have Michael's DNA on it. Catherine lay down, and a sad smile crept over her face as she drifted off to sleep.

After a while she woke up and packed her suitcase. Christopher called to see what had happened, then said he was at the pub near the Churchill and would come right over to the hotel.

Catherine went to the front desk, and was handed an official-looking letter as she paid for her room. She stuffed it into her purse. She and Christopher exchanged the latest information; Catherine wiped Christopher's tears with her new handkerchief and gave him a hug, then climbed into a taxi. Christopher could almost have been David:

such a devoted friend. He seemed to bow in slow motion as he closed the taxi door behind her, but she noticed a twinkle in his eyes as he glanced into hers for the minutest second. He saluted to her as her taxi drew away from her hotel. Catherine wondered if she would ever see Maureen or Christopher again.

Just before she arrived at the airport, Catherine took out the official letter and opened it. It appeared, to her surprise, that she was being ordered to be present at the Old Bailey for Michael's trial. She was asked to stay in the country for the time being. Catherine stopped the taxi driver just before he drove into the airport taxi drop-off lane.

"Please take me back to the Churchill Bed and Breakfast," she said.

"Of course, ma'am," he said, his face bored and disinterested as he turned back toward London.

"Thank you!" Catherine spluttered. It was all too much.

Back in her same room, she closed the door, took off her shoes, and flopped onto the bed.

Maybe it was true: Maybe it was an accident with David and Michael. Michael had stoically visited her for twelve years. There was constancy there, possibly not from guilt over a killing, but shame at his cowardice at not challenging her sentence; from his own necessary selfishness. Perhaps Michael was a man with some kind of conscience. Then again, maybe he was a murderer, as well as an angry sibling of David's. Half of him contained David's DNA, his genes; and half of him probably loved his brother. The other half carried on the family feud, which might never end.

Michael had followed her for weeks around London, possibly just shoring up the courage to tell her the truth, or maybe a lie. Her journey was not yet over. There were things still to do.

The next day, she ordered a cab to take her to Scotland Yard.

"I would like to visit Michael Evans," she said to the young policeman at the front desk.

"Who are you, then?" he asked. "Only relations allowed at present."

Michael probably had no relatives now besides his nephews and nieces, who didn't even know of him.

"I'm his sister-in-law," she lied. It was partly true, and true enough to be challenged. She waited an interminable time, until a man in a uniform came in and greeted her. She didn't stand up. No need to be at attention before this young man.

"Mrs. Evans," he said confidentially, bowing very slightly, "speaking off the record, you understand, I have to say it looks like we've got the real murderer now." He leaned close to her ear and whispered so quietly she could hardly hear him: "Terrible injustice done to you back then."

His words hit her body like a thunderbolt. There was no compensation she could have possibly wished for more than those words from Scotland Yard.

Catherine had to wait another twenty minutes, and then finally Michael sat across from her–in silence. She sat, looking down–in silence. Twelve years' practice made this strange bond easy and natural. Neither spoke; everything had been said. But there was that silence between them that seemed so familiar.

When she got up to leave, he stood up and started to walk away, then turned back to her and said, "I didn't kill David." How many times had just those words come from her lips over years and years; occasionally said, but mostly swallowed? How many people believed her? How many thought her a liar? How sad she had felt not to be trusted when she told them the truth.

Catherine sat in her room in a kind of endless silence. In her mind her whole life flowered before her. David seemed alive. She imagined him begging her on his knees. What was the memory of David trying to tell her? She thought of his beautiful grandson, Henry, and wondered at what secret level this young man contained the grief of thinking his step-grandmother had murdered his grandfather? Did he ever talk to his friends about it? Had he conveniently hidden it from himself up to now and had it thrust into his consciousness by her appearance in England?

As her own death one day became evident to her, she wondered about the children left in the wake of this carnage. What was worse, a stepmother and step-grandmother, supposedly murdering their father or grandfather, or an uncle murdering his brother? What fact would wound them harder, longer; even for generations to come? She thought of the Indian concept of karma. It was something like that.

Scotland Yard had all the DNA they needed. But it was all still circumstantial. It put both Michael and her at the scene of the crime.

Maybe they were eager to capture him and acquire his six silver cups as well as hers, as a result? Didn't the paper say they already had his cups? What did Scotland Yard know about the Italians who had followed her? Probably everything: She could imagine the deals going on between the governments.

# A KEY WITNESS

**Catherine telephoned** Christopher and Maureen to let them know she was staying in England. She sat alone in her room, flicking on the television while she waited for the day of Michael's trial. It seemed that every other day more people were found to be innocent of crimes that they had been accused of, once their DNA had been tested and compared with the DNA on the evidence.

The telephone rang. "Hello?" she answered.

"We will need you as a key witness in the trial of Michael Evans," said the official-sounding voice.

"Me? A key witness?" Catherine struggled to sit up in bed. The voice reminded her that she would not be able to leave the country until after the trial.

Catherine got out of bed, dressed quickly, and immediately taxied out to Maureen's for tea.

Their street and front door looked so familiar to her by now that it felt like home. She knocked, and Maureen let her in. There was a bright feeling to the long hallway that had not been there before: two small, new watercolors in the front of the hall, full of reds and yellows, not far from the Constable and Turner prints. It was strange how these colors lifted Catherine to a higher plain, a positive place where she stood a little taller, walked firmly, and felt an easy smile come upon her face.

"Come in, me love, sit down and have a nice, hot cuppa tea, and tell me all about it," Maureen said.

They walked into the warm kitchen, and Catherine went for her favorite chair.

"That Gracie," Maureen said. "Rough breed, always was: harboring that murderer all the while."

Maureen chattered to her budgie for a bit, then asked, "Don't you miss your home, then, Mrs. Evans? It's been awhile. You plan to wait for this bloody judicial system to chug along? You ought to fly home and come back when they're ready. Must be getting very dear at that Churchill B and B, an' all."

Catherine pondered the truth of it. Once they set a firm date, she could make her plans.

"They don't want me to leave until after the trial, so I expect we won't have to wait too long. I've got enough money, so that's not a concern for a while." Catherine pondered quietly. "David would have wanted me to be comfortable during this period. I'm spending part of the money his mother left to me, so it should be used to help me close this case once and for all, for him, for me, and for Mr. Smith, I mean, Michael Evans."

"That bleeder's guilty," Maureen said. "It's one of them open-and-shut cases." She brushed the crumbs off her palms like the story was over and done with. Maureen opened her cardboard box of newspaper articles and lifted one out. It was cut out from *The Daily Mail.* She smoothed it down in front of Catherine. "It's 'im," she stated triumphantly.

Catherine stared at the black-and-white newspaper photo. Maureen was pointing at young Michael, the one who had visited them in prison. But Catherine was shocked to see the young man he was standing with, holding up a silver urn. The caption read, *"Portobello Road Enthusiasts Discover Genuine Silver Chalice."*

At first, Catherine was so shocked she could hardly comment, but then she said, "The other young man is definitely David. Look, Maureen: Their arms are around each other. They look like good friends sharing a life-long interest, not fighting siblings!"

"Go on," Maureen said. "Your David what got murdered? Blimey! He looks like he likes that Mr. Smith!"

"They don't look like mortal enemies, people who would kill each other. They look like brothers, excited like they'd caught a big fish together."

"Read it, then," Maureen said.

*"Michael and David Evans,"* Catherine read aloud, *"have discovered a valuable chalice at Portobello Road, the antique finders' center of London. The brothers have pored over the jumbled contents in each barrow for years, said Michael, finding little of value. This chalice could be worth all their patient hunting.*

*"The young brothers both spotted it at the same time, according to David, and they agreed to split the proceeds once they found a buyer. The brothers have shared this lifelong hobby since childhood, when playing together at their grandfather's farm, showing that patience is their best virtue."*

Maureen stared at their faces. She pulled her magnifying glass over the top of Michael's face. "Same eyes: Only here they're happy. Must be mid-teens, I'd say."

Catherine took the magnifying glass and held it over David's face, then Michael's; then back to David's. From the look of their young faces, this chalice was found a year or two before they bought the silver cups.

"Sometimes," Catherine said quietly, "brothers fight just because brothers fight."

She rested the magnifying glass on the chalice in the photo and fell deep into thought. She didn't relish a cold winter in England, but she was as warm and comfortable at the Churchill as she could be. Had Michael killed David or was it an accident? His voice saying, "I didn't do it," followed her around as if he were present.

A week later she received a phone message from the clerk at the Old Bailey. The trial would be held the following week. It seemed that the Italians needed some finality about Michael Evans and his cups before they could take all twelve back to Italy. Catherine guessed the Italian government's request had pushed the date much closer.

She visited Michael the day before his first scheduled appearance at the Old Bailey. The newspapers had blown up the whole story. Her own photo was on the front page, but of her face in 1956. She was still incognito.

# THE TRIAL

**Out for an early start** the morning of the trial, Catherine sped along in a shiny new taxi, no longer square-shaped, but curved, feminine. They drove through Trafalgar Square and on to Fleet Street. The taxi circled around so many narrow one-way streets, Catherine wondered if the driver might be taking advantage of her American accent.

"Turn left here," she said, to let him know she knew the roads of London. He stopped the taxi right outside the Old Bailey. How different it looked this time. Few people were around. Catherine paid the driver and aimed her body toward the building that had betrayed her. In the distance she saw a van with a camera on top. Shielding her face, she ducked into the courthouse and studied the day's agenda. Walking over to a far corner, Catherine, trying to look invisible, pulled out *The Daily Mail,* which had been delivered to her door at the hotel at her request. The horoscopes fell open as if begging her to study them.

First, she checked Aquarius. Why she should care about his fate over hers, she couldn't fathom. It said, *"Be ready for a turn of events that will change the rest of your life."* Mr. Rutherford had written that. She turned to her own sign and read: *"Stick to your original purpose. Justice must be served."* Mr. Rutherford must be keeping a close watch on the trial. She turned to Gracie's horoscope. *"Prepare for dramatic changes."* Catherine smiled at Mr.

Rutherford's probable attempt to tell her a story with his hints. She wondered if the stars really said all that to him. Certainly, her stars only said there were many worlds beyond this small earth, and who knew what there was out there? Why would the stars care at all about one individual's day, when there were whole universes to ponder?

Cameramen were now outside the front door, setting up their tripods; probably looking around for people like her. She was the first one inside the courtroom. An official seated her near the witness box, as required. Her body would be temporarily erect on that witness stand, and there she would proclaim to the world that she was innocent.

Every seat in the courtroom was taken. There was a bubble of conversation downstairs and upstairs. The judge appeared at the far door wearing a wig, and the buzzing crowd was hushed to whispers.

"May it please the court, all rise!" said a male voice by the door. Catherine pulled herself up. After they all sat down and the judge mumbled things to the barristers, he turned toward Michael.

"Michael Evans, you are here on suspicion of murdering your half-brother, David Evans, on November 3, 1956. How do you plead?"

"Not guilty, m'lord," Michael said, humbly.

Catherine could just see Michael's eyes as he sat there in that truth chair. They were the eyes that she had memorized for twelve long years. She shuddered, remembering that cold prison, her loneliness and anger; his welcomed silent visits. If he were innocent, how could she stand by and let him go to jail? But what if he were the murderer?

Catherine's hand went up to her forehead, remembering the day she visited Michael at Scotland Yard. A person who said, "I didn't kill him," the way Michael did, couldn't be guilty. Catherine knew the sound of guilt and innocence better than she knew her own voice. She looked at Michael sitting there, a man who had spent an early life with a brother finding antiques in Portobello Road; fighting over an inheritance; fighting over ownership of the silver cups; tending to two well-loved family members who needed Michael until their deaths. His eyes felt like they were peering into her very soul. Twelve years of silence beamed across the room, a language of no spoken words, but messages nevertheless: kindness, empathy; maybe even love.

Catherine stared at her shoes for the longest moment then quietly stood up, and in as loud a voice as she could muster, bellowed, "I killed David Evans and spent twelve years in prison for my crime. Michael Evans is innocent!"

The packed courtroom broke up into pandemonium. Several news media reporters ran from the courtroom.

Michael's face was covered by his palms. His shoulders were shaking. He wiped his face on his sleeve.

"I killed my husband. I paid the price. That's all there is to it," she said clearly, then turned and shouted for all to witness, "Michael Evans is innocent!"

Michael smeared the tears across his cheeks as he jumped up and bellowed, "Catherine Evans is innocent, m'lord. She wasn't there when her husband died. I was. But it was an accident. David accidentally fell on his knife. I didn't touch it. My fingerprints weren't on it. But I was there. Mrs. Evans was not. She is completely innocent!"

"Order," yelled the judge as pandemonium broke out. "Order in this court!"

Journalists at the back pushed through the door and out into the street.

"Do you swear that you are telling the truth, Michael Evans?" the judge asked.

"I can't see that poor, innocent woman going to her grave, the whole world thinking she's a murderer, when she's not. She adored her husband. I swear that this is the truth; everything I have said. I swear it!"

The judge seemed to go into a trance, his brain obviously straining to remember hundreds of trials before. His eyes finally focused, and he banged the gavel hard and boldly said, "Case dismissed."

"All rise," said a voice. The remaining crowd stood, whispering, and the second the judge was out of sight, the people scurried and pushed out the door with the news.

Catherine plowed her way through the crowd. As she exited the door, flashes blinded her. Reporters yelled at her. "Give us your statement, Mrs. Evans."

"I am innocent, it's true. But so is Michael Evans."

Christopher and Maureen stood right there at the front of the pushing crowd, cheering. Christopher helped the police hold the crowd back, then opened the waiting taxi door for Catherine.

"Well done, Mrs. Evans!" he yelled. Christopher seemed to understand her better than anyone else she ever knew.

The taxi sped her back to the Churchill Bed and Breakfast. Now the whole of England would know her face. As soon as she could get to the phone, she called her airline.

"Hello, Virgin? I'd like a seat. Yes, Catherine Evans: same as my last order. Tomorrow morning would do nicely. Goodbye."

The next day, when she looked at her photo closely in *The Times,* she saw Christopher and Maureen cheering in the background.

# THE LETTER

**A few weeks** after she returned home to Vermont, Catherine opened a letter from Peter. It was an article written by Mr. Rutherford in *The Daily Mail.* It said: *"...Michael Evans was freed on a technicality. A judge and jury will never try him and never pronounce a different verdict. Mrs. Catherine Evans attempted to say that she was the murderer. Then Michael Evans swore she was not. DNA evidence from cat hairs puts Michael Evans at the scene of the crime. He says it was an accident, a fight with his brother. It is of the opinion of this writer that Catherine Evans did not murder her husband, but confessed to it in order to prevent her brother-in-law, Michael Evans, from going to jail. Although he swears he is innocent, he also swears Catherine Evans was not even present when her husband died.*

*"Nobody will ever know who really killed David Evans or if he died by accident. Michael Evans could also have been unjustly accused. One thing is clear, however: Twelve years have been served for it, probably unjustly. This writer would go so far as to say that in coming forward in Michael Evans' trial, and proclaiming her guilt in order to save him, Catherine Evans is hardly a murderer. More important, however, is the fact that Benvenuto Cellini's silver cups have been rediscovered. This is an enormous find for Europe and the world in the community of art and its treasures. This is a fitting end to such a dramatic case, which cost Catherine Evans her psychological welfare, and which included spending years in Holloway Prison for a death resulting from a fight two brothers apparently had over these cups."*

Catherine put the article inside a clear plastic holder and laid it in the box with David's things. The case was closed. If her relatives needed reassurance, here it was in black and white: She was a saint. For her own part, she didn't really care what anybody thought now. Some things just did not matter that much–not anymore.

Maybe Michael had told her the truth; maybe not. Perhaps he'd paid for it all the years he visited her at Holloway Prison. His son and wife had died. In his freedom, he had still pursued the cups. To her, the cups were a symbol of David's love for her. To Michael, they seemed to be a treasure to grasp.

A few weeks later Catherine received another letter. It was snowing outside. The Connecticut River's ice floes floated by between the twinkling bare branches outside her window, but she was warm by the fire. The letter was from England and in handwriting she didn't recognize. She opened it using her carved wooden letter-opener.

*Dear Catherine Evans,*

*I don't know how to thank you for what you did. It was a magnificent gesture, and probably saved me from going to prison. I know you still might not believe me, but I do want to reassure you that you did the right thing.*

*But now on to the best news. I have made good friends with Peter and Henry who kindly wrote to me after the trial, and have become such good friends with Mrs. David Evans that she has invited me to board in a room at her house. Gracie gave me up the minute she found out I didn't have the money from the cups.*

*Henry asks about his grandfather and loves to hear how we fought. I take him to Portobello Road once a month to search for treasures. Peter stands quietly in the background listening when he comes by. Perhaps I am an adopted father to him. He never really knew David, so I am as close as he can get. He reminds me a lot of David, but at least we don't fight! He is a wonderful man and nephew.*

*I hope this letter finds you happily back in your abode in Brattleboro. I am sure it was a very trying time for you in London. I suppose you heard that they found cat hairs on my shoes: your cat. The cat Mrs. Evans has is a direct descendent of your cat! Put me right at the scene of the crime. But you knew that.*

*Once again, I swear to you I didn't kill David. But I am devastated to this day that you had to sit in jail for so long because I was such a coward. Can you ever forgive*

*me? I think that with your courageous voice in that courtroom you showed amazing*
*forgiveness. I will never forget it.*
  *I do wish you all the very best.*
  *Your brother-in-law, Michael*

Catherine read the letter over and over, and thought now of Peter, tall, his blond hair hiding the white at the temples; he walked like David, even his deep voice was David's; even his gestures, his very English way of holding back, not speaking up, observing others. He had the qualities of a good private investigator. His search in the world seemed to be his wish to right wrongs, find culprits, and perhaps keep his nose available all those years for sniffing out hints of his father's demise. Peter: the image of how his father might have been had he lived; who would possibly never quite believe it was an accident, but who grew to love Michael anyway as an excellent substitute grandfather to Peter's children.

She slid the letter back into its envelope and put it onto the table, and placed the wooden letter opener on top of it.

Visions of silver cups haunted Catherine's dreams: crabs, human-headed horses, balances, bulls, lions, fish, scorpions, Capricorns, Aquarians, Aries; entwined and tumbling together among the stars in the sky. The fish lay lifeless on the balances that were carried in the crab's claws and teetering on the horse's back, which charged the oncoming bull. Surrounding her misty dreams the drums beat and the violins were so high-pitched they almost woke her up; but the cymbals crashing at the end of this dream shook the crab, the horse, the bull, the lion, and the fish, and scattered them into the sky and over the distant hills and into the rocks and the sea, where the waves rolled and disappeared into eternity.

When Catherine woke up, a vision of Michael as a young man hung before her, filling her memories with his eternal guilt, his finger held before her and the sign saying NO TALKING, and his wife with her cane and sad face, and somewhere a Down's syndrome boy, whose imagined sweet smile of gratitude was Catherine's only consolation for twelve lost years.

A year after she had arrived back in Brattleboro, an invitation arrived in Catherine's mailbox from her father's family over in Connecticut; for proper English tea, it said; in one week, it said. Here was Catherine's chance to put things to rights, to smile, broadly; perhaps to be hugged. Maybe apologies would filter through her ears for the long years of silence and neglect. Maybe a little grand-nephew would reach for her hand, not knowing of her agonizing past, and walk with her toward the swings, giggle and yell, "Push me higher!"

Maybe Catherine could grab the little life left to her now and act like a woman whose name was finally cleared, whose sense of injustice had been bandaged and healed. She could visit her father's family, who could finally find the time to invite her to tea.

Maybe one day, before she couldn't travel that far, they would invite her to dinner.

# FOURTEEN YEARS LATER

**There is** a pride in Catherine as she is tucked up in bed. Her sleepy eyes blink lazily as her caregiver, Nancy, pulls the covers up over Catherine's cold nose. Nancy's kind face moves toward Catherine's. She puckers her large lips, gently kissing Catherine's wrinkled forehead as she has done now for the past three years following Catherine's stroke.

Winter is approaching in Vermont. The sunsets have given way to gray skies and freezing air. The orange leaves on the ground have hardened, turned brown, broken up.

Nancy pulls the shades down and closes the curtains. "Now, my dear, take your heart pill. It's time to sleep."

Catherine holds out her frail good hand, closed in a fragile fist, and her helper, Nancy, encircles it warmly with both of her hands for a moment. As Nancy holds up Catherine's head, she lays the pill on Catherine's tongue, Catherine sips the water from the glass Nancy holds and swallows the pill. Then she smiles as Nancy lays her head back upon the pillow then leaves the room and closes the door quietly behind her.

As she drifts into her final sleep, Catherine hears the roar of the sea crashing against the purple rocks, sees the spraying mist land on strange faces of people with names she had never heard of or known until she read David's manuscript: Benvenuto Cellini, Caruso, Carey, George,

Hawthorn, John, Harry, Ronnie, a woman doctor, little Christine, Nurse Pritchard; names that somehow she feels have also touched the silver cups on their journey into her own life. Now they are gone from her; gone like David and prison and all her attempts to make a life without a family.

What are left to her in her last night are the stars: There they are. Now they are hazy; really mostly a memory of years of looking up and studying their spatial distances; but they are there, steady, reliable, like a part of her that never changed. The rest is the shadow of memories that may or may not have really happened. She feels herself drifting and floating like a million particles of dust, up now, toward the sky, blown away by the breeze and scattering over the ocean somewhere off the coast of England to be held by the waves that roll in and out, past the pier, past the sailboats, forever and ever, just dust and stars; dust and stars.

The End

# EPILOGUE

**Real life is full** of coincidences, not just fiction. During the writing of this novel, the most amazing coincidences happened to me.

Once I had finished the novel, I really needed verification of a few details from a rag-and-bone man from the 1940s and a taxi driver from the 1950s. In the summer of 2008, I flew to Oslo from London. The man sitting next to me had been a rag-and-bone man in the 1940s and a taxi driver in London in the 1950s. He told me the exact call he used, "rag and bone, rag and bone, any old iron," and he confirmed that taxi drivers then all knew each other and might well remember a strange delivery thirty years before in, say, the Brick Lane neighborhood, where many Cockney working-class families lived then.

The next coincidence was in the fall of 2008, on my way up to Highgate on the bus. I sat next to a woman who told me that her mother had been the Director of Holloway Prison in the 1950s and she, herself, had been the Director in the 1960s. So she told me, among other things, that it had been remodeled, but it was just after Catherine had left prison.

After I had written the book, I found out that Rudyard Kipling lived in Rottingdean and Brattleboro.

The most amazing coincidence occurred when I had finished the novel and it was just being emailed back to me by my line editor. That day a friend sent me a great photograph of Cellini's astrological chart. I loved it and then I noticed that it said that Cellini was born on November 3. That was the date that I had picked two years earlier for the "murder" to take place.

Wendy Bartlett
Berkeley, California 2009 (updated 2021)

# ABOUT THE AUTHOR

Wendy Bartlett currently lives in Berkeley, California. She lived in England for thirteen years and visits her family regularly where she haunts the places she writes about like the Old Bailey, the River Thames and Rottingdean. She re-published her novel *Broad Reach* in 2019 and has published four children's books recently, including *The Flood*. This new edition of *Cellini's Revenge* is now Book One in a trilogy.

Wendy has written much poetry, seven novels and one screenplay that has become an audio play called *Girl with a Violin*. She is excited to work on her writing every day, telling great stories.

# The Elizabeth Books
## Written and Illustrated by Wendy Bartlett
### Available through Indiebound.org, bookshop.org, Apple Books, Nook, and Kobo
### as well as other print and ebook retailers worldwide

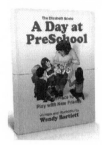

A beautifully illustrated book for children attending preschool showing all the activities children do in preschool: meeting new friends, listening to stories, swinging on the tire swing, playing table games, singing with a guitar, hammering, riding bikes, and playing in the sand. Teachers, parents, and children will love this book because they can point and say, "We go to a school like that!"

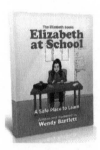

First grade is a challenge with new friends, maybe a new teacher and a feeling of advancement into the world of reading and writing. It is a time of friendship, sharing, learning and playing. It is a place where children come into their own, a secure leap into the world of math and science, and the beginning of learning to spell and sound out whole sentences. It is fun!

My mother sketches me all over Paris, whether of me eating an ice cream cone under the Eiffel Tower, or washing socks in the bidet, or going on the merry-go-round. It is lots of fun being her model! It takes many turns for me on the merry-go-round for her to finish her drawing. I don't mind a bit! Paris is amazing!

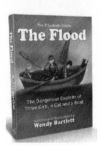

When eleven-year-old Elizabeth is left to babysit her four-year-old sister one rainy night, neither of them expect the adventure that unfolds. Their parents don't return home, and by morning there is a flood that fills the first floor of their house. Elizabeth must take initiative and make an agonizing decision: whether to stay put where her parents might find them, or to be brave and leave home to go in search of their parents. Dangers loom in either scenario.

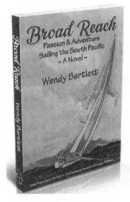

With her only child off to college, Sarah, a divorcée, is overwhelmed with emptiness. Here home overlooking San Francisco Bay is quiet, and her work with young children is routine. Most of all, her heart has become an excruciating vacuum.

When she meets a very sexy and charming Englishman tending his sailboat, Sarah makes an impulsive decision. It takes little to persuade her to join this mysterious sailor for an around-the-world cruise as his second mate, despite her amateur knowledge of sailing.

At first, warm winds, lust, and romance fill her days as they journey to the South Pacific. Soon her romantic idyll is rocked by the stormy seas as the dark side of her captain is revealed against the harsh backdrop of sailing. As life on the water becomes unforgiving, Sarah finds herself plunged into an abyss of fear and confusion, and ultimately, the greatest challenge she has ever faced.

Broad Reach *is engaging, real and powerful. While most sailing stories romanticize the experience, this gripping novel explores the hard, cold, nitty-gritty, crazy-making, dark side of small-boat ocean cruising. A must read!*
—**William McGinnis, author of *Sailing the Greek Islands, Whitewater: A Thriller, Gold Bay, The Guide's Guide, Whitewater Rafting* and more.**

# COMING SOON

# Cellini's Revenge

## BOOK 3

**This trilogy is about the mystery of the disappearance of the twelve silver cups that were made by the silversmith, Benvenuto Cellini, in 1527 and spans many stories of the cups for about five centuries until the early 21st Century. The cups bring bad luck to those who own them, unless and until they are returned to Italy.**

**Book 1**: Catherine, David's wife, is blamed for David's murder and is sent to Holloway Prison for twelve years. When she gets out, she decides to find out who the real culprit is, and travels to Rottingdean to find the cups, where she finds out David's secrets.

**Book 2**: Peter, who wonders who his father is, meets Jeannie, a wild young woman, whom he marries. They have endless troubles, and Peter thinks it must have something to do with the cups, perhaps still in England. *Available Now.*

**Book 3**: Peter, now a single father, meets Susan when the plane crashes at Heathrow and their children survive. He works through his life's tragedies, and is frustrated by his parents who are still spellbound by the Cellini cups, as he chases them to Italy and back. A mysterious man turns up from the past.

# BOOK CLUB QUESTIONS

1. What was Catherine's original method of finding the murderer?

2. What was the sound that was so familiar to her when she met Christopher's mother, Maureen?

3. What was Catherine's disappointment in her 'perfect' husband, David?

4. What was your favorite chapter throughout the story that took us to the history of the silver cups?

5. Did the astrology make sense to you through her quest?

6. Did she believe in astrology?

7. Did you like Mrs. Angela Evans' son, Peter?

8. What was your favorite part of this novel?

# LETTER TO MY READERS

Thank you very much for reading my novel, *Cellini's Revenge: The Mystery of the Silver Cups*.

I appreciate your interest and hope you found it as exciting and fun to read as it was to write.

I would so appreciate your taking a moment to please write to me at wendyberk@aol.com and let me know what you think.

If you would like, you could also write an honest review wherever you bought this book online, like Amazon. Here's a direct link to my author page on that site. amazon.com/author/wendybartlett. Just click on the gold *Cellini's Revenge* cover.

Book 2 of *Cellini's Revenge* is now available and Book 3 will be published soon. If you would like to be on the notification list for my books, please go to my website and sign up.

Thank you very much again for reading my novel.

Gratefully,

*Wendy Bartlett*

Wendy Bartlett, author
wendybartlett.com

Made in the USA
Middletown, DE
30 June 2021

43423697R00177